An Unfamiliar Kindness

ALSO BY DANIE BOTHA

Be Silent
Be Good
Maxime
Young Maxime

An Unfamiliar Kindness

Danie Botha

https://www.daniebotha.com

Published in the United States by Charbellini Press

ISBN-13: 9780995174870 paperback
ISBN-13: 978-0-9951748-8-7
ISBN-10: 0995174870

For Charlize and Clara-Li

Author's Note

UNTIL THE LATE 1970s, connections between Britain, Europe, and South Africa were maintained by sea for passengers, cargo, and mail. The large ships completed the fourteen-day journey with considerable ease. One such liner was the *Windsor Castle*, a British Royal Mail Ship (RMS), which completed the journey between Southampton and Cape Town on a regular basis, always departing on a Thursday at 4 p.m. Only during the latter part of the 1970s did the arrival of the jumbo jet make air travel not only faster but also cheaper than ocean liners.

"The Troubles" refers to the thirty-year period of conflict from 1968 to 1998 between elements of Northern Ireland's Irish Nationalist community (mainly self-identified as Irish and Catholic) and its Unionist community (mainly self-identified as British and Protestant). The goal of the former was to end British rule in Northern Ireland and reunite Ireland and create an Irish Republic. During this time, more than 3,500 civilians were killed.

The Women's Liberation Movement in the UK that kicked off in early 1970 was a second-wave feminist movement, which followed the suffrage campaign of the nineteenth and early twentieth centuries. It pushed hard to improve the conditions and quality of life in general for women. It succeeded in getting several laws passed, such as the Equal Pay Act in 1970, the Sex Discrimination Act in 1975, and the Domestic Violence Act in 1976.

Even though *An Unfamiliar Kindness* is woven around these historical facts, it remains a work of fiction, and all the characters and most of the incidents are imaginary and bear no reference to individuals alive or dead.

The letter. Oxford, UK. 29 July 2000.

EMILEE WAS AFRAID, not of dying, but of picking up her mail.

This had to stop, she realized—her being so terrified. Each time the heaviness choked the life from her. All these years—all the therapy sessions—wasted.

Friday afternoons became a calculated dance, rehearsed to precision. Only in the safety of her apartment, the doors locked, two fingers of Dún Léire on the rocks later—would she sort through the postal pieces, berating herself for being such a coward.

And the therapist claimed I'd outgrow my angst. Well, she knows nothing.

It started as a game. He was smart. Serious. A complex man. She loved the challenge, in spite of the intimidation; the elaborate daily test. The changes were subtle, so slight she didn't notice. Her insecurity grew under his ridicule. It turned into a maelstrom, from where there soon was no escape. And, when he got ill, it blossomed into full-scale dread—of living with an unpredictable man. From the mountaintops he plunged into valleys of desolation, the momentum hauling her along. She loved him and yet learned to fear for Caitlynn and herself when he became aggressive, vindictive. Then, one night, they disappeared; without word, without warning. No last kiss.

The search was a stillbirth from the start. Caitie's red jacket was discovered a week later a mile downstream. Nothing else. How does a heart heal when it is denied farewell, denied closure, even a burial? It was three years later when Emilee filed for an annulment. For the declarations of presumed death, she had to wait seven.

She remained hopeful to receive word—a letter, a notice in a newspaper, a sign—even a body.

There was nothing.

When the official documents arrived, after seven years of waiting, seven years of hoping, she could begin her grieving.

Emilee surprised even herself as she bolted away from the counter, her face drained. The high stool crashed over, and her mail scattered as she glanced around the room. Shivering, she shook her hand with the letter as if to free itself of the calamity that had entered her house and from the horror that had attached itself to her fingers: a handwritten envelope with no return address.

They were dead. Connor and Caitie are dead. It was official. The courts had confirmed that all those many years ago. In the end, she believed it to be so.

And even if that were no longer the case, how could he have known my mailing address? If he found my address, then he knows where I live. Why an old-fashioned letter? He must be outside, watching the house. She shuddered. *But he's dead, Emilee. And Caitie? He must know what happened.*

She scrutinized the letter under the glaring spotlights of her breakfast nook. *It is him. The way he curled his n's. He must have a tremor now.* The post office stamp was legible: 27 July 2000. Unmistakable. It had been mailed in Slough. *So he went back.* Still clinging to the unopened letter, she grabbed her cell phone and darted through the house, again checking the front door.

Emilee slipped the Yale lock into place one more time and turned the key in the second lock, then raced to the back for the kitchen door and turned the key one more time, then through to the living room where she yanked the sliding door open and stepped onto the small, open-sided porch. She glanced around then jumped down three brick steps. She paid her only row of blooming roses little attention as she dashed toward the garden gate on the side of the house. It was a wooden contraption built from split poles—like the fence, six-foot high—and covered by a trumpet creeper over its entire length. The creeper was late that year with flowering. The padlock was in place, and she gave it a confirmatory tug.

Her heart skipped another beat. *The water. He can come along the water, along with the Castle Mill stream!*

She raced through her backyard toward the twenty-foot stretch of dock, which had been built flush with the riverbank. She tried to tiptoe to the dock's edge, but her momentum made her do a butterfly dance not to end up in the water. Once she regained her balance, she peered up and down the stream, cupping her hand against the glare. There was no traffic on the canal, not even a water snake to disturb its surface. It was too quiet for that time of the afternoon. She cocked her head. Water lapped against the undersides of the wooden dock. She inhaled the reassuring smell of water grass, rotting wood, and stale water.

Something yellow caught her eyes: the tip of her kayak, safely tucked in along the cast-iron fence to the side of the property, underneath a long, rectangular black tarpaulin she had strung to protect it.

She could not recall being in such a panic—not since she had moved back here to Rewley Road in 1983. At first, she had rented, but then she bought the place. She had never been afraid—not to this extent, not since they disappeared. Not since the courts had sent her the certificates.

Dare I hope again? Caitie would have turned twenty-seven in May.

She stepped through the patio door on her way back and heard thumping on her garden gate. She jumped. Someone had called her name.

She paused before slamming the door closed behind her with a scream, only to open it again and jut her head out. "Francois?"

The thumping was more assertive. "Emilee!"

"Hold on. I'm getting the key!"

She fumbled in the kitchen. The key was not hanging on its usual little hook. She dropped the letter and hurried outside. She could see narrow slices of her friend through the slits in the gate. "I'm sorry, but I can't seem to find the key." She stopped to catch her breath. "Come around to the front door."

"*What's* going on?"

Running back toward the house, Emilee hollered, "Try the front door!" She slammed the patio door shut and locked it, scooped the letter from the floor, and made for the front entrance. *Why could Francois not have phoned me like other civilized people, to say he was outside? The poor idiot. His head is still in Africa.*

She jerked the Yale lock back and turned the second key, swung the heavy door open, and grabbed her startled guest by his jacket. She dragged him inside, kicked the door shut, slipped the Yale back in place, and turned the key. She spun around and took his face in her hands and kissed him smack on the lips. His face was one big frown.

"*Francois.*"

Francois Moolman took hold of Emilee's shoulders as tears ran down her cheeks. He tried to dry them with his thumbs, stroking upward on each cheek, but failed. He inhaled her fear.

He hesitated, then kissed her pale lips. "*What* is wrong?"

"You won't understand, this . . . this . . . ." She shook the condemning letter, which had grown to her skin.

He pulled her closer when she gave a sob and hugged her, her tremors shaking them both. "When I spoke to you earlier today, everything seemed fine."

"It *was* fine. I received, or rather discovered, this letter only minutes ago among my stack of mail." Emilee stuffed the letter into his hand.

And everyone thought I was mad for having this obsession about picking up my mail.

He broke the embrace and pulled her behind him into the house. "You don't mind if we go in and perhaps sit down?"

He plopped onto her couch and studied the letter. "Isn't it amazing that there are still people writing letters by hand and then with an ink cartridge?" He began reading aloud. "Mrs. Emilee O'Hannigan." Francois glanced at her. "You never told me your married name. I much preferred Emilee Stephens." He turned the envelope over several times. "This was written by an individual who is sure of himself, or, perhaps not. The writing is a bit unsteady. It was written with a fountain pen, was mailed two days ago in Slough, and it has no return address."

Francois held out his hand. "Come sit, Emilee O'Hannigan. Please."

She took the letter from him as she sat down, their thighs touching, but she continued shaking. "Thank you, Mr. Sherlock, but I already know all that." She struggled not to smile through her tears.

He studied her eyes, the face of the woman he had put on a plane in Windhoek, Namibia, four months ago. She had then seemed at peace with herself and her world.

"You plucked me through your front door like a Navy SEAL on a mission and then locked everything in a panic. Why are you so terrified?"

"This letter was written by Connor O'Hannigan." Emilee took several breaths. "But he's dead, or rather, *was* dead. I was married to him for four years during the seventies. He was involved with the Unions and *The Troubles* in the North. His involvement was much deeper than I had ever suspected. Then he disappeared one day, *with* our daughter. They were declared deceased by the courts in nineteen eighty-three, after seven years of hoping and waiting."

"You had *a girl*?"

Emilee nodded.

"What . . . has he *done* to you?"

"It's not that simple."

"Did he *hurt* you?"

She shook her head but avoided his eyes.

"He *must* have," Francois insisted, lifting her chin.

"When he got angry, which was often, he would break things, but he *never* hit me," she whispered. "Although, he taught me, taught us, what fear was. He was a master."

CHAPTER 1

The RMS Windsor Castle. Cape Town, South Africa. 7 December 1969.

EMILEE TIGHTENED HER iron-grip on her friend's hand and elbowed their path open to a spot next to the railing, apologizing as they went. She bestowed a sweet smile on everyone who frowned on their uncivil pushing to get to where they could have an unobstructed view of the dock far beneath. She was determined to make visual contact with her family before their ship sailed. Taken aback by their boldness, young and old, male and female, found it impossible not to take a step back to allow the two girls thoroughfare.

Caroline Washington had little control over her blushing, which only intensified as they approached the railing. She loved her friend but was equally exasperated by her forwardness. Her free arm was engaged in keeping herself decent as she smoothed and held down the hem of her summer dress that took flight in the breeze. Wearing the miniskirt dresses was Emilee's idea. "Something cool and complimentary for our departure," she had said.

Still attached to Emilee's hand, she whispered, "That was *so* embarrassing."

Emilee only laughed. "No, it wasn't. *There* they are!" She pointed at her parents, brothers, and Caroline's family, who stood huddled together on A-berth, waiting on the two girls to appear.

Emilee took a step back from the railing as the subtle stench of spilled sewage, salt water, dead fish, and ship's oil shot up at them. Far below, gentle waves washed against the steel hull.

Their families heard them calling and answered their beckoning. Everyone waved. The moment they had dreaded and dreamed about had arrived.

The wave of hands intensified. Some waved with handkerchiefs, shouting endearments as the PA system behind the girls warned, "The ship is sailing." The horn sounded. Dockworkers called in warning. Seagulls screeched excitedly as they dipped toward the water.

As the horn sounded a second time, the screws started turning. The bow—in no apparent hurry—righted in the direction of the open sea. Later, it would point at Southampton. The people on the wharf-side grew smaller, the separation taking place in slow motion until they were beyond hearing distance. Neither party had the heart to cease waving, not even when infinite specks were all that remained of them. Emilee clung to her handkerchief, waving, refusing to concede.

One by one the passengers left the railing in search of their cabins, but the two friends held fast, unwilling to say their final goodbyes. Wrapped in its cloud-blanket, Table Mountain towered behind Cape Town as the RMS *Windsor Castle* left port.

Emilee squeezed her friend's hand, leaned against her, and whispered a last goodbye to Cape Town and good old Africa.

Caroline repeated the farewell and wrapped her arms around her friend's slim shoulders to slow her shaking.

She pondered whether they would ever see their folks again, or their country, and whether that would happen before they were both old and senile.

Together they swayed with the roll of the ship, leaning into the breeze.

They remained there until the mountain and the continent faded into the sea and their tear-streaked faces had dried.

Their haven for the ten-day journey was a two-berth cabin, number 54, in Tourist Class. Since it consisted of two bunk beds, they had to toss a coin on Emilee's insistence, "in order to be fair." Caroline spun the coin and Emilee called it. Emilee chose the top bunk.

Except for a single red chair, everything in the cabin was mint green.

Emilee immediately responded, "It's *hideous*. It looks like bile!"

"Bile is yellow. This is called mint, and the bedspreads have beautiful hibiscuses. They're gorgeous and match the chair."

"It's still hideous," Emilee said, giving her final verdict. "Our cabin smells of abandoned rugby boots too."

As she bent forward and stretched out on the hibiscus-print spread, Caroline stared at her friend of five years, baffled by her random outbursts of cynicism. She closed her eyes and imagined smelling the flowers. *Rugby boots.* They had both graduated three weeks earlier from Wynberg Girls High in Cape Town and were on their way to Oxford, where they would study with scholarships.

She was so proud of them both—they had worked hard for this, to get accepted—and yet so afraid. England had seemed all safe and secure and not far at all on the map.

But just now, when Table Mountain finally dropped off behind the horizon, the ten long days on the open sea sunk in. It was quite disconcerting. They were scheduled to berth in Southampton on the seventeenth, with their interviews for college placement, as per special arrangement, at 9 a.m. on Friday the nineteenth. Her hopes were to study law, and Emilee was obsessed with immersing herself in English literature and modern languages.

Emilee bounced to the floor. "*Come on*, Carrie. Enough of this self-inflicted cabin-arrest. I'm not waiting until suppertime. Let's go find something edible."

They locked the door and bolted down the hallway as Emilee bellowed, "Last one to reach the Promenade deck is an old maid!" They ran neck-to-neck until Emilee overtook her friend as they rounded the corner, where they crashed into a crewmember, sending them all careening to the floor. The poor man went down without so much as a squeak.

Caroline had seldom seen Emilee crimson and in search of words. She was stuttering as they picked themselves up and straightened their clothes. The young man had gathered the small stack of papers he was carrying and pushed his fingers through his hair before he put his cap back on. He glared at Emilee.

"Is there an emergency that the captain should know about, Miss?" he managed with a straight face.

"No . . . not exactly," Emilee stuttered, catching her breath. "We were being silly. I'm *so* sorry."

"Not at all. Do you play rugby, Miss? That was a brilliant tackle."

Emilee laughed and flushed. She was not blind. He was striking—a virile young man. He smelled of shaving cream. "You're making fun of me, sir. Please forgive us."

"I'm afraid I can't. I'll have to report you to the First Officer on deck. No running is allowed on this vessel."

"*Excuse* me? That's a *joke*, right?" Emilee said.

"It is *not*. This is a Royal Mail Ship. We discourage any frivolity during the journey due to the precious cargo in the hull. Your name, Miss?" The man took a small notebook and pen from his pocket but failed to hide his grin.

Emilee groaned as she grabbed Caroline's hand. "Come, Carrie! This man is not accepting our apology and takes us for fools." She scrutinized his nametag. "Excuse us, Mr. Harding." She spun around, no longer embarrassed but furious.

He capitulated immediately and called after them, "Ladies, I'm sorry! I've been an ass—it was unpardonable. Please allow me to make it up to you."

Emilee turned back. "Pardon me, Mr. Harding. First you refuse to accept my apology, and the next moment you make a pass at me. I would say that *is* unpardonable. Come, Caroline. Perhaps *we* should go find the First Officer on deck."

Mr. Harding remained only one step behind them as they went up the staircase. "Please accept my apology, Miss. But I still don't know your name."

"Perhaps it is better that way, Mr. Harding." Emilee hollered, "We prefer *anonymity*," and they ran off toward the dining hall.

CHAPTER 2

—◊◊—

At sea. 8 December 1969

IT WAS LUNCH hour the following day before Douglas Harding had success in locating the two young ladies from cabin 54 who had run him over. He chastised himself for not being able to extract the anonymous one's name from her before he had to sound the retreat. He stood behind the buffet tables armed with a small stack of menus, which he had reprinted late that morning.

He bided his time. He could not afford another fumble with the redhead. There were over eight hundred passengers on this vessel, with scores of young ladies, and he had to choose these two. If he caught him here, his boss in the printing shop would demand his head.

He approached their table and leaned in next to Caroline's chair. "Excuse me, Miss Caroline, I hope I'm not too late. I printed a couple of fresh menus for your table. I was hoping . . . ." He offered the blushing Caroline two of the menus.

"Thank you, Mr. Harding," Caroline stammered.

Emilee leaned forward and hissed, "How did you *find* us? Are you a *stalker*?"

"No, Miss," Douglas said. "I only brought you those, as well as this," and he took a folded sheet from his back pocket. "Perhaps, if you missed the daily news-sheet."

Caroline slapped her friend's arm, "Stop it, Emilee. It's a peace offering."

"Stalker," Emilee insisted.

He ignored her comment. "Thank you, Miss Caroline. I have to go. Have a pleasant meal. Please excuse me, Miss Emilee, Miss Caroline." He hesitated, took the news-sheet from Caroline, scribbled on it, then handed it back to Emilee, bowed, and took his leave.

"What did he write?" Caroline cried as she tried to take the news-sheet, but Emilee pinned it down on the white tablecloth.

Misses E & C, please meet me at the entrance to the smoking room at 4 p.m., aft side. Douglas Harding.

"He *likes* you," Caroline purred as her friend let go of the sheet and she inhaled the fresh printer's ink. She closed her eyes.

"Oh please, he's a pip-squeak who stalks us." Emilee leaned back in her chair as they waited for their order. "I think we should rather socialize with the engineers or radio operators. That sounds so much more exciting and sophisticated than *printing-shop assistant.*"

Caroline gasped, "You *are* a snob."

"Or better still," Emilee laughed, "what about the sonar operator?"

"Be careful what you beg for," Caroline said. "The sonar guy might be a blubber of a sailor with a stubble beard and missing teeth. If you wish to meet the upper class, we'll have to hang out in the dance hall every night, or go on hourly excursions with the captain—if you can convince him."

—⚬—

As soon as they left the dining hall, Emilee made them search for two unoccupied deck chairs. "Please let me lie down—my sea legs feel all wobbly. I'm not used to this constant heaving." She dropped down on the first open canvas chair. Her complexion was similar to the mint color of their cabin.

Caroline was easy to be alarmed. "Shouldn't we rather go to the hospital? Let the ship surgeon attend to you."

"No . . . no doctor. It will pass. Let's rest for a bit."

Emilee broke the silence after two minutes. "Aft. Is that at the rear, the stern?"

Caroline laughed. "It's the rear. He's a stalker, remember? Now you want to go and *meet* with the man."

"He's only a boy. It will be bad manners if we don't show up."

"A beautiful boy. He looks twenty, though," Caroline mused.

"Nineteen, max. He has such a weird accent."

"He's British, silly. They must think *we* speak funny." She turned on her side facing her friend. "Somebody's smitten."

Emilee snapped upright. "I feel better already. Smitten? Who's silly now? Let's grab our swimming gear and do laps in the pool."

—ﾠﾠﾠﾠﾠ

Their hair was still damp from the swim as they hovered outside, close to the stern entrance to the smoking room, leaning against the outside railing, trying desperately to look old enough to hang around a bar facility.

Douglas Harding was on time, to the second, and walked over with a wide grin. He had changed out of his uniform. "Miss Emilee, Miss Caroline, I am honored—you both came."

"We didn't want to hurt your feelings, Mr. Harding," Emilee said. "Please, can you drop this *Miss* thing. We are not princesses." She curtsied.

"Shame on you!" Caroline chided.

"I see milady mocks me," Douglas said.

"Well, stop acting like a fool. And what's it with the smoking room? None of us smoke."

"Neither do I."

"So, is this really the *only* place on the ship where you can meet a young lady?" Emilee asked.

Caroline tried to put her hand over her friend's mouth.

"Very few people actually smoke inside," Douglas said. "Children are not allowed in here, so there's no one who can run you over, and besides, they have a decent bar. You'll love it. Both of you are eighteen, aren't you?"

Emilee blushed. "Touché, Mr. Harding. Yes, we're over age. Sorry for being such a bitchy female." She held her hand, which he took and squeezed.

"That's a contradiction of terms, but you're forgiven," Douglas said. "Let's go inside."

Fresh-poured liquor, tobacco smoke, and leather upholstery greeted them as the three found seats at the far side of the bar counter. The two girls got lost in studying the cocktail menu. Caroline bumped Emilee's elbow, whispering, "*What* are you going to order?"

"Tequila sunrise."

"It sounds like a breakfast drink."

Douglas laughed. "It would be wiser not to start with that in the morning."

"Well, it's healthy. Got tons of orange juice in it," Emilee replied.

Caroline continued whispering, "You never drink. Where did you learn all this about cocktails?"

"I did some research before we came, in the school library."

"You learned about mixing cocktails in our *school* library?"

"One only needs to know *where* to look."

They were thirsty from the swim, and Emilee finished her first sunrise with three gulps. She immediately ordered a second one and downed it on the spot. Caroline sipped on her first one with caution. Douglas said nothing as he nursed his drink, his hooded eyes resting on them.

"*Wow*! I can feel the orange juice *surging* through my veins," Emilee said.

Douglas raised his brow, and Caroline touched her hand. "That's not the orange juice you're feeling. Slow down."

Emilee bubbled over, "Oh no, Carrie, I am filling up with vitamin C," and she laughed with unfamiliar abandon.

They sipped in silence for several minutes, but as soon as the tequila and vitamin C found equilibrium inside her, Emilee turned in her high seat, all sweet and nice. "What exactly are you doing on the Windsor Castle, Douglas Harding?"

"I chaperone unescorted young ladies from the Cape of Good Hope all the way to Southampton and deliver them in one piece to the doorstep of her Royal Majesty."

Emilee snorted in her drink. "Douglas, you Philistine! Not only are you a stalker, you are a charlatan." She turned toward Caroline. "See why I need to be hard on him?"

Douglas laughed and clinked their glasses. "I've been employed on this Royal Mail Ship for the past twelve months. I started as a cleaner in the dining hall, which I didn't enjoy. I got to meet all the passengers, but they all, especially the young ladies, took me as a fool because of my low status. I transferred to the printing shop, where I am now the first assistant, my day job, and I *love* it."

"And first printing assistant has status?" Emilee asked.

He pulled up his shoulders. "I enjoy it."

"And what is your other job?" Caroline asked.

"Oh, that is my chaperone portfolio, my extracurricular activity, from after work till I start again the next morning. But I don't charge for the service. It's free."

Both girls turned scarlet.

"That's not what I *meant!*"

Emilee jumped off her chair, "We've heard *enough*. Carrie, let's go. He's indeed a charlatan. Thanks for the drinks, Mr. Harding. Please excuse us." Emilee took Caroline by the arm and they made for the exit.

Douglas was quicker and bolted ahead of them. "Ladies, that was *unfair!* I said nothing improper. I was pulling your legs. You act as if I run an undercover white slave-trade business on this mail liner."

Emilee pouted her lips. "For all we know, you do."

"Let's at least finish our drinks," he pleaded.

"My friend feels I've had enough," Emilee said.

"Remember that it's not water, and sip it slower," he said.

The girls took their time to return to their drinks at the bar counter and slipped back onto their seats, eying their companion with suspicion, not touching their cocktails.

He threw his arms up in mock surrender. "Why are you guys glaring at me like that?"

Emilee jumped up again, this time with her drink in hand. "There's an open table in the back. Come along."

Once they sat down, she downed her third drink with little hesitation, hiccupped twice, and giggled. She leaned forward in an unhurried fashion and murmured, "Douglas Harding, did you think just because we wear bell-bottom jeans and our hair all long and wavy that you could bring us here, get us all tipsy, and then make love to us?"

Caroline gasped. Douglas choked on his drink.

"Make *love*?" he whispered, still coughing.

"Yes, Douglas, have intercourse with us—one after the other. I can see you are young, fit, and trim. You could do that."

Douglas Harding was pale when he stood up, keeping his voice down. "Is that what you want?"

"No, Douglas," Emilee said, "that's what you were hoping for. Two for the trouble of one."

Although she had temporarily lost her tact and sensibility, she was still able to read his expression, witnessing the extent of his turmoil. She immediately regretted her words. Not once since they'd met (even in the most awkward fashion on the hallway floor when she'd run him over) had she found him staring at her in a gawking or lusting fashion, undressing her with his eyes, as many of the other males on the vessel had done with both her and Caroline. Although, he had openly demonstrated an interest in her, which was, she realized now, an appreciation of her unbound spirit, of her fearless honesty.

His eyes and mouth showed the unexpected hurt: a mixture of shock and disappointment, but also a declaration of hope that he was not wrong in his initial assessment of her character. Those fleeting expressions confirmed his noble intent: that he was innocent of what she had accused him—the betrayal was all hers.

"Miss Emilee, you're not used to alcohol, to cocktails for that matter, and definitely not on an empty stomach." Douglas's voice was hushed. "You're probably a little drunk. Why would I want to make love to you? Sorry, that came out wrong. You are both alluring females, two exceptionally gifted individuals, and I was . . . ." He blushed, coughed, and continued.

"A man can dream—but that was not my intention. I thought you were *different* from all the other girls on the ship who only care about fancy nails and designer clothes and five-course meals and copulating. They don't make love—they have nothing between their ears. I thought you were of a class apart. You have such a fresh and effervescent spirit. I was wrong. *Excuse me*, ladies."

He bowed and stormed from the smoking room.

CHAPTER 3

A storm in the Atlantic Ocean. 8 December 1969

CAROLINE BOLTED UPRIGHT and implored her friend to meet her eyes. "I don't need to tell you—that was low. Shameful. I give you a formal time-out. I'm going for a long walk outside. Don't try and follow me. I do *not* want to see you, and I do *not* want to talk to you. I only want to see you *once* you're truly sorry."

Emilee jumped up, her eyes wet. "Carrie, don't go . . . I'm sorry . . . ."

"No, you're not! Sorry comes too easy for you. I am extremely upset with you. You're more than a little drunk. Ask the barman to help you with a black coffee." She marched out without looking back.

Caroline followed the railing toward the stern, glad to escape the stale confines of the smoke room. The wind gusted round the superstructure, taking her by surprise, billowing her clothes; it forced her to cling to the railing. *This stupid long hair.* She lurched into a doorway, pulled the hair out of her face, and knotted it into a ponytail before grabbing the railing again. *Just imagine if I had a dress and platform shoes on. I'll show Emilee. I'll finish my walk. I need some distance from her.* She went down a set of stairs and had difficulty telling where the dark sea ended and where the gray skies began.

She wasn't certain for whom she felt the most sympathy: for Douglas, for herself, or for Emilee. She hauled herself along, struggled against the wind, and moved with the roll of the ship. *And they boasted about those stabilizers down below!*

Only during their last year in Waterloo House, the hostel at Wynberg Girls High, did they receive half a glass of wine each, on three separate occasions, and once at a wedding, when they had champagne. She realized now how pitiful and inadequate the parental and adult educators' guidance had been in all things men: falling in love, relationships, marriage, making love . . . contraception.

The word *sex* was seldom used. It was hushed—referred to but seldom uttered. The same went for smoking, alcohol, and recreational drugs, believing it would suffice to inform them, "Ladies of good upbringing abstained from such things, since it destroys lives." As if that would be good enough.

Emilee's parents still worked in the Caprivi in Namibia, so she had spent every weekend in the hostel, except for the few compulsory weekends out, when she would stay with Caroline's folks.

Limited. That was the extent of their knowledge and exposure to alcohol—and to boys. The few times she had tumbled around with them, the farthest they'd ever got was to fondle her breasts. She never allowed their hands *down there*.

She liked the Harding boy. He was more than sweet. To use his own word, he was *different*. In spite of the unruly wind that tugged at her, she found herself glowing as she thought about the first printing assistant on the *Windsor Castle*. He wasn't a stalker, only a tenacious young man. She liked that. She was so ready to fall in love with such a man—someone who cared.

She was certain Douglas had taken the trouble to print the extra menus for their sole benefit, at great risk to himself, if only to impress them. She could still smell the fresh printers' ink when he handed her the menus. Their fingers had touched for the briefest of moments, sending a current through her—it gave her goose bumps all over again.

Wake up, Caroline! He did it for your friend, before he realized she had a two-forked tongue. Now he will have nothing to do with either of us. We've barely been on this liner for twenty-four hours and already we've sunk to the bottom of the popularity list.

In the five minutes she had been outside, the wind had increased in force, and she had to pay attention and guard each step. Every second step, a spray of seawater rained down on her. She licked her lips. The saltwater stung. Gone was the nauseating odor of the harbor and docks in Cape Town.

Her path became slippery fast. The railing and deck were as if coated with soap. She lost her footing once. Then a second time. *Emilee will be the death of me. But I am not ready to go back.* She passed a pair of deckhands dressed in orange oilskins. They were tying down some of the big ropes on deck and securing everything around it. They mock-saluted her, pointed toward the ominous grayness above them, then pointed below. They yelled something at her. The wind stole their words.

"Excuse me?" she hollered back.

"*Back!* . . . You should turn back . . . Inside . . . ." She lip-read.

One of them shuffled across and was slammed into the railing next to her. Once he regained his balance, he grasped her by her upper arm. She was surprised by his immediacy and physicality and tried to yank her arm free. He smiled at her but held tight and yelled close to her ear. She smelled his hot breath and inhaled his oilskins and sweating torso. His lips brushed her ear. "Storm coming . . . Let me help you . . . This wind . . . Not your friend."

He refused to let go of her arm and helped her work her way back, both of them clinging to the railing until they reached an outside door where she could slip in. He held the door steady against the wind and tugged her inside. She was surprised how immediately quiet it was in the hallway—safe and warm and dry.

"You'll be fine now, Miss. Just follow the hallway all the way to the center of the vessel."

"Thank you," Caroline piped.

The sailor grinned at her, gave a half-salute, and, with an almost inaudible "Ma'am," disappeared back into the storm. She pushed the door tight behind him.

Caroline leaned against the steel bulkhead to catch her breath. She was cold. *Too bad about the wet blouse. I am not returning to our cabin. I'm not ready to face Emilee.*

Setting off at a brisk pace, she hoped to warm herself with the walk but had to slow down. Like-minded passengers, all forced indoors by the storm, congested the hallways and stairs. The temptation for a bite became overwhelming when the aroma of fresh bread wafted from the gulley. *It will have to wait until Operation Bridge is completed.*

She rubbed her arms as she clambered the stairs and waited outside the door, shivering, peering inside.

Most of the bridge was visible. Officers and crew moved about with purpose, adjusting instruments and devices. No one noticed her. The glow of embarrassment crept up her neck. *What were you thinking, Miss Washington? That you're still an eight-year-old whom the captain will show around as a treat?*

As she turned to leave, the door slid open and a man asked, "Can I help you, Miss?"

She spun around, her face glowing. *This man is even more handsome than Mr. Harding.* The arctic white uniform suited him. He was too young to be the captain—perhaps one day.

"Miss?"

"Oh yes, I . . . wanted to see the bridge."

He hesitated, and the hint of a smile appeared as he stood back. "Sure, but you won't be able to stay long. With the storm brewing, things are hectic around here. By the way, I am the third radio operator." He gave her an amused look over. "It seems you have already tasted the tail end of the storm?"

She touched her wet hair and followed his gaze, regretting having chosen a white silk blouse that morning. Her nipples strained dark against the now-transparent, damp fabric. She clasped her arms across her chest and met his eyes until he looked away with a smirk, then followed him around the bridge, not hearing a single word he said. She prayed the churning sea would swallow her.

The trance only broke when he introduced her to the helmsman, who asked, "Would you like to spin the wheel, Miss?"

Mesmerized, she nodded and took hold of the large wheel, clutching it in a death grip. "Does *this* steer the ship?"

"Indeed, ma'am. Why don't you relax your grip and give it a spin?"

"Spin it?"

"Yes, ma'am." He showed her and she spun it.

Emilee would never believe that she had steered their colossal vessel during the storm. The third RO then showed her the intricacies of the radiotelephone, the gyro compass, and the radar monitor, as well as the functions of the multitude of dials against the one wall, but she was still navigating the RMS *Windsor Castle* through a storm in the Atlantic, off the coast of South West Africa, with a crew of 475 and some 821 passengers depending on her—Captain Caroline Washington—set on a course, north by northwest.

CHAPTER 4

Doing penance.

THE ACT OF penance should not be undervalued, my child. Caroline recalled her grandmother's words of last summer when they kneaded dough side by side in her kitchen. Then she had added, *But the punishment should not be worse than the transgression, and never throw away the key.*

Thank you, *Ouma*, for making *me* feel guilty.

Caroline had returned to their cabin, finding it empty. She rushed through a shower and changed into dry clothes. *Miss Emilee is playing the martyr game, forcing me to go look for her.*

She found Emilee sitting at a different table, in the corner of the smoking room, with three empty coffee cups in front of her. Emilee cringed and whimpered—a pathetic mess.

"*What* are you still doing here?"

"I'm doing penance," was Emilee's meek response.

"By hiding in a bar, drinking black coffee?" Caroline squeezed her friend's shoulder only to jerk her arm away. "You're *drenched*. Why did *you* go into the storm?"

Emilee's shoulders shook as she glanced at her friend, her hand clasped over her mouth to silence her sobs. She shivered uncontrollably.

"Poor *thing*." Caroline swooped in and cradled her friend, pulling her upright. "*What* happened? Let's get you out of these wet clothes."

She gripped Emilee's shoulders and pulled her along, waving at the barman as they left.

"No need to cry. Douglas will survive the insult—he's a big boy. *Enough* of this self-pity. You need a warm shower."

Emilee was inconsolable as Caroline steered her from the aft deck inside and down hallway after hallway.

"Why did you *follow* me on deck?"

Emilee shook her head, trying to catch her breath. "I tried to get away from this man in the bar. I ordered a fourth sunrise after you left when this asshole joined me."

"Why didn't you call the barman?"

"I was embarrassed. We were both a little drunk. He was witty when he sat down, but then he started gawking down my shirt, making all kinds of vulgar suggestions."

Caroline unlocked their cabin door, pulled her shivering friend inside, kicked the door closed, and peeled Emilee's wet clothes from her.

Emilee wept louder as she allowed her friend to steer her into the soon-steaming shower, her teeth chattering. "I ran off. I couldn't think clear . . . just to get away from him."

"*Here*, take the shampoo." Caroline passed the container around the shower curtain. She averted her eyes. She had to maintain an illusion of modesty. It was irrelevant that she had seen her friend unclothed before and that she had undressed her now.

"The bastard followed me onto deck and then *groped* me."

"Didn't you cry for help?"

Steamed filled the small room. Emilee poked her head around the curtain. "You were outside—it was useless. The storm gave him perfect cover." She laughed through her sobs. "But I hit him."

"That's my girl!"

"He held on and fondled my—"

"Did he touch . . . ?"

Emilee yanked the curtain open for her friend to see.

Caroline gasped. Her friend's chest was nine inches from her face. Both nipples were engorged and sienna-red from the steaming water. She had always been jealous of her friend's perfect bosom—not too big, not too small. Two flawless peaks. Bruises the shape of deft fingers marred the left globe.

"The *bastard!*" Caroline whispered.

"He wouldn't let go. I hit him again. He was so strong. Held me from behind, kissed my neck, and shoved his hand inside my jeans. He hollered something that sounded like 'teach you a lesson.'"

Emilee spun back into the shower, her chest heaving as she let the curtain fall in place. She sobbed louder behind the plastic drape.

"Did he . . . did he manage . . . ?"

"The ship rolled and caught him off balance. That's when I struck him a third time, this time between his legs, and shoved him into the railing. I escaped and raced back to the smoke room."

"He didn't go overboard?"

Emilee shook her head. "He was down on his knees when I left him."

"Will you recognize him? Was he a passenger or crew member?"

Emilee turned the water off, stepped out, and allowed Caroline to wrap a towel around her. She shook her head and whispered, "I don't know. He had civilian clothes on . . . I think."

Once Emilee was dressed, Caroline made her sit down in their only chair, grabbed a second towel, and rubbed her hair down. "The *scoundrel*. We'll *hunt* him down. Douglas must help us. We'll go see the Captain. He can—"

"The Captain will *laugh* at me. I was *drunk*."

"Drunk doesn't mean you said yes."

Emilee took the towel and faced her friend. "I was such a fool—baring my inexperience with liquor for the whole world to witness. I embarrassed you, my dearest friend. I must have mortally wounded Douglas Harding. And I became an easy prey for that drunken jerk. I'm certain Douglas never wants to see me or speak to me again."

"*Nonsense.* It was a misunderstanding. I told you, he's a big boy. Let's go find him—he's a decent man. He'll listen. And, we must tell him about the guy who assaulted you."

Emilee clambered to her feet. "I'll apologize to him, but not tonight." Her lower lip trembled; her eyes brimmed. "I'm not ready to tell Douglas about the groper. He'll then lose *all* his respect for me."

It was late afternoon on December the eleventh, and the peace between Mr. Harding and Miss Stephens still had to be made. The latter found a reason (or fabricated one, according to her roommate) on a daily basis for three consecutive days not to visit the printing shop. In her defense though, it was noticed that since they'd left port in Table Bay, at least once a day, sometimes even twice, Miss Emilee was seen hanging over the railing retching (or over the sides of the hand basin in their cabin), her complexion mint-tinged, struggling to find harmony between her empty innards and the incessant rolling, heaving, and dipping of the *Windsor Castle*, stabilizers in spite.

Emilee refused to say a word further about the man who had assaulted her on deck. She refused that they report the incident to the Captain or port authorities.

Caroline felt compassion for her friend. When they had crossed the imaginary line in the ocean that morning, leaving the South and entering the North, the realization dawned on them of the infinite distance that had been put between them and their families. The sea journey was all excitement on the surface, but at night in their berths, when neither of them could sleep, they would listen to the hum of the engines, taking them farther away from where it was safe and familiar, and closer to the vast unknown.

That Thursday afternoon, Caroline cornered her friend in the coral lounge. There would be no further excuses or procrastination tolerated. Seasick or not, peace had to be made.

"Emilee, you broke a promise."

"I don't know what you're talking about. Please let me pass."

"No, not until I receive a solemn undertaking from you."

A light blush crept into Emilee's face. "He'll refuse to speak to me."

"You didn't commit a crime. He didn't think what he was saying, and you got the tequila to speak on your behalf." Caroline then leaned forward and pressed down on her friend's shoulders, forcing her to sit.

Caroline lowered her voice. "You never told me. Did you secretly hope Douglas would take us to our cabin afterwards and have sex with us—well, at least with one of us? He definitely likes us." She giggled and turned crimson as she leaned closer.

Emilee's blush intensified. She mimicked their headmistress's voice. "Miss Washington, it is unbecoming for a young lady of your class and upbringing to have such carnal thoughts."

"You didn't answer my question."

"Caroline, he's a beautiful young man, but it would have been wrong. We're not married. You know that."

"I don't know anymore. Douglas is not like the other boys—it might have been different." Caroline gave a longing sigh.

Emilee took her friend's hands, held them tight, and kissed both. She was relieved that Caroline could not read her own confused mind, which at that moment had longings all of its own. She was longing for someone strong and lithe who would fall in love with her. She blushed again when she thought of the word Douglas had used—*copulating*—that had so little meaning. She needed commitment. A special person who would love her, hold her, without hurting her. She was so scared for a man to touch her again, touch her *there*. Her secret place was not to be taken by force—only to be given by her.

She pulled the now-standing Caroline closer and hugged her. *My dear, dear friend.* This someone would have to take great care—be a master of patience. But it wouldn't be Douglas.

"*You* fancy him." Emilee stated the obvious.

"It's *not* true."

"Miss Washington, you have my blessing."

"What are you talking about? Come, enough babbling. We have to go find him and get you to make peace."

They reached the printing shop without another word.

"Go inside," Caroline urged.

"Come with me." She took Caroline's hand. The smell of printer's ink and freshly cut paper was overwhelming inside the compact shop.

They asked to speak to "first printing assistant Douglas Harding."

A gentle cough behind them made both girls jump and turn around. The first printing assistant didn't say a word.

"Douglas," Emilee started.

Caroline slipped past her. "I'll wait outside."

Emilee met his gaze. "I apologize for what I said the other day in the smoking room. I must have hurt you."

He laughed. "My sensitive ego has recovered."

"You must think I'm a heartless wench."

"Many guys would have taken that as an open invitation. I was intrigued by your fire and your overwhelming innocence."

Emilee held out her hand. "Can we be friends again?"

He transferred the pages in his hands and shook her hand. "Friends."

She stood on tiptoes and planted a kiss on his cheek without letting go of his hand. He gave her a quick hug before she stepped back.

"Miss Emilee, don't ever change." He swallowed. "Here are two copies of tomorrow's program, with my compliments."

"Thank you, *Mr. Darling*," she giggled as she slipped out.

CHAPTER 5

Las Palmas, en route to Southampton. 14 December 1969.

IT CAME AS no great surprise that Douglas Harding was entrusted with the responsibility of unofficial tour guide for their day visit to *Las Palmas* on the Canary Islands. Since a peace deal had been reached on the eleventh, he spent most of his time after work in the company of both Caroline and Emilee—perhaps more time with Caroline. He had little trouble in convincing them that his private tour of the town would by far overshadow the official outing planned by the entertainment group on Her Majesty's mail liner. As a bonus, if they got lost, he even knew a few Spanish words.

Douglas completed his commitments in the printing shop in advance, making it possible for him to stand at the railing between the two girls as the RMS *Windsor Castle* approached the middle island of the archipelago. Tucked over his shoulder was a substantial knapsack filled with items for a picnic, which he had obtained from his contact in the gulley. His mission for the day was to please.

The early sun was at their backs as the liner approached the harbor. The highest point of the island, a naked gray mountain, towered a thousand feet behind the city. On the short strip of beach, early walkers waved at them as the ship navigated past the marina, which was spread open like a giant fishbone, with anchored boats bobbing in the ship's tidal wave on their way to the pier.

"*Look*. The houses!" Caroline called out, pointing.

Behind the scattered businesses and apartment buildings of the city center, close to the harbor, were clusters of houses that covered the foothills, all in soft yellows, whites, beiges, pinks, blues, and earth tones.

"*Bienvenidos a Las Palmas, señoritas!*" Douglas said, arms around their shoulders, planting kisses on their cheeks.

They both stuck their tongues out at him. "Jolly good for an Englishman," Emilee muttered.

He bowed as he took their hands. "Come, ladies. Not a minute to be wasted. We've got twelve hours."

They had barely stepped forward when he halted them. "A moment, Emilee. What's in that shoulder bag of yours? It's stuffed to the brim."

She pulled her hand free. "How dare you? It's none of a gentleman's business what a lady has in her bag. Girlfriend?"

"If you *do* have to know, we followed your instructions and packed swimming attire and accessories," Caroline said. She pressed her wide-brimmed hat firmer on her head as the wind picked up.

"Last one on dry land is a sailor with a wooden leg," Emilee called out as she dashed forward.

The two girlfriends soon discovered that flattery could persuade their tour guide to deviate from his rigid plan. Despite

Douglas's effort to explain that now was not the time, the girls wouldn't hear of it; they had to walk barefoot on the small beach next to the marina. Ankle-deep in the surf, they chased each other and the odd gull that ventured too close. The overbearing stench of a busy harbor was absent. They basked in the gentle scents of rotten seaweed, sand, shells, and crushed crustaceans.

After half an hour of running, laughing, and shoving one another in the shallow water, they were salt-sprayed and part wet and dropped down on the low wall at the beach's end. Douglas pointed at the sun and then at his watch, but the girls shook their heads, leaned forward, and kissed him.

It was time for breakfast; the contents of the knapsack would be kept for lunch. Democracy ruled in the choice of a street café. They found an eating house one street up.

"How much farther do we have to walk up this hill to go look at a stupid old church, *Señor* Harding?" Emilee complained soon after they had stepped off the bus, following breakfast at the harbor.

"Come on. You can already see its spires through the trees and palms."

"I need a rest, Mr. Harding. My heart is pounding." She sat down on the low wall to the side of the sidewalk at the last turnoff toward the San Juan Bautista Cathedral.

Caroline joined her in the shade. "Rest with us." She beckoned their guide.

"We'll rest at the church." Douglas remained standing.

For a moment, their sore feet and the steep hill were forgotten as the three friends drank in the panorama.

"It's like *home*," Emilee muttered, waving at the banana plantations, the palm trees, and the bougainvillea, which flanked them on all sides.

It was impossible not to hear the fondness with which she spoke of her birthplace. She told them about Katima Molilo in the Caprivi. She told them about the young friends she'd had at the Mission school. She told them about her parents, who were teachers, then went quiet.

Caroline squeezed her hand. "Tell him about the drunk on the ship."

Emilee caught her breath as she clung to her friend's hand, swearing her friend to silence with her eyes. She shook her head and jumped to her feet, forcing a laugh. "Enough. Let's go see this *glorious* cathedral."

They walked around the imposing building with its innumerable gray spires, stone columns, and column heads, arches, and lead-glass windows. At the front were two solid wooden doors with thirteen steps, and, at the back, two identical doors with only three steps. The doors were all locked.

Emilee raised her hand. "Permission to speak, Mr. Tour Guide."

Douglas laughed.

"Shall we fire you as our guide because we took all the trouble to walk up the mountain to get here only to find the doors locked, or should we kiss you out of gratitude?"

He bowed. "You decide."

"Shame on you, even if we can only look from the outside. It's *gorgeous*," Caroline quipped.

"It's *ugly*. It's depressing and drab. An almost *black* building," Emilee said.

"It was built from local *Arucas* stone. That's why it's black. It's a pity we can't go in," Douglas remarked.

"It's a blessing. Can we go *back* now?" Emilee asked.

She turned around and took a few steps toward the narrow street. "There's the harbor! I can see the *Windsor Castle* and the ocean." She ran and jumped on the single bench and beckoned Caroline to join her, gesturing toward the sea.

The two friends clung to each other, balancing on the bench, eyes glued to the harbor.

"*Thank you*, Mr. Darling!"

"We aim to please, Miss Emilee."

The bus took them back toward an ocean-fronting street a block higher than the harbor road where they'd had breakfast. They would have their picnic lunch in a small town square while watching the *Jota* dancers.

The pulsing Latin music reached the trio as they followed a narrow street leading toward the square. They snatched the last open table at the very back, their eyes on the dancing couples who swayed their hips and arms in time to the music: step-step, clap-clap, and turn and turn. A male band member sang his song to Emilee in unintelligible but very sad-sounding Spanish. She and Caroline soon stood up, moved behind their stools, and mimicked the dancers, swaying and clapping and turning with the rhythm.

Emilee whispered to Douglas, "If we borrowed you one of the men's outfits, will you join us dancing here in the square?"

"You expect me to dance in a white kilt, puffed sleeves, and a waistcoat in this heat?"

"You're British. You must have worn a kilt before, and we promise there will be no bagpipes in the band. Only guitars, lutes, and castanets," Caroline coaxed.

"Then I'll have to teach you the difference between a Scotsman and an Englishman."

"Promise you'll spare us that," Emilee pleaded.

"As you wish. But keep in mind, in three days' time, once you set foot on British soil, you'll be confronted with a bigger dilemma: What's the difference between a Scotsman, an Englishman, *and* an Irishman?"

As both girls stuck their tongues out at him in answer, Douglas grinned and excused himself to find them something cold to drink.

An hour later, when the folk dancers took a break, the three friends sauntered down a different street to catch a bus to their last stop, a visit to the *Las Canteras* beach.

They paused under the king palms on the beach walkway to find a vacant spot on the vast collection of sand. The beach stretched endlessly in each direction, wide, level, and white, running into a tranquil surf, the sun blinding on the wet zone touching the water. Hundreds of sun seekers armed with beach chairs and umbrellas in red, yellow, and blue, were scattered across the hot sand.

Once they found a spot, the girls slipped out of their wraparounds, ready for the water. They'd already changed into their bathing suits earlier that day.

"Coming *with* us, Douglas?" Emilee called.

"Not quite yet. Run along. I'll join you later."

He propped himself up on the beach chair and took his notebook and pencil from his bag. His eyes did not leave the figures of his two companions who made their way toward the foaming surf, their bikinis hugging their lithe figures. He sighed and started writing, searching for his friends every few minutes. He joined them an hour later after their tenth attempt to lure him into the water.

Hours later, all sunburnt, sanded, and windblown, they sat on the stairs leading up the beach walkway, each licking an ice cream. Their contentment was difficult to hide.

Caroline leaned back, craning her neck. "Will you show us what you wrote, Douglas?"

His smile waned. "It's not much. Really."

"Douglas, come on," Emilee said. "You write in that notebook every spare *minute*. Will you *one day*, when you're ready?"

"When I'm ready."

CHAPTER 6

—∿—

Southampton. 17 December 1969

THEY STOOD AT the starboard railing facing the European mainland, where the promise of daylight had already arrived, as the *Windsor Castle* entered the English Channel. They were off the coast of France, having steered between the outskirts of the Celtic Sea in the north and the Bay of Biscay to the south.

Emilee had required little coaxing to get Caroline to join her on deck. Their two-berth cabin with its punishing bunk beds, their haven of the past ten days, had become too confined. They hadn't slept well, as on so many nights before, despite having grown used to the humming and rolling of the ship as it stayed its course.

It was their last day on board, which was reason enough to cherish the remaining hours. As the girls waited for day to break, so did they also wait for their friend from the printing office, who had promised to observe the sunrise with them. They voiced their discontent with the unreliability of men, and printing assistants specifically, when he showed up behind them, making them shriek in surprise.

"You're *late*," was Emilee's chilled response.

"It's only *starting* to light up over the mainland," Douglas countered, giving each girl a quick kiss on the cheek.

"You're still late."

"Never mind her," Caroline crooned. "She's been miserable with me since she kicked me out of our cabin at six. It was so dark out here we had to feel our way around, *and* in this bitter cold." She hooked in with him.

"It was *quarter past six,* and you often don't know what is good for you, Missy. See how *beautiful* it is now." Emilee hooked in on his other side, trying to hide from the nip in the air. The warm temperatures of the Canaries belonged to the past.

They watched as the sun inched out above the horizon. The bow of Her Majesty's mail carrier, as if by an invisible hand, righted itself west-northwest, toward the Isle of Wight.

It was already midmorning when Douglas joined the two again at the portside railing from where more land had been sighted.

"The Isle of Wight," Douglas pointed out.

"I told you he talks funny," Emilee laughed. "Who would give an island the name *right*?"

"It's *Wight*." Douglas said. "Your *pronunciation*."

Both girls snickered. "Wight or whong, Mr. Harding?" Emilee mocked as Douglas grabbed them around their necks and wrestled their heads together.

"I predict endless suffering for both of you until you learn to speak English in a proper fashion!" Douglas called out.

Emilee, who had leaned over the railing, turned silent, then turned to her friends. "I'm scared."

"How can you be?" Douglas said. "It's going to be one marvelous adventure, an exploration of grand proportions. A whole life lies ahead of you. You're both bright and bold and gorgeous."

"Still, I'm scared," Emilee said. "I may appear brave on the surface, and I usually have an opinion on everything, but *this*—it's intimidating." She pointed toward starboard where England was approaching. She turned toward Caroline. "Do you have *any* idea how far we are from home at the moment?"

"Six thousand miles?"

Emilee lapsed into an elaborate explanation that though they were physically only separated by a mere continent-and-a-half, plus an ocean, two seas, and a bay, and, yes, the six thousand miles, the crucial thing happening to them was: they were in the process of cutting themselves off. They were being severed from their people, their families, their land, and their previous lives.

Caroline exclaimed that her friend's observation was skewed. They were severing nothing; they would always phone and write and visit by ship or plane. Nothing was going to change.

"No, Caroline," Emilee whispered. "*Nothing* will be the same—ever—it has already started."

"Welcome to our world Miss E. You're growing up." Douglas said.

"That was so heartless," Caroline cried out.

"Sorry," Douglas said. "There's no easier way to put it: grow up." He raised his hands in defense and took several steps away from them. "Please don't throw me overboard. When are your interviews? Friday morning?"

They both nodded.

"You have thirty-six hours in which to grow up."

When both girls charged at him, he sidestepped them with a chuckle, sat down on a deck chair, and beckoned them to join him.

He raised his brow. "The world you will walk into in less than two days' time demands this of you: to be mature in many things. Close your eyes and picture Shakespeare's England. Then picture the time of the Crusaders on their way to the Holy Land. Now, picture a world between those two periods. *That's* what you're walking into: the thirteenth and fourteenth centuries."

"You're such a charlatan, Harding!"

"Close your eyes, Miss Stephens!"

He continued. "You will step back into an old world, into ancient history, into a thriving community and culture that's been hundreds of years in the making, carried by centuries of Catholicism and Reformation, becoming part of a living history. You will become part of the past yourself, and, at the same time, write a new history, with modern paraphernalia and aids, immersed and surrounded by old institutions and traditions and hundreds of academics. And you will compete with the brightest and most ambitious individuals in the world."

Emilee groaned. "I never realized you're *that* smart, Douglas. To know all *this*." Then she croaked. "I'll never survive inside a museum, hoarded up with a bunch of Einsteins."

She jumped from the chair. "Caroline and I should go speak to the captain about taking the four p.m. mail run tomorrow on the *Windsor Castle's* sister ship out of Southampton back to Cape Town."

Douglas snickered.

"Before it's too *late*," Emilee groaned.

"Shame on you, Harding. You dreamed this all up to unnerve us!" Caroline called out. "One could swear you've been there yourself."

"I think you've been *lying* to us all this time," Emilee said.

As they wrestled him off his deck chair, he was quick to point out that he had an older half-sister who had studied there in the mid-sixties and who had spared him no small detail about her university experiences.

"Remember," Douglas said, catching his breath, "during the interviews on Friday, they have already been briefed on your academic ability, but they are dying to know what your academic potential is. They need to know whether you will *do* great things—especially generate money and enhance the reputation of the institution, one day. If you can convince them of *that* and continue doing that, then you're in and will remain in. It's that simple."

"Thank you, Professor Harding," Emilee mumbled, "for such a sobering speech." She clapped her hands as she rose from her chair.

"Will you excuse me? I have to go and speak to the captain. I'm definitely taking the four p.m. out of Southampton—bound south!" Emilee turned to leave.

Both Douglas and Caroline jumped to their feet. They had learned that their friend could very well be serious.

"The captain won't allow it." Douglas said.

"Will you then take the train with us to Oxford?" Emilee pleaded.

"You don't need a babysitter."

"Come, friend. Let's go and speak to the captain concerning a return passage on Her Majesty's mail liner tomorrow afternoon. Douglas is right. We don't need a babysitter; we need a friend."

An Unfamiliar Kindness

Mr. Douglas Harding accompanied Miss Emilee Stephens and Miss Caroline Washington that same afternoon on the train from Southampton Central bound for Oxford. The journey lasted all of eighty minutes.

CHAPTER 7

Oxford at last. 17 December 1969.

WHEN THE TAXI dropped the trio off on Catte Street at the address Emilee had provided, it was almost 5:05 p.m. and completely dark. The mid-December chill immediately settled in as they found themselves next to a tower of luggage at the entrance to Hertford College. The girls were to have their interviews there, as well as find accommodation for the short term.

The moment Emilee noticed the distance from the sidewalk to the front door of the college in the anemic glare of the street lamps, she pleaded with Douglas to help them with their luggage, which consisted of only two large pieces each, she said, plus hand luggage—the extent of their earthly possessions.

He hesitated while eyeing the mountain of luggage, but she was immediately ready to remind him that they were fortunate enough that there was no snow on the ground, only the snap in the evening air. Douglas, a born and raised Brit, could but chuckle as he listened to the opinionated lass from Africa. As he maneuvered the awkward pieces along their path, she confided that she'd never seen snow in her life but had read the weather report.

Every single building was from a former era—grandiose, even in the poor light—and intimidating at the very least.

Emilee grew mute as reality set in along the path. She found herself expecting people to wear Shakespearian costumes. They had stepped into a never-ending museum it seemed. It was no longer a dream. They were walking on foreign soil. The nightmare—or was it the adventure—was about to begin. Only at the front door did she find her voice. "Are you certain it would not be *too* much trouble to meet us here on Sunday, Douglas?"

"Not at all milady," he said. "I've arranged to stay with my sister, who lives on the outskirts of town. I'll take the two of you to lunch, send you off on your way, and return to my mother in Southampton for a few days. She suffers from incurable overprotectiveness."

Emilee kissed his cheek.

He smiled. "She almost had a heart attack when I phoned her before we docked to inform her of my change in plans: that I would accompany two young ladies—damsels in distress. Charlotte, my sister, was ecstatic with the news."

"We were *not* in distress," Emilee said, "but wanted to witness, perhaps for the last time, true chivalry in action."

Douglas laughed as he hugged each girl and planted a light kiss on each one's lips. He mock-saluted them and ran down the stairs, waving.

The girls waved until their friend had disappeared down the path they'd come.

Emilee, bag in each hand, heart pounding, approached the front doors. "Come, Carrie. Let's step through the looking glass, into the Middle Ages—*if* we can believe the first printing assistant."

Since many of the students were away during Christmas break, the girls would be accommodated in Hertford College until a final decision on their acceptance was reached. They had both opted for open applications. Neither of them wished to express a preference for one particular college—better to leave that decision in the hands of the assessors, the Dons, and the administrators.

Once the lots had been cast early during the following week, as per special arrangement because they were both from overseas with scholarships, Emilee was accepted to Magdalen (pronounced *Maudlen*) College on Longwall Street. Caroline had an initial advantage: she was accepted to Hertford on Catte Street, where they were staying at the moment.

If they were surprised at what they found inside once they crossed the doorstep, neither let on. The centuries-old, wood-paneled hallway, oiled to dark perfection, reflected the scant light falling through lead-glass windows. Their relief showed when they encountered young ladies, students their own age, dressed similarly to themselves, who immediately lent a hand with their luggage. One helped them locate the administrative assistant, who was expecting them.

She put them up for the night after a light meal. The fine print would be inked out first thing the next morning.

Hours later, alone in their room, they enjoyed the gift of proper beds solidly planted on an unmoving floor in the mansion-like dormitory. There was little concern of knocking their heads against steel bulkheads.

Emilee waited, almost longing to hear the groan of steel walls with each roll of the hull. It would take time to get used to this absolute silence and lack of movement. She watched as the moon, unhurried, shifted across the room with bands of pale light. She recalled seeing Father and Mother, on the wharf in Table Bay, her parents standing next to Caroline's family. The white of Mother's handkerchief was the one thing she could still see long after their respective greetings became unintelligible. The handkerchief became a gesture, a beacon, a white speck of surrender. Overwhelmed by the finality of her departure, it bored down on her with unexpected force.

She shifted in her bed. The pressure in her chest made breathing hard. The faraway *one day* had arrived, mind-numbing and ferocious.

Emilee glanced at their room. She was covered in goose bumps. *What a strange place. A museum, a palace and a monastery, all in one—and we're expected to live here. Improbable.*

"Friend?" she whispered. "I don't think I'll be able to sleep. My heart is pounding. Today was so—"

"Unparalleled," Caroline muttered.

"You read my mind. Can I wiggle in beside you?"

As soon as she heard her friend move over, Emilee carried her pillow and nestled in. The curtains weren't pulled. Moonlight now stroked the foot of the bed—ample light to read faces in. Their smiles said enough. Words were obsolete.

Emilee huddled against her friend with whom she'd shared half a decade.

She strained and listened to the sounds of the ancient English town, cocking her ears for anything familiar, for friendly sounds. All she heard, as did Caroline, was the thumping of their own hearts. Emilee jumped when an owl hooted nearby.

Far away in a tower, a bell chimed the hour.

"I'm not scared, only cold," she murmured, as she snuggled and spooned with her friend until sleep stole them away.

43

CHAPTER 8

Oxford University. January 1970.

MUCH TO EMILEE'S surprise and less so to Caroline's, it required more than a week to fall into the rhythm of college life. Since they resided in different colleges, they vowed to see each other, if not during the week, then on every Saturday and Sunday. They faithfully kept this schedule for the full extent of their first years at Oxford, each time savoring the camaraderie and kinship they were accustomed to and craved.

As Emilee discovered on her fifth morning of waking up in her room at Magdalen while it was still night outside—a light tapping on her door and a muffled voice calling her name had woken her—it was possible to overcommit. As she fumbled for the door, she wondered how wise it had been to join every club and society on campus based on falling in love with its name and mission statement. It was 5:50 a.m., the second week of January. She opened the door for Emma Davis, her coach and slave driver for the next hour.

They had to be in the gym and ready at 6:00 a.m. Since she was a novice, Emilee had to learn and master the basics of proper rowing on an indoor machine, as per the rowing coach. "We will have to build up your condition, Miss Stephens," she'd said when

An Unfamiliar Kindness

Emilee had joined the Magdalen College women's rowing club three days earlier. "And, it will require hard work."

She was supposed to row for forty-five minutes in the gym and only *then* go down to the boathouse, where she could get a feel for and see the coxed eight fine boat in action, depending on outdoor conditions.

Emma was the assistant coach who had taken it upon herself to instruct Emilee and another newcomer, Rachel Lloyd, on the essentials of rowing on dry land. Four-and-a-half minutes later, Emilee joined the other two down the hallway, at Rachel's room. They had a minute to spare by the time they'd reached the rowing machines. The head coach held strong beliefs about punctuality and commitment, especially in her absence.

"Remember girls, rowing is not pulling with your arms," Emma Davis said as they clipped their feet into place.

"Rowing is using your *legs* and your *body*," Emilee finished her sentence.

Rachel laughed.

"Exactly, Miss Stephens. Let's see whether you paid any attention yesterday. I want to see those backs remain straight during the drive as well as the recovery phase. Enough talking."

It was still five degrees Celsius when they went down to the boathouse close to seven that morning. A solid mist had settled on the water as the darkness shifted. Still glowing from the indoor rowing, they were unconcerned by the crispness of the morning as they blindly peered into the twirling fog.

Emilee still had to learn: Oxford fog had a distinct savor.

They required only ears to see where the boat was. The catch of blades in the water mixed with the coxswain's monotone wafted toward them, guiding their eyes. They huddled on the dock, listening to the sound of ghosts approaching.

—⚏—

Emilee found it difficult to explain how she had stumbled upon the suffrage campaign of the nineteenth and twentieth centuries. It happened in the last week of January, during one of her daily library reading sessions in preparation for her Victorian literature tutorial. She believed in destiny. "The plight of women in society—" She clasped her mouth once she noticed the look of disapproval from nearby library users. She must have uttered something illegal.

They—women—weren't taken seriously. Over the centuries they had been shunned and forced into the shadows of their male counterparts, always to be reminded of the lowly status of their inferior sex, as if they were cursed, secondhand citizens simply for being born female. No, she realized—not *they—us—us, women.* Oh, the injustice!

At the first opportunity the next day, when she saw her classmate Tracy Russell, she shared her epiphany.

Tracy only laughed. "Today it is called the Women's Liberation Movement, the 'second wave feminism.' Why don't you join me next month? The movement has a weekend conference at Ruskin College. It's the college behind the John Radcliffe Hospital. It may change your life."

Emilee had difficulty waiting until Saturday when she would visit with Caroline to share her latest passion. She loved the sound and feel of the word on her tongue and, above all, its meaning. *Suffrage.* Every spare minute she had that week was invested in additional research on the first wave feminist movement. She had little doubt that Caroline would be as fascinated, especially with her future heading into jurisprudence. The movement could definitely benefit from a supporter to rewrite the laws of the land one day, giving women more legal protection and a push toward a more balanced and fair society.

They caught the nine-to-five bus that took them across the Thames to a coffee shop near the railway station, where they were to meet Douglas Harding at ten. It was the first time they would see him since the Sunday before Christmas.

"Emilee," Caroline said, "how is it *possible* that you found the time for additional research on women's conundrums during the previous century? Don't you have ten books to read every month? *And* you have committed to the six-mornings-a-week rowing schedule. I fear for you. To think I promised your parents I would look out for you."

"Girlfriend," Emilee laughed, "it's a wonderful roller coaster! Not a minute of my day is wasted. Doesn't it move you—the plight of women in society? Roll the phrase on your tongue: the *plight.*"

"You fell in love with an idea. It's only a novel concept. If you allow yourself to be distracted this much, you might soon experience the *personal plight* of Emilee Stephens and *not* that of the poor women in society. You do remember the *conditions* of our scholarships? You sound like a *philosophy* major and not an English literature student."

"My dear Miss Washington, *thou* fret too much. I'm up to date with *all* my tutorials." She jumped up, almost knocking her cup over. "Douglas is outside." She gulped her coffee. "I'll go get him."

Each girl received a solid hug and a kiss on each cheek before Douglas took the remaining chair. He complimented them on their striking appearances, an indication that college life was not as overwhelming as he had feared; although, they did need some sun. Their sickly pallor was cause for great concern.

"Mr. Harding, you don't look too shabby yourself. You even smell nice. But you *remain* a charlatan. Sickly pallor. *You* had the good fortune of spending a week basking in Cape Town's summer weather on your land pass before returning to the Isles, and now you dare lecture us." Emilee laughed as she waved the waitress closer.

Once their hot drinks arrived, it did not take Emilee long before she shared her excitement about her discovery of the suffrage movement with their friend from the RMS *Windsor Castle*. Caroline sighed and rolled her eyes.

Douglas's demeanor changed as he leaned forward. "Miss Stephens, I've made you aware in the past that you are special, unique to an extreme degree." He looked at Caroline for support. "Don't tell me the Women's Libbers have made you their latest disciple."

Both girls choked on their second cups of coffee, glancing at Douglas, Caroline in pleasant surprise that she had a soul mate in the first printing assistant and Emilee in disbelief. She smelled betrayal.

"It's not a religion," she hissed.

"It's damn close. How much do you *know* about this new Women's Liberation Movement? Really know?" Douglas asked.

"Only what I've read in the library and what Tracy told me. And I don't think you can call it a movement at this stage. It might be premature. But I'm planning on attending a meeting of theirs next month. Then I will be able to fill you in." She relaxed. The relief washed over her that her friends, if they didn't share her interest, were at least sympathetic toward this newfound love of hers.

"I know a little about them," Douglas confided. "My big sis was also into it. She *was*. What they tell you and what you see is probably only the tip of an invisible colossus. I don't want your heart broken one day when you obtain clarity and see the crude gears of their big machine—when you discover all the ulterior motives."

Emilee assured him that *that* would never be the case since she had a good feeling about the whole thing. She needed the strength of such a body, such an organization, to achieve what she could never achieve as an individual.

Douglas argued that she required no organization. She was one of the most headstrong and determined individuals he had ever encountered, and he met hundreds of people every month.

Emilee shook her head. "You *don't* understand."

Her body grew rigid. She shivered, her eyes wet as she turned toward Caroline and took her hands, then looked at Douglas. "I didn't want to tell you. Someone assaulted me on the ship . . . after our disastrous meeting in the smoke room . . . after you and Caroline had left."

Douglas leaned closer. "Why didn't you tell me? A *man*? We could have—"

"I felt so ashamed." Emilee lowered her eyes. "I was drunk. I had hurt you. I dared not tell you. I believed it would heal on its own."

She clung to both her friend's hands and wept.

Douglas waited for a minute before excusing himself to find their waitress for three fresh espressos on an urgent basis. By the time the coffee arrived, Emilee was in control of her sorrow again.

Douglas moved closer and took her hands. "Did he . . . Did the man . . . ?"

Emilee shook her head. "He bruised my . . . breast." Crimson crawled up her neck as she touched her chest. She swallowed, glancing from Douglas to Caroline. "He only got his hands inside my pants, breathing down my neck."

Douglas cupped her and Caroline's hands.

They remained seated long after the coffee had grown cold. The tears on Emilee's cheeks had time to dry.

Douglas convinced them that they did not need the bus to get back across the Thames. The walk would warm them and give them more time to talk, which they did. By the time the three of them reached Hertford College, Emilee had the understanding from both her friends that they would accompany her to the February meeting of the Women's Liberation Movement.

As they passed through the college gate, Douglas turned toward his female companions. His face beamed. They would have to go to the February meeting without him. "That's the whole idea of the Women's Libbers! We, us men, are *verboten*!"

CHAPTER 9

Life in Oxford. February 1970.

Six days a week, at six in the morning, Emilee showed up in the gym without a word of complaint and got to work. She loved the discipline and reveled in her new skills. Her dream was to be promoted to a coxed eight sweep boat—a real boat. She'd do anything, *anything*, to escape the stale confines of the indoor rowing and training facility.

Once she received confirmation of being promoted to the boats from Coach Davis, it became impossible to pay attention in class. For two entire days, she had to attend classes with a straight face, pretending nothing had happened.

The night before Rachel and she were to try out the fine boat on the river with six other rowers, sleep evaded her. Her usual, packed-to-the-ceiling daily program left few idle minutes, causing her to always lapse into a coma when her head made contact with the pillow. But not that night.

She watched as the moon crawled into her room on the second floor. She always pulled the curtains aside when she turned the lights out. The bands of yellow light shifted across the furniture without bringing comfort or rest. It was hopeless. Emilee grabbed her nightgown and tiptoed toward Rachel's room. She crossed her fingers that her rowing mate would also suffer from rower's-anxiety insomnia.

A hesitant knock and a whisper followed. "Rachel . . . it's Emilee."

She had to repeat the knock.

The door opened to a darkened room, its owner remaining in the shadows. "Miss Stephens, shouldn't you be *sleeping*?" Rachel giggled and yanked her into the room.

Emilee plopped into a chair. "It's *impossible*. Any suggestions?" She couldn't see her friend's face.

"Sex would have fixed the 'can't fall asleep problem,'" Rachel murmured, "but it's out of the question—unsuitable candidates. I suggest swimming."

"Making love? . . . Excuse me . . . *Swimming*?"

Rachel chuckled. "Without any doubt—swimming—it will relax us. The swimming pool isn't locked at night. Come." She turned her bed lamp on and gathered her swimming gear. "We'll change in your room. Let's hurry. We do need *some* sleep."

Emilee did not turn the lights on in her room; the moonlight was ample, allowing them to slip out of their sleeping attire. She stared—mesmerized—as the naked Rachel changed into her bikini. She had seen Caroline before, but Rachel was different: taller, firmer.

Rachel laughed. "Hurry up!" She wrapped her towel around her as the scarlet Emilee followed.

The poolroom was empty. They dared not turn on any lights for fear of discovery. Scatterings of moonlight reached in through the window blinds. After twenty laps in fast succession, they rested on the stairs.

Emilee giggled as she stepped out, drying herself. "I believe sleep will come to me now, Miss Lloyd. Much obliged."

"Wouldn't you like to come more often? We can always come late at night for half an hour."

Soon it became their routine: go swimming at ten thirty in the evening three times a week, pushing the twenty laps to thirty, then forty, before they would eventually head back to bed.

Caroline accompanied Emilee and Tracy Russell on the last Friday evening in February to attend the opening of the Women's Liberation Movement Conference at Ruskin College. They had decided to walk. Late winter had bestowed them with a sunny ten-degree Celsius day, boosting their confidence in their light coats' ability. Emilee and Tracy chattered like starlings, constantly increasing their pace to keep up with their heated discussion of their expectations for the evening.

Caroline bit her lip as she kept up, keeping to herself, intrigued by her companion's excitement. Her enthusiasm had waned as the days passed following Emilee's emotional breakdown in the coffee shop—the day Douglas had visited. Several times that morning, she had considered phoning Emilee to excuse herself. She was willing to fake illness. In the end, loyalty to her old friend won the battle. She had few illusions of what to expect but surrendered herself to the moment. This was her gift to her friend: the evening belonged to Emilee.

Caroline, who had fallen a pace behind her friends, knew she would never tire of the town, of the narrow streets, as they headed down Dunstan Road. She had fallen in love with the place the day they had arrived. Stone walls, blackened by age, lined each property. Only the rooftops of the private homes were visible, and only if one walked on tippy-toes. Creepers and ground cover flanked the walls and sidewalks, reaching as far as the tarmac. Having left the busy streets behind, filled with tourists' and students' footsteps, it became possible to hear birdsong, a lonely turtle dove cooing and a warbler competing with a starling, or was it a blue tit?

The moment the trio crossed the doorstep to the college, the pulsing enthusiasm of the attendees swept them along. After having received colorful pamphlets detailing the evening and the remainder of the weekend, it was easy to jump in and follow the throng through the foyer and into the hall. Caroline even stopped biting her lip, fascinated by the collection of females around them, women of all ages, shapes, and sizes, and, apparently, all different levels of society.

Emilee grasped her hand as they entered the big hall. "Isn't this *incredible*, girlfriend? There must be hundreds of women here. One can *feel* the energy!" She shivered in anticipation as she clasped Caroline's shoulders, who tried to pull free.

They found seats in the middle of the meeting hall and sat down as attendees kept pouring in. The meeting started more than half-an-hour late as the overwhelmed organizers scrambled to find and carry more chairs into the hall. Their expectations had been exceeded.

Caroline craned her neck as she watched the chair-carrying volunteers—all female. She found it strange. Even at their girls-only high school, there were males on staff who performed those tasks, the hard and heavy and sometimes menial things to do—not that they were ever made to believe they were princesses. Their headmistress was too down-to-earth to promote such a fallacy. She encouraged working with one's hands, even tilling the soil, preaching that they were never too delicate to get their hands dirty. And yet—this evening was strange.

Around them, the friends could hear women whispering "historic," "unprecedented," "freedom from bondage," and such things as "an end of the era of victimization is nigh." Caroline sighed and lost count of how many times she'd rolled her eyes.

Silence settled once the chairwoman went on stage and took a position in front of the lectern with her arms raised. Caroline was reminded of their pastor back home who would spread his arms over the congregation in a similar fashion prior to giving them the benediction.

Caroline held her breath. It was clear: for Emilee, this *was* a spiritual experience. But it was wrong to feel this way outside a church building. Caroline listened as the chairwoman welcomed them, sketched their vision, and explained their *raison d'être*. She explained how over the ensuing two-and-a-half days they would look at and discuss the contemporary position of women in society. They were encouraging attendees, imploring them, actually, to question the conditions of their lives and their relationships with men, with other women, and with their children.

Caroline gawked at the enthralled Emilee, who nodded her head each time someone nearby murmured, "Oh yes," "Exactly," and "Amen to that" in response to the effervescent presentation at the lectern. The cardinal question according to the speaker was: "What does it mean to be a woman?" That answer could no longer remain an individual issue hidden in private homes or behind business doors. It had become a collective and a social matter, one that affected them all.

The five hundred attendees came to their feet as one and applauded. Emilee took hold of her two companions and danced with them in front of their chairs, shouting in unison with many others, "Hear, hear!"

However, as the speeches droned on, Caroline felt more and more disconnected. She knew how a proud parent would have felt as she looked at her invigorated friend, basking at her side. She was glad for Emilee but failed to grasp the speaker's point.

She, Caroline Washington, had no illusions or unease about *what it meant to be a woman*. She was convinced it was an immense privilege to be a nineteen-year-old *young* woman in 1970—and not a curse as the dressed-up lady at the lectern made it sound. She was glad she was a girl and not a boy. She had always been grateful for the fact that she had two breasts and a vagina, and that was *that*. She didn't need an organization to tell her to feel insecure about herself.

CHAPTER 10

Late-night swimming. Oxford. July 1970.

EMILEE CONTINUED TO excel in fine-boat rowing, English literature, and reading. Caroline again, joined her college's tennis team to find fulfillment outside the classroom. They met each Saturday. Once a month, Douglas would take the train to visit them in Oxford. Then, once every three months, the two girls made the journey to Southampton to visit Douglas.

With unexpected pleasure, they had discovered little villages and towns previously unknown to them, clustered along the rail line, running south in a zigzag fashion through the English countryside. There was Abingdon, Didcot, Cholsey, and Streatley, which led to the bigger town of Reading. Then followed Basingstoke and Winchester and, as their final stop, Southampton Central, where Douglas would be waiting. It always amazed Emilee as they stepped onto the platform that it would be 9:30 a.m. exactly. He was always on time: not a minute early, not a minute late.

Without formally deciding to do so, the three friends chose to talk less about the "plight of women in society," although Emilee remained a spirited supporter of the WLM. She attended the monthly Oxford chapter meeting with her equally enthused soul mate in matters of women's suffrage, Tracy Russell. They fed off each other's dedication, involvement, and most recently accrued knowledge, and they found inspiration in the growing knowledge that it could become possible one day to implement change in their society.

Over the course of their first year, Emilee realized that Caroline had no serious intention or interest in bringing her legal knowledge to the table. Emilee would have to study the law by herself in order to understand and grasp the extent of, or lack of, specific laws in her new country.

Changing these laws, which existed only in a limited fashion, for the protection of women and children in a male-dominated and male thought-out society was a seemingly impossible task, making her even more set on it. She had tried to explain to Douglas in the coffee shop why she needed the support of a bigger and more effective body lest she be doomed to failure.

—⚬—

Evening swimming with Rachel became part of Emilee's week, the seal on a day's hard work of rowing, study, and lectures. It became the rule for Mondays, Wednesdays, and Thursdays, and remained, without their intention, a covert operation. None of the other students were aware of their late-night ritual taking place in the pool often lit by moonlight only.

It was toward the middle of the year, after one of their always faster and more furious forty-lap swimming sessions, that Rachel swam over to the far side of the pool. She called Emilee to follow. By that time, swimming goggles were their routine. Specks of moonlight brushed the water. They required little light. They knew the pool.

Once Emilee had reached the deep end, her friend called out, "I want to show you something, partner! Dive to the bottom, then look." Rachel had moved toward where the moonlight played. A moment later, she disappeared below the surface.

Emilee took a breath and dived. Shafts of light and bubbles surrounded her only to be disturbed as Rachel came racing at her, bands of light playing over her as she slid past and shot toward the surface. Emilee swallowed a mouthful of water when she registered that her friend only had on her swimming goggles.

"You can't swim in the nude!" Emilee gasped, still coughing. Her friend's breasts had passed mere inches from her face. She could have touched each part of her body had she put out a hand.

"It's called skinny-dipping, silly. It's no big deal."

"You'll get us *expelled*!"

"Come on, Emilee. It's 1970. *You* are usually the one who pushes the envelope. Students have been doing this since the Middle Ages. No one comes here at this time of the night. I *dare* you to do the same."

"You're shaved down there."

"So?"

Emilee was grateful for the darkness where she clung to the side. It was impossible for Rachel to see her crimson face. Still, she hesitated.

"Come on."

Emilee treaded water as she slipped out of her two-piece and placed the strips of wet fabric on the side, close to Rachel's bikini. She swallowed and followed her friend.

Strong strokes took them down toward the bottom. They took turns turning onto their backs, dipping, arching, and diving, appreciating their fit, bare limbs and torsos and flowing hair, revealed in all its hidden parts, caressed in each curve and fold by moonlight and bubbles.

They would later bob to the surface and float next to each other, only to take a deep breath and dive again, touch the bottom, turn around, and cut through the water in never-ending loops and shafts of light. Around and around they went, faster and faster, touching a finger, an arm, a limb.

When at last they reached the side, out of breath, their hands touched in the dark. Emilee inched away.

Rachel sighed. "How *was* it?"

"Strange," Emilee murmured. "The water touched *everything*. My body's glowing—in spite of the cold."

Rachel chuckled.

Emilee clung to the side, her goggles pushed back on her head. She wiped the water from her eyes. Her right hand ventured out in the dark and touched her friend's wet hair. She trailed her hand down her friend's face, following the contour of her brow, her nose, brushed past her lips, and traced her slim neck till she reached her collarbone.

Rachel sighed, stabilizing herself against the side. With her free hand, she took Emilee's hand and guided it to her chest. Both girls gasped, their faces inches apart. They could feel each other's breath.

"What are we *doing*?" Emilee whispered, retracting her hand.

"Come." Rachel pulled, first herself, then her friend, out onto the side. "It's too cold out here. Let's go change in my room."

They tiptoed back to Rachel's room, towels wrapped around their shivering bodies.

In the bedroom, they stripped the wet pieces off and rubbed their goose-bumps-covered bodies with uncommon vigor. Rachel produced two more towels and threw one at Emilee.

"Rachel," she whimpered, her teeth chattering. "I'm still so *cold*."

"Let me help you." Rachel clambered onto the bed behind her and took the extra towel and toweled Emilee's hair at the back. They continued shivering uncontrollably.

"Only *one* solution for hypothermia. Get under the covers," Rachel instructed.

She draped the damp towels over a chair, turned the lights out, and pulled the curtains apart before joining her friend. "Move over and turn on your side, away from me."

Their limbs made hesitant contact, testing the foreign proximity. They shivered now from lowered body temperatures and unspoken anticipation. Rachel traced Emilee's shoulder and arm until she reached her hand, then laced their fingers together. She pulled Emilee in against herself, each body fitting into the hollow and curve of the other, skin against skin. Time ceased. Dampness and chill were driven from their interlaced limbs. Soon, sleep overtook them.

Moonlight playing over Emilee's face woke her. She was still in her friend's embrace. She disentangled herself, turned around, and rolled the half-asleep Rachel on her other side, reversing roles, making Rachel face away as Emilee wrapped her now-glowing body around her friend's. Emilee's fingers traced the curve of her friend's thigh and followed it to her ribcage, then slid forward toward her chest.

When Emilee woke again, she remembered what she had seen in the pool. She thought about Douglas Harding and Caroline when they were on the ship in the smoking room. Her fingers paused. *Is this what he could have done for us if I hadn't been so ignorant? But he belongs to Caroline.* She closed her eyes. The smooth shaven skin felt unfamiliar. She paused. Rachel mumbled in her sleep.

Sometime during the middle of the night, Emilee awoke and extracted herself, gathered her clothing, and returned to her own room—back to a cold and empty bed. She was aware of an unnamed void as she waited for her shivering to cease and sleep to pull her in.

CHAPTER 11

The London March. 6 March 1971.

THEY CAME BY train, bus, car, and on foot—droves of them—women from all over England, for the National Women's Liberation Movement march. They aggregated at Hyde Park Corner, a pulsing, buzzing, throng of bodies sprouting as the minutes passed.

Then, as if prearranged, the procession moved when the first snowflakes sifted down. Feeding off each other, the March took on a life all its own. It throbbed and ebbed as it wormed its way toward Trafalgar Square. The snow became a benediction, an unending veil, draped over their heads and shoulders as they forged ahead.

Emilee and Tracy, along with dozens of supporters, had left Oxford Station at 5:30 in the morning. Fortunately, Tracy, at that stage the more practical one, had had the presence of mind to listen to the weather report and made Emilee turn back for a larger shoulder bag to house something warm for the cold: gloves, a cap, something to eat, and an overcoat for if it snowed, just as the weatherperson had predicted for London. In Oxford, the sky was sullen and heavy, the temperature hovering around zero when they boarded.

It was as if the humming of the city had ceased. All that existed was them, the marchers. Snow dampened sound.

The two friends marched alongside each other, shoulder-to-shoulder, faces upturned, celebrating and defying the snow-flakes that floated like confetti as they followed the flock through the streets of London.

Emilee noticed the different attires of her fellow females under their overcoats. Indeed, the cold and the snow were equalizers, hiding expensive boutique-bought dresses and designer pants and blouses from more modest garments obtained from Goodwill storefronts. They marched united, if only by way of their sex.

Without a doubt, under all those layers, if stripped to the skin they all shared a similar anatomy: two breasts, and below, a triangular mount. In all other aspects, especially personality, they would prove to be so different. Some were tall, some short, some slim and lean, others broad and big-boned, obese and all round, and yet some were infinitely small and petite.

And there, as they marched, side by side, they were: professors and spinsters, young girls and old mothers, widows and midwives, housewives and students, some doctors and nurses, a judge and some lawyers, even dockworkers and cleaners and, for whatever good measure, a forgotten hippie or two.

Curious observers lined the streets who would pause to watch: some mere onlookers, a few women with children, and then the occasional TV cameraman. Most of them were men dressed in warm weekend clothes, with some in practical work clothes, others in fine-tailored suits, together, observing the marchers with varied expressions. The men's faces a study: from curious to intrigued, from amused to annoyed, from sympathetic to naked contempt.

Many women brandished posters as they marched and sang and cried with their sisters, pleading to be freed. They chanted and paid slight heed to gentle admonitions by dozens of Bobbies, all dressed up in black, with cone-shaped helmets, guarding the peace. Their presence was necessary as some spectators spat bitter obscenities into the crowd.

As the march progressed, it became apparent that scores of female onlookers took courage from their passing sisters and slipped in and joined the ranks. Even the occasional male was witnessed to join their division in blatant support of a global awareness: the plight of women universal.

As they reached the square, the snow, as if by divine intervention, subsided enough for the event organizers and marchers alike to restore an element of finesse and decorum to the unstitching of their ranks. They did, after all, want to show the world the power of what women united could do. TV cameras rolled as the women encored, raising their posters up high, cheering the MC as she took to the platform. The message was clear: "Women unite! All women, *unite!*"

Many of the speakers weren't trained orators, but they spoke from within, from where they hurt the most. The first lady related how she had battled, not only to find a good job, but also to hold one, as she had to compete with her male counterparts—not because of her competence, but because of her female sex. Females were inferior, even feeble, her boss had proclaimed.

Emilee and Tracy jumped up and down and cheered at the end of the speech to demonstrate solidarity, but more to warm their chilled bodies.

The next speaker related how her boss had called her in one day. "No complaint about your quality of work," he had said, but still he'd laid her off. He'd received word that she preferred women in her personal life. "It could prove to be embarrassing for the company's image, you see." How could it concern him whom she loved if she did it in private and in good taste? The crowd applauded and chanted en masse, stomping their feet and waving their arms and placards.

Emilee frowned when a man dressed in a tailored tweed jacket appeared out of nowhere, right at their side, and took part in the stomping and waving of arms. He glanced at her once and nodded with a grin before paying attention to what was said in the front.

She touched Tracy's arm to draw her attention to the new supporter—a male, of all things. She was surprised by the degree of annoyance she felt. *He simply has no right to be here. No right to share these moments—it belongs to us.*

Tracy laughed at her friend's displeasure as Emilee hissed, "I'm *certain* he's gay. What else has he lost here?"

To which the young man immediately replied. "*Gay* I'm not, Miss. I'm always fascinated by people who dare to stand for *something* worthwhile, *something* morally defensible."

He put out a hand. "Connor. Connor O'Hannigan, at your service, ma'am." He bowed his head in their direction.

Emilee snorted but took his hand. He had long, slim fingers. His eyes held hers with a sudden intensity. She stammered. "Emilee . . . Stephens . . . And this is my friend . . . Tracy Russell."

He touched the rim of his wool cap, which was pulled halfway down to his eyes, with a matching scarf wrapped around his neck. "Miss Stephens, Miss Russell—the pleasure is mine."

As they cheered the next speaker, Connor O'Hannigan stepped closer. "Do you ladies drink coffee?"

When they both nodded yes, Emilee with more reluctance than Tracy, he immediately spun around. "Don't go *anywhere*. I should be back in less than ten minutes." He casually slipped past the clusters of women around them, whispering "Excuse me, excuse me," and fast disappeared.

"His English sounds weird," Emilee insisted.

"Irish," Tracy said. "He must be Irish."

Emilee sniffed with annoyance. "What do the Irish know about matters *morally defensible*?"

"Why don't you ask him?"

"Oh, I will!"

CHAPTER 12

—⟋⟍⟋—

Mr. O'Hannigan. 6 March 1971.

CONNOR O'HANNIGAN RETURNED nine minutes later with two paper cups, each three-quarters filled with coffee. The rest had spilled over his hands. He handed over the cups, shook his hands, and wiped them dry with a white, ironed handkerchief from his trouser pocket.

He remained unapologetic at the reduced contents of the cups, stating that the coffee shop was at the far side of the square, and not all the women out there were ladies, you know.

Both women whispered their thanks as they felt the eyes of their sisters around them, who were trying to listen to whatever the next speaker had to say.

"My pleasure." He was immune to the glaring eyes surrounding them. "I didn't know, so I added two sugars to each. I thought it quite brave of you two, well actually you *all*, to stand here today and face this miserable weather, unmoved by the scorn and ridicule of so many spectators along the way."

Emilee eyed him over the brim of her cup, trying to wrench any remaining heat from the paper cup. "*That* was quite thoughtful of you, Mr. O'Hannigan. *Thank you.*"

Her eyes kept dropping to his hands. She had never seen such slender fingers.

He nodded, and she added, still whispering, "I wasn't aware the Irish had noblemen among them."

"I would love to enlighten you, ma'am." He touched the rim of his wool cap again and leaned in. "Why don't you two meet me at the coffee shop at the southern tip of the square once this whole thing is over, before you guys return home? It's cold, and I will ensure that the coffee is piping hot then, and not too sweet—not lukewarm like this stuff. They might even have fresh scones."

He willed her not to look away—implored her—peered into her soul until her breath caught. He wasn't asking.

When she still hesitated, he added, "Please. I'll wait." The next moment he was gone.

"The *nerve*," Emilee stuttered.

"Irish. I told you he's Irish," Tracy whispered, as if that explained everything.

It was early afternoon when the crowd dispersed, and the two friends made their way toward the southern part of the square, never discussing that the way to the train station was north.

He waited on them as promised, having secured a table inside, off to the back, where it was less crowded. The warmth of the room wrapped around them as they entered. Ground coffee and fresh-baked bread sealed the welcome. It was impossible to miss his raised hand. He rose and pulled their chairs out, then pushed each one back as they sat down, and he placed paper menus in front of them. It was obvious he knew his way around the establishment.

"I've asked the proprietor. There *are* fresh scones—still warm." He sat back and allowed them to study the menus.

"Do you *work* here?" Emilee asked.

He shook his head.

Emilee studied the menu with renewed fervor. When she looked up, his generous mouth was drawn into the shadow of a grin, which seemed never to leave his face, his eyes unblinking, holding hers, as if amused—perhaps bored. She had trouble reading him, uncertain how much of his demeanor was a well-crafted façade, a mask she had yet to decipher. She lowered her eyes and memorized the rest of the menu, waiting on Tracy to place her order first. She will prove this Irishman wrong—thinking Oxford girls are easy.

She could play shy. She could even play dumb, more than he could ever imagine. *The man needs a lesson, strutting his gall so in the open.* She appreciated assertiveness but arrogance—especially naked arrogance—made any man a has-been in her books. He required immediate execution by the firing squad for unsuitable suitors. This man with the freckled nose thought they were two brainless women's libbers. She'd love to shake his faith in himself a little.

As soon as Tracy looked up, he said, "Ready to order? It's on *me*."

"Thank you, Mr. O'Hannigan, but we have our *own* money," Emilee said, touching Tracy's hand.

Tracy looked at her friend as they placed their orders. That's it then. The gauntlet was thrown. Connor O'Hannigan let it slip.

"I'm still convinced you're gay, O'Hannigan," Emilee said.

"Do you have a problem with that?" he asked.

"Not at all, because then we can relax. I knew it the moment I smelled your cologne and laid eyes on your all-too-perfect wardrobe—everything matches. It's colorful, and the quality is exquisite, even down to the shoes. Italian leather? You didn't buy it at the Goodwill store around the corner."

"They're called Oxford shoes. If I may, neither did *you* see the inside of the corner store."

"So? *You're* the one under suspicion. We came here today to support the WLM. We have *no* hidden agenda. There's *nothing* to explain," Emilee said as their coffee and scones and her hot chocolate arrived. She often opted to skip the coffee.

Tracy kicked her friend under the table and pleaded with her eyes to ease off their guest. Connor O'Hannigan noticed the interaction and chuckled, busied himself with spreading jam and cream on his scones, took a small bite, and chewed without saying a word, daring Emilee to continue her assault. Emilee turned silent but held his gaze. Tracy waited along with her friend.

Connor conceded defeat, though he had never developed a taste for it. He held up his hands in surrender, claiming he too had no agenda and nothing to explain, that he happened to be a curious onlooker who had become intrigued by the march and eventually joined it, ending up next to two lovely ladies.

"Curious onlooker!" Emilee exclaimed. "You take us for *fools*. It's insulting! What's your *story*—your mission here today? We could leave, if you're going to lie to us."

His laugh came easy. She noticed for the first time the hint of mint in his irises.

"Please stay," he said. "I told you, I came today because I am moved, inspired, motivated when I see people stand up and take action for something they believe in, especially if it's a matter of public interest and for a cause, a morally defensible one."

Emilee snickered then laughed. "You're good, O'Hannigan—sweet-talking unsuspecting ladies like this. Perhaps you're not gay, but only an opportunistic Don Juan. Just imagine: thousands of women to pick and choose from. Charm them with coffee in the cold and with a clever story and they'll eat from your hand—you were hoping."

He shook his head. "You're mistaken." Then he stood. "Pardon me for a moment. I need to go wash my hands."

"Sorry," Emilee continued once he returned. "I still don't buy your BS. *Where* do you fit in? Where do you live?"

"Oxford."

Emilee snorted, more audibly this time. "You came *all* the way from Oxford to watch thousands of women march in the snow?"

"Yes, your Honor." Again, the easy laugh.

"Then why didn't we see you on the train?" Emilee touched her friend's hand. "Tracy, what do you think? Is this Irishman lying? It sounds *too* good to be possibly true. Bollocks—that's what he's talking."

Tracy laughed her bell-like happy chuckle. "I am afraid, Mr. O'Hannigan, you have *not* convinced us."

Emilee added that she believed Mr. O'Hannigan was an undercover journalist, government official, or someone from the establishment who was trying to befriend members of the organization under pretenses, especially since he was much older than they were—he couldn't be a student—all in an effort to obtain material for his skewed story.

Connor O'Hannigan claimed he was innocent of all the accusations. It must be obvious to them that he couldn't be a reporter. He had no camera on him, not even a pen, and couldn't possibly be someone from the press since the WLM had their own people out on the street during the march.

"I thought your movement wants the *whole* world to see, to get the word out!" he added.

"O'Hannigan," Emilee said, "the movement will do its *own* reporting. We've seen during the last year how the established media omitted facts and misquoted and misrepresented many things we said and did. And, most importantly, we *women* will do it. We do not *need* you—*men*. Although," and she chuckled, "we've not established that fact one hundred percent, but you *do* come across as a male."

He remained nonplussed. "I never said I came by train. You have a fascinating philosophy about many things. And you're definitely not shy to share your opinion. You two must be students. Let me guess. Miss Stephens: you're studying law? Which college?"

Emily got up. "You're mistaken—about many things. Come, Tracy, our train's not going to wait. O'Hannigan, thank you for sharing your coffee table with us. Please excuse us."

He jumped up as well and followed them to the cashier where they each paid, then followed them outside onto the sidewalk. "Miss Stephens . . . I am not used to pleading . . . The name of your college . . . Please?"

The girls crossed the street without answering. Connor O'Hannigan remained standing in front of the café, visibly at a loss.

Emilee turned back and hollered across the traffic, "Ruskin College, Mr. O'Hannigan. Ruskin College!"

She took her friend's hand, and they laughed as they ran together onto Trafalgar Square.

CHAPTER 13

───── ◈ ─────

Mr. O'Hannigan's visit. 13 March 1971.

EMILEE WAS BUZZED to the reception of her college early Saturday morning, minutes after eight. She had a guest. *This is so strange. Weird. Nobody calls at the front desk anymore.* She had just finished showering after her rowing practice earlier that morning and combed her damp hair with her fingers as she made her way down. It was too early for her appointment with Caroline and Douglas. They were meeting with her at noon at the usual place. Rachel would have come to her room. The same went for Tracy.

He stood in front of one of the windows, close to the front doors. It was the man from the march. Even though the light haloed his silhouette, it was unmistakable. *How dare he?*

"How did you *find* me?" Emilee whispered, upset that he made her blush.

He bowed. "Good morning, Miss Stephens." As he stepped away from the window, she could see parts of his face. Again, that bored grin.

"How *did* you find me?"

"That's what I do: *find* people." He laughed. "Come on— give me some credit. Oxford is not that big, and when Ruskin College couldn't help me, I did some research of my own. I have contacts."

"Never mind then. But you are aware of the time, O'Hannigan?" she said. "The sun is barely out."

He chuckled. "My impression of you was that you're not a person who sleeps in—not on such a glorious day." He pointed at her hair. "You had a shower. Probably following rowing practice?"

"It *was* nice out on the river this morning," Emilee mused. "We rowed through the sleeping town, our boat hidden by a blanket of fog the entire route. If anyone was up, they could only hear us. We remained invisible." She suppressed a smile.

"Coxed eight?"

She nodded.

"I was wondering . . ." he started.

"The answer is no."

"Your whole Saturday can't be booked already. It's only eight fifteen. I'm only asking for an hour at the most."

Emilee left through the front door with Connor on her heels. It was too dark inside to her liking. She had to see his eyes, all of his face. She paused outside on the stairs.

"Mr. O'Hannigan," she said. "I'm a sophomore this year. I'm always busy. I have to work hard—bursary commitments. You already know that I row six mornings a week. I have several tutorials to complete. I have an appointment at noon, and I still have to dry my hair, which would not have been the case if you hadn't bothered me."

"I do apologize," he said, "for being responsible for the damp hair. But how would four this afternoon work for you? Your hair should be dry by then. I can meet you here. You seem to prefer the outdoors."

"Connor O'Hannigan," she said, "the answer is still no. I don't date older men, and I especially don't spend time with arrogant individuals—not if I have a choice. If, and this is a big if, *if* you change your attitude, I may be able to meet you here *next* Saturday at four, at the foot of these stairs."

He chuckled. "I'm only twenty-six. Next Saturday then, Miss Stephens—complete with a humble attitude, outside here on the stairs—at four." He mock-bowed and took his leave.

"Hypocrite!" Emilee called after him as he went down the stairs. "You don't *do* humble, O'Hannigan. But, I'll give you *one* more chance next Saturday. *Surprise* me."

—◊—

Douglas Harding waited in the coffee shop that morning. His train from Southampton made good time, and there wasn't any snow or ice on the ground, making getting around easy. As he walked from the station, he could smell the earth for the first time that year. Even the fallen leaves' muskiness was welcome. Spring was holding its breath.

To have Caroline all to himself for the remainder of the day, after coffee, without offending Emilee, was his most pressing dilemma. He would have to be *über* diplomatic. The three of them had become used to doing most everything together, and Emilee was prone to being hypersensitive. He hadn't even told Caroline about his plan. He had so much news of his own. He still had difficulty believing his recent promotion. Perhaps he should have phoned her at least, to warn her. His feelings for Caroline had changed.

He got up when his friends burst into the shop.

Emilee, always the more boisterous of the two, was even more hyperactive than usual. She planted a quick kiss on Douglas's cheek and barely allowed Caroline to kiss and hug their friend from the RMS *Windsor Castle* before she sat down and let the server take their order.

"Douglas," Emilee blurted, "when we visited Las Palmas the year before last, you promised us that you would teach us the difference between an Englishman, a Scotsman, and an Irishman. Can you do that now?" She grabbed his hand. "Please? Right *now!*"

Douglas laughed at her urgency. "I was fooling around. It's not that simple. It's something subtle."

Emilee leaned forward and kissed him full on the mouth. "I'm serious. Stop your BS. You *have* to tell me." She turned crimson.

"You're a crafty one, Emilee Stephens," Caroline called out. "What's his name?" She hugged her friend. "Out with it!"

Emilee shook her head, still blushing.

"Douglas," Caroline said, "she's smitten."

Emilee raised her hands in defense. "Not true—the smitten part—I've just met the man. Only last week. O'Hannigan is his name. Connor O'Hannigan. I met him in London during the march." She faced her friends. "Then, out of the blue, he dropped by uninvited early this morning." She quickly added, "and he's so *arrogant*."

"He's definitely Irish," Douglas said.

"Why?" Emilee asked. "Because he's arrogant and invited himself or because he speaks funny?"

"Because he's *O'Hannigan*," Douglas said.

Emilee kicked his shin. "I'm serious. You have to tell me: are *all* Irishmen arrogant?"

Douglas laughed as he rubbed his leg.

Caroline leaned forward and kissed Emilee's cheek. "*Smitten.*"

CHAPTER 14

———— ◦◦◦ ————

The peculiar Mr. O'Hannigan.
20 March 1971.

EMILEE DIDN'T WAIT for reception to buzz her but stood waiting, long before four, to the side of the stairs, as casual as possible, at the front door of her college. She fumed all over, recalling her most recent visit with Douglas and Caroline. They had mocked her. She has *no* feelings for the pompous Irishman. He was firing-squad-for-unsuitable-suitors fodder. She was only *curious*.

If she hadn't done her research in the library the past week, she would not have been the wiser about all things Irish. She snorted. And she, in her naivety, believed all this time that Douglas knew the difference between the English and the Irish. As if *anyone* knew the difference—least of all an Englishman to the likes of Mr. Harding. She wandered away from the stairs.

"Emilee."

That voice. She snapped out of her reverie. *Emilee—slow your breathing, close your mouth, and, for heaven's sake, stop blushing.*

"Hello, Connor." She noticed the care he had once again taken with his attire, from his jacket down to his sneakers. It spelled money, taste, and comfort. She wasn't certain she liked that.

"It's four o'clock," he said. "I'll have you back by five, exactly. Come." He took her by the elbow and steered her toward the front gate. "I have a vehicle outside."

She pulled her elbow free and walked beside him. He was about four inches taller. None of them said a word until they passed through the gates and he pointed at his car.

"*There* she is."

"She?" Emilee called out, glancing around. "It's only a car." She remembered her dad's 1959 Chevrolet truck back home in the Caprivi: black and sturdy, the only car she had known. So, this was Connor's pride and joy—she heard the smugness in his voice—a navy blue, two-door sports car parked on the side of the street in all its polished glory.

"It's not *only a car*," Connor said, emphasizing every syllable. "It's a 1970 MGB roadster, MK two." He added with a cough, "It has an eighteen-hundred cc engine, manual shift."

Emilee walked around the vehicle and looked at its owner, her brows cocked.

"Does she have *a name*?" She was hoping to be wrong.

"She does. Mary Gabriella. MG for short."

"How original. Is one allowed to *touch* her?" She put her hand on the black canvas soft-top above the passenger door and gave it a gentle pat.

She could hear Connor exhale with relief. "The canvas top is okay. It won't leave prominent fingerprints." He laughed as if embarrassed. "Our skin—our fingers—have natural oils that leave marks on the body of the vehicle. It can blemish the polish, the paintwork."

Emilee paused, processing what she had just learned. She shook her head, glancing at the bemused Connor.

"O'Hannigan," she said, "if you're planning on having me back by five, we should get going." Then she added, "Are we allowed to *drive* with her, or is she only for looking at?"

"Sorry!" Connor called out as he ran around and unlocked the door. He took care not to touch the navy blue body but only the chrome door handle with a white handkerchief, holding the door open. "Your carriage is ready, ma'am." He bowed.

Emilee laughed as she slipped in and settled into the black seat. She closed her eyes and leaned back. The bucket seat hugged her back. The interior brimmed with the scent of treated leather and car polish—not entirely unpleasant. Her eyes flew open when Connor coughed next to her. He still held the door ajar, then bent down and pierced her with his look.

"*What?*"

"Your shoes," he said.

"You're not *serious?*"

"You'll notice the small black bag next to your left foot. Take your shoes off and place them in the bag, please." The green of his eyes had black flecks. He straightened and closed the door.

Emilee seethed. She knew he was arrogant and he talked funny, but he was Irish—he couldn't help that. She had her reservations about him being gay—how he smelled and the way he overdressed compared to most other young men his age—which was fine by her. Then she would have one less thing to worry about.

But this—this was crossing the line. This was a disease. There were names for what he had, she was certain. *It is a stupid car.*

She slipped her shoes off and placed them in the provided cloth bag while he walked around and unlocked his door, returned his handkerchief to his pocket, and folded himself into his seat. Slipping the key into the ignition, he gave her a beaming smile when he noticed her bare feet.

She swallowed several times before she spoke. "Why don't you take *your* shoes off, if the car is so holy, Mister?"

He laughed as he started the engine. "It's not holy, and I need to keep my shoes on in order to protect my feet from the pedals." He leaned closer, looking into her eyes. "I'm not crazy, as I can clearly see you think. It is only *a silly car*, but I pride myself in looking after what belongs to me. I take care of my property since I work hard to earn every penny."

He put the car in gear, glanced over his shoulder, and pulled away. "There's no shame in taking pride in that now, is there, Miss Emilee?"

"You have a serious problem, Connor O'Hannigan!" she yelled above the engine's din. "There's looking after and there's *looking after*. This is *not* normal!"

Her companion laughed above the churning of the engine as he turned down a street and raced down to the next stop sign.

"Where are we going in such great hurry?"

"It's a surprise."

"You may just as well slow down then. I'm not impressed— not by the car with its wooden steering wheel, and even less with the speeding. But I *am* curious. What do you do for a living? A mighty fine living by the looks of it. Is there a rich daddy?" She turned to face him. "Or do you belong to a crime syndicate? Oh, I know. You probably run the cartel."

He pulled into a parking spot before he answered. They had arrived at their destination: the same coffee shop Caroline and she had always visited with Douglas. There was nothing wrong with their own taste then.

"There's no rich daddy. I haven't seen him, my parents for that matter, in five years. The alienation is from his side." The bravado had left his voice. "He expected me to continue the family tradition. He's a family physician in a remote coastal town, like my grandfather had been and my great-grandfather before him, all in the same goddamn village, off the face of the earth. And when I wouldn't, he cut me off. Stopped all financial support as well."

He turned off the engine and wiped his face. "I had to get away. But I miss her—Mother—she's completely under his spell. She . . . she's not as strong as him." He sighed. "I'm a shop steward. A union rep, if you wish, at British Leyland, over in Cowley." Then he added, "I work very hard, picking up overtime whenever I can. I've been doing the shop steward part for the past year. Before that, I physically assembled the vehicles, worked the floor."

When he saw her blank face, he continued. "Cowley, the big motor plant, is on the outskirts of town, east of the town." He laughed. "Come on. It's southeast of your famous Ruskin College!"

"I think I know where that is now," Emilee said. "They must be paying you a handsome wage, O'Hannigan. Perhaps I should abandon my English studies." She peered at him. "Do they have a vacancy on the factory floor?"

He grimaced as he opened his door. "You do *not* want to work there."

"How can you know what I like? It must be a terribly boring life, though. All work and nothing else? Horrible."

He let go of the door again. "It's not what you think—me only working. I have a bicycle and a kayak. I sometimes sneak out before dawn." He laughed. "I can find my way on the river and the streams, even in the fog." He patted his upper arm and smiled, "One has to keep in shape."

The next moment he walked around and held her door. "Come, let me make it up to you. I'll treat you to a proper afternoon tea—with *all* the trimmings."

He waited as she slipped her shoes back on, folded the small black bag, and placed it where she had found it. The white handkerchief was ready in his hand, holding the chrome door handle.

CHAPTER 15

─ⁿ⁰⁰⁰─

The concern of friends. 8 May 1971.

IT SOON BECAME her weekend routine: sweep rowing at six, meeting up with Caroline at noon and then with her Irishman at four. Precisely on the hour, when the bell tower chimed, he would stand at the stairs to her college, waiting.

Connor stuck to a visiting time of exactly an hour, priding himself on having her back by five. He gently insisted that they make use of Mary Gabriella as their sole mode of transportation, frequenting the same coffee shop for tea, with refreshments, which Emilee tolerated for the time being, each time rolling her eyes and gnashing her teeth. That was, until the novelty wore off.

That morning, Caroline and Douglas Harding had been particularly relentless. Caroline would not let go of the facts that Connor O'Hannigan used a white *ironed* handkerchief to touch his car's door handles and insisted that Emilee take her shoes off and stow them in a small black cloth bag. Emilee regretted ever having shared the information, embarrassed with herself for tolerating the eccentricities of her new friend.

"Douglas and I are concerned about you," Caroline said.

Emilee brushed it off with a laugh, "Oh, it's nothing. He's only a little possessive about his car."

"You're a dear friend. You know that. But we cannot stand here and let you remain blind to this obsessed man with all his insecurities. 'A little possessive?' Don't you see? He will smother your effervescent spirit. He will strangle your liberated soul. You don't see any of this because you're infatuated."

"Infatuated? You haven't even *met* the man!"

"Then *introduce* us. *Both* me and Douglas."

Douglas nodded in silent agreement, trailing Caroline's hand.

Emilee noticed for the first time the way Douglas and Caroline made frequent eye contact and would touch one another in passing. That was no accident. It was different from the old days, when the three of them would fool around together. So, their platonic friendship must have been elevated to the next level.

When did that happen? And right under my nose. Carrie was right—I've been so blind.

Emilee snapped upright. She'd show her friends, even prove them wrong. "If you guys *do* care so much, why don't you meet his Irish Highness this afternoon? We can surprise him. I have my f-f-fixed appointment," she stammered, "with Connor at four. He always meets me on the steps outside Magdalen."

Caroline looked at Douglas. "When do you have to be back on the Windsor Castle?"

When he stole a glance at Caroline, Emilee added, "Sorry, if you had other plans, we can try it again at another time, perhaps?"

They were both blushing now.

"Carrie . . . are you and Mr. Darling . . . Is there something . . . ?"

Caroline smiled red-faced at her friend.

"I've been so *obtuse*. You're right. I've been preoccupied with my own things that I've allowed this development to slip through." Emilee jumped from her stool, almost knocking it over, shrieked, and kissed Caroline on the lips and cheeks, yanking her halfway across the table. She waved the waitress away who had stormed closer in alarm.

Next in line for hugs and kisses was Douglas, who resignedly allowed it.

Emilee turned back toward Douglas. "*When* did you ask her? You *are* a charlatan!"

Douglas smiled, lacing his fingers with Caroline's. "I don't know . . . It happened gradually . . . over time."

Emilee spun toward her girlfriend. "Out with it! When?"

Caroline laughed, turning crimson. "If you insist on a date, it was on Valentine's Day, a little over two months ago."

"And you thought you could keep it a secret? Shame on you." Emilee pulled her friend's hands free from Douglas's and inspected Caroline's fingers, raising her hands. "Where's the ring, Harding?"

Both her friends laughed. "There's no ring. We're only good friends—that's all."

Emilee leaned across the table and squeezed both of her friend's hands. "Good friends. I wonder. I bet he's a good kisser, Carrie. Is he?" She beamed at Douglas, who only smiled in embarrassment.

Caroline groaned. "Is there nothing sacred?"

Emilee waved their waitress over and insisted on another round of liquid refreshments on her tab. Once the order arrived, she leaned closer. "You have my blessing, Caroline Washington. I actually gave it when we were still on the Royal Mail ship on our way from Cape Town." She paused. "All right, my two lovebirds, back to the matter of Mr. Connor O'Hannigan." She cleared her throat and looked at Douglas. "You haven't answered my question, Douglas. Will four *this* afternoon work for the two of you?"

Douglas chuckled. "Relax." He glanced at Caroline. "If I may speak on Carrie's behalf, we'll be there. We can do that for an old friend. I'm *so* glad you haven't lost your consuming intensity, the fervor with which you approach everything. It's quite draining, but at the same time, so invigorating."

Emilee leaned in again. "Old friend, my foot. Remember, four o'clock, *exactly*, the outside stairs to Magdalen's main building. *Don't* be late. We don't want to upset the Irishman."

Caroline laughed. "*See?* Do you understand why this intervention is necessary? Your eyes will be opened to the glaring insecurities of your Irish friend."

CHAPTER 16

———— ∿ ————

Exposing Mr. O'Hannigan. 8 May 1971.

DOUGLAS AND CAROLINE did not disappoint Emilee. They arrived five minutes early. The three friends waited at the bottom of the stairs for the bell tower to chime the hour. Standing there, Emilee pondered their plan to test Connor—perhaps she had lost perspective. For a moment, she felt sorry for him.

"Emilee?"

How did he always manage to sneak up on her?

"*Connor.*" She stepped forward and took his hand, turning him around. "Meet two of my friends, Douglas Harding and Caroline Washington."

He nodded in acknowledgment, shook their hands, then took her elbow to steer her away.

Emilee pulled free. "Would you mind if we're not back by five and rather *walk* to the coffee shop? *With* Douglas and Caroline? I would love that."

Connor's smile appeared strained. "*You* would love that," he murmured. "You mean *walk* all the way to the coffee shop?" He glanced at the three friends. It was clear that was exactly what she meant. "And leave Mary Gabriella—my car—out on the street? That will take *hours.*" He straightened out a wrinkle in his tailored trouser leg.

"Nonsense." Emilee grabbed his hand. "I've done it many times. And nothing will happen to your fancy car. It'll be safe. The students respect a thing of beauty, especially a classic."

His eyes bored into hers, unable to tell if she was mocking him. His brow knotted.

She smiled up at him, not letting go, and only pulled with more effort.

Caroline and Douglas were already several steps ahead of them when Caroline turned and called, "Come on, Mr. O'Hannigan. Emilee couldn't stop boasting about how fit you were and how much you loved the outdoors, that you're kayaking. We were *so* impressed. We'd better get going if we want to be back by six."

"Six?" Connor inquired as he fell in pace with Emilee. He hissed through clenched teeth, "Nice setup, *Missy*. You're all dressed for walking, while I came in my weekend-best."

Emilee increased her pace. "I told you not to overdress. It doesn't impress me. None of your fancy stuff does."

By the time they had gone through the main gate, Connor had slipped out of his deft blazer and draped it over his shoulder, throwing a last forlorn glance at his sportster. He mumbled, "You are *so* wrong about me. I'm not trying to impress you. I dress for myself."

Emilee chuckled as she skipped ahead, catching up with Caroline and Douglas. "What's your hang-up, O'Hannigan? You don't walk and you don't do laundry. You dress fancy, you prefer driving to walking, and you send everything to the dry cleaners!" She hollered and grabbed his hand again, swinging it with force.

He struggled to smile. "I said I own a bicycle and a kayak."

"So you lied to me?"

He laughed for the first time. "Come on. Stop painting me as this arrogant snob with a broomstick up his ass. I do my *own* laundry, and yes, some of the clothes *have* to be sent to a dry cleaner."

Emilee caught up with Caroline. "Did you hear that, Carrie? My Irish friend has confessed to sending all his washing to the cleaners, like the Royals!" Laughing, she sidestepped Connor when he tried to smack her bottom.

"I said I do my *own* laundry."

Caroline chipped in. "We heard you refer to yourself as a 'stuck-up snob with a broomstick in the behind."

Connor's face became more drawn the farther they walked. The constant barrage and bickering were at his expense. He was out of his league to fend off such unrelenting verbal bombardments. It was a linguistic jousting tournament—something he wasn't accustomed to. At work, he had a position of power, of prestige. He was looked up to. No one would dream making fun of him—not even the Union bosses.

He was the master on the factory floor. He negotiated the price for each shop-floor job. He had the power to slow down the entire production line or even implement a full strike if he had good reason—until the workers' demands were met. Now he had to swallow these silly remarks of Emilee and her off-kilter friends. They were weird—so shallow. Perhaps he had misjudged himself with the redhead.

They reached the coffee shop and found a table, the trio's usual one, and placed their order.

Enjoying herself, Emilee inhaled deeply. She could never get enough of the aroma of freshly ground coffee and baked treats wafting around them. She turned to face Connor. "Since we brought you here against your wishes, O'Hannigan, the bill is on us."

When he objected, she continued. "We insist. It's a token of our appreciation for your willingness to face such hardship."

He had no option than to join in the laughter and hilarity that washed over him.

Caroline winked at him. "You'll have to loosen up if you want to remain friends with her."

—∞—

It was half past five by the time they returned to Magdalen College. By then, Connor had resigned himself to his fate. He allowed the trio to horse around and mock him out in the open. All his life he had tried so hard to prove himself, to please his father, to be good enough.

This was different. He finally enjoyed the bantering. He had never experienced it at home or at work. The guiding principle in his life had always been: life was deadly serious. This was a foreign experience.

They could see the college buildings down the road when Emilee called out, "Do you agree, O'Hannigan? Were we success-ful in pulling a portion of that broomstick out from your royal bottom?"

They walked side by side, hooked in at the elbows, and Emilee leaned over and gave Connor a peck on the cheek. He grinned as her two old friends cheered their approval.

Connor smiled. "You're an exasperating treat." He kept up with their brisk pace, emboldened by the afternoon, and hollered,

"What you need, Missy, is *someone* to put you in your place. There's *nothing* like a few good slaps on a woman's behind." Then he added with a laugh, "Nothing like *teaching* a woman a lesson or two." He gave her a firm smack on the behind.

Emilee gasped, yanked her arm free, her face pallid as she came to an abrupt stop, rubbing her bottom. "That hurt."

Caroline sucked in her breath and silence fell on the group. No one moved.

"Connor O'Hannigan! You have *no* idea what you've just said. How *dare* you suggest raising your hand? Even in *jest*. The whole afternoon we've been fooling around and, yes, joking. You've crossed *the line*. You know so little about me . . . You know *nothing* about me. Slapping . . . hitting a woman. It can *never* be right. *Never!*" Emilee struggled to catch her breath.

He stammered. "W-w-what did I say wrong?"

"Please!" she called out when he raised his arms in defense. "It's called *abuse*. You have to go." She sobbed and stepped into Caroline's embrace, turning away from the shocked Irishman, who was still speechless at her outburst.

"Please *go*," Emilee whimpered.

Connor stepped closer, his hands outstretched toward her. "I'm *sorry* . . . What did I do *wrong?*"

Douglas took his arm, turning him away. "You *heard* her, O'Hannigan."

Connor swung back. "Please, Emilee. That's not what I *meant.*"

Douglas Harding wouldn't let go of the man's arm. "O'Hannigan! *There's* your vehicle. Leave *now*." Douglas shoved him toward the blue sportster.

As the three friends, now huddled together, entered through the college gates, the Irishman remained standing next to his vehicle, his face unreadable, his hands balled into fists, his eyes not for a moment leaving the retreating figure of the slumped-forward redhead.

CHAPTER 17

The factory floor. July 1971.

FOR FOUR SATURDAYS in a row, until mid-June at exactly 4 p.m., Connor O'Hannigan had called the Reception of Magdalen College. Each time, Emilee had refused to make an appearance. On the first two Saturdays, he'd left a bushel of red roses accompanied by a letter. The roses immediately ended up in the garbage can, along with the unread letter.

Soon, Emilee had made a special arrangement with the staff at Reception not to bother her whenever this particular gentleman—the well-dressed young man with the freckles and green eyes—called. He was *persona non grata*. She found a safe haven in The Old Library.

Despite unwavering support from Caroline and Douglas in the matter of all things Irish, it did not ease her agony. Emilee remained bothered by the status of affairs.

"He's bad news. He's a *bad* apple," Caroline cautioned.

Their assurance that hundreds of other decent and well-adjusted men were around and available did not help. Emilee found it improbable that she would ever forgive the arrogant shop steward or reconcile with the woman-bashing. Sleep now evaded her at night.

Tracy was so upset when Emilee had shared her ordeal that she immediately declared herself battle-ready. It was a call to arms. "Emilee, I'll activate the local chapter of the Women's Liberation Movement. I'll use all my contacts. They know me. Hell, they even know you. This man has to be put in his place. *Neutralized!*"

Her dramatic although not unexpected response startled Emilee. She wasn't certain what she wished for, but she wasn't ready to fight the man. *Neutralized* sounded aggressive. It could imply altering his anatomy. She begged Tracy to do nothing of the kind.

Emilee's friend Rachel shrugged her shoulders and laughed at her rowing mate's predicament. "What've I been telling you? You thought I'm a *man-hater*. I'm a realist. That's what the bastards do: charm the ladies, sleep with them, get them pregnant or give them diseases, and then dump them. And those they don't dump, they abuse, if not physically or sexually, then emotionally and financially. They treat women like *trash*. I don't have time for that."

Alone in bed, Emilee watched the moon complete its entire cycle most nights, its bands of pallid light shifting through the room, the bell tower measuring the hours, while she struggled to reconcile her curiosity about and aversion to the man. It was in equal measures.

On the third Saturday of June, Connor stopped calling, dropping off roses, or leaving messages.

By the time July arrived, Emilee had her mind set on visiting Connor's workplace, the factory floor of the motorcar assembly plant in Cowley. What she hoped to learn there, she couldn't explain. Perhaps, she could find clarity, though she secretly hoped it would reveal his flawed character and she could condemn him on the spot. Maybe this visit would help her decide and close the case.

Every time they parted, Caroline warned her, "He's not your soul mate, Friend. He never will be."

Tracy remained as determined to take physical action the moment Emilee granted her permission.

Rachel reaffirmed her resolution that all men should be viewed with suspicion insofar as the integrity of their intentions were concerned. Their sole mission in life was to score with a girl.

On Friday morning, July 2, Emilee only had an early class. It would be the perfect day for executing her plan. She pedaled down Cowley Road with a tiny backpack clipped in place on her bicycle carrier. Her research had convinced her that a bicycle would grant her greater freedom of movement than taking the bus since she did not own a motorcar.

She pondered the wisdom of her decision as she peered at the menacing clouds in the east mushrooming in the direction she was heading. It required concerted effort to remain to the side of the road out of harm's way as traffic rushed past, as increasing crosswinds gusted around her, threatening to topple her, billowing her raincoat in all directions like a schooner at sea. The humid air was pregnant with the promise of rain.

See what comes from making hasty decisions, Emilee Stephens? This was a silly plan. You should have taken the bus.

Emilee winced when a thunderbolt cracked high above her. The sky had turned jet-black. The few raindrops that struck her face as she reached the entrance to the motor plant only increased her resolve to see it through. The large wire gates were pushed open, but a lowered boom was still in place, forcing her to dismount and push her bike to get past. She ignored the gate guard and started around the boom.

"Miss, a moment!" The guard trudged closer with a clipboard in hand.

She played deaf and slipped past the boom, preparing to mount the bike, but the guard was quicker. He jumped in front of her bicycle, forcing her to stop. "Sorry, Miss. I need your particulars!"

Emilee's face glowed. She only then realized how hard she had been pedaling. Her heart pounded, partly due to annoyance for being apprehended.

"What *is* your problem, sir? I'm only a visitor."

The man held the clipboard for her, scrutinizing her from head to toes. "That's fine, but I still require your particulars, please."

"Why? This is not a military base."

"It's still private property, Miss. *Who* are you visiting?"

Emilee leaned her bicycle against a post and mumbled, now blushing. "It's none of your business."

The man laughed. "You have to write down a person's name."

Emilee snatched the clipboard and scribbled a name.

He took the clipboard back and wrote the time in, glancing at her entry, then at her face. "Oh, the shop steward, Mr. O'Hannigan."

She smirked.

"His girlfriend?"

Emilee turned crimson. "*No,*" she hissed. "I have a *personal* message to deliver. That's all. *Excuse* me." She slipped her leg over, jumped in the saddle, and pedaled hard to get away. Several more drops splattered against her face and coat.

She could hear the guard laughing as she took off. "He never told us his girlfriend was *so* gorgeous. Second building on the right, Miss!"

Grateful for the rain that gave her a reprieve, Emilee stood her bicycle against the outside wall to the side of the entrance of the indicated building. She unclipped the backpack and made for the door. She paused in the entrance hall for her eyes to get used to the darker interior. She fought to catch her breath as she glanced from the entrance to the array of doors leading from the foyer.

Dear Lord, I have no business here.

Offices were to her left it seemed. She had no interest in explaining her presence to the administration. A sign above a double door to her right stated *Employees only.* That must be it.

Emilee pushed the door open and let herself in, immediately stepping to the side where she wouldn't draw attention. Bombarded by a kaleidoscope of colors, odors, and sounds, she took a deep breath and clasped her hands over her ears. The smell of new plastic upholstery, barely dry body paint, and fresh engine oil was overwhelming. A pounding metallic clatter and whining hydraulic devices and power tools engulfed her. The factory floor, a cavernous hall, flooded with fluorescents, stretched out in front of her, the size of four football fields. A high roof with open steel support beams with tall windows across the breadth of the building towered above her.

As far as the eye could see were rows and rows of half-finished identical cars, with giant C-shaped clamps that held the bodies in place, dangling from above. Men in brown dust coats milled around each vehicle.

She stumbled a step backward but remained inside the door.

The tableau was unexpected. Between two and six workers, each in brown, attended to each vehicle. Some of the men, those in navy blue overalls, slid on close-to-the-floor car-creepers, darting in the middle underneath the cars.

Everybody had a specific function and was performing a particular task.

She noticed a small number of men in white coats with clipboards who moved from vehicle to vehicle, checking and saying a few words, then making notes on their clipboards. They had to be higher up in the hierarchy—managers, perhaps.

What did Connor call himself—a shop steward? No, that wasn't what the white coats did, she decided. She sighed again. How would she ever find him in this ant's nest, with all the cacophony and hundreds of workers scuttling around?

After half an hour of silent observation, she had figured out the inner workings of the nest. She couldn't believe that nobody had noticed her. They were definitely working the men too hard.

At the bottom of the ladder were the "blue overalls," the guys on the sliding car-creepers. They were visibly dirty, covered in grease. Next were the "brown-coats." Their job seemed a cleaner one, and they were in the majority, responsible for attaching and tightening everything. Next in line were the "white-coats," the clipboard-brigade, who were probably supervisors of some sort.

Connor and his peers, being the link with the manager and Union bosses, were likely above the white-coats. Emilee grinned, they were probably dressed in fancy shirts and ties, indicative of their importance in the system.

She startled and panicked when a siren went off mere feet from her, high above the wall. Within seconds, the clanging and banging and drilling ceased, then went quiet altogether. Some yelling could be heard a few rows over from where she stood. Then silence. She could hear her own heartbeat.

The workers abandoned their posts and moved in the direction of the heated conversation—angry voices, it seemed. Emilee snuck behind the car bodies and followed the men, keeping her head low, keeping a row of partly assembled vehicles between her and the workers. It soon became clear that a verbal confrontation was taking place between a white-coat and a suit-person. She was right. That had to be a shop steward or someone equally important.

Oh no. She ducked behind a vehicle when the suited man turned and glanced in her direction. Connor O'Hannigan. *He must have seen me.* He returned his attention to the man in the white coat in front of him. A circle of white-coats had surrounded the two men, with brown-coats and blue overall men flocking closer and pushing forward.

The leading man in the white coat, a good six inches taller than Connor, towered over him and waved with the clipboard. Was he hoping to intimidate Connor?

"Mr. O'Hannigan, you do *not* have the authority to halt production."

The shop steward stood his ground. "You're mistaken, Smith. I *do*." Connor stepped within six inches from the face of Mr. Smith, who retreated a step. "That's what the Union pays me for. You were warned on Monday, then again on Wednesday, that the unit price for this final assembly job is too low. The ultimatum was that corrections to the workers' wages would have been agreed upon by nine this morning. It's past eleven. The adjustments have not been made. Therefore, the production *will* be halted. The workers will lay down their tools until management agrees to our ultimatum."

The white-coat's voice raised an octave. "We've had over a hundred strikes already this year, Mr. O'Hannigan! It's a disservice to the company and to the country."

"Be glad this is the first strike this week, Smith. My first priority is to improve the working conditions of the men, and that *includes* remuneration." Connor had taken another step closer toward Mr. Smith. "Don't play the patriotism shit with me. You embarrass yourself. You have till noon to produce the signed documentation, or the men walk off the job—indefinitely."

Then he added, "And they *will* be paid for this hour until noon and beyond, pending your handling of the situation."

Mr. Smith still protested, "But Mr. Hall isn't—"

"Mr. Hall is here, hiding in his office. I've checked. You have forty-five minutes to convince management, Smith."

Connor spun around and addressed the workers. "*Gentlemen.* All tools are down till noon. You *will* get paid. Be back at your respective stations by five to noon please!"

The next moment he stepped through the throng of men and darted in Emilee's direction, who was momentarily frozen in concentration. She spun around and made a beeline for the double doors where she had slipped in, dashing between the rows of cars. *Damn. He did see me.*

Connor was more familiar with the factory floor and gained on her.

"Emilee, wait!" he reached for her as she grabbed the door handle and swung it open, sidestepping him and crouching through the narrowing gap between the two doors.

She hollered over her shoulder, "Let me be, O'Hannigan!" as she sprinted toward the front entrance and slipped outside, making for her bicycle.

Connor kept up with her.

She had swung her bicycle around when he stepped right in front of her and took hold of the handlebars. She ripped the handles free, "Let *go.*"

He laughed as he stepped closer and took the surprised Emilee's face in his hands and planted a kiss on her lips, his mocking eyes burning into her.

She staggered back with her bicycle, regained her balance, and slapped him across the cheek. "How *dare* you?" she hissed.

He rubbed his cheek, still laughing. "Then why did you come and spy on me?"

Emilee was crimson. "I didn't spy. It was *research.*"

"So you *do* care." He smiled. "I was worried, since you've been avoiding me like the plague."

"I had every reason to be upset about what you said," she countered.

"I apologized on the spot. I never intended malice." He paused. "Why *did* you come to the factory floor?"

"I d-d-don't know . . . I . . . was hoping to see you in a real life—"

"Did you *find* what you came looking for?'

"I still don't know. It seems you care a great deal about the workers."

Again, the easy laugh. "Is that a bad thing?"

She swung her leg across and slid onto the saddle. "Never mind. Goodbye, Connor."

He jumped forward and cradled her face a second time and kissed her for longer. "Goodbye, Emilee-who-cares."

This time she gave a dry sob as she pulled away from his lingering kiss.

The Irishman stood, smiling, hands on his hips, and watched as the redhead raced toward the boom at the gate, before he turned back to face management.

CHAPTER 18

───── ⟶〰〰⟵ ─────

Signing a truce. August 1971

IF ANYTHING, CONNOR O'Hannigan learned a lesson in his dealings with Emilee: it was wiser not to mess with a she-lion. He had to be more cautious, bide his time, make her wonder about his intentions.

He stayed away. Applying such self-control was hard. He could not recall when last he had met someone, a woman, who intrigued him, who would challenge him so relentlessly. She cared. Why else did she cycle all the way to the factory floor in the rain? She didn't slap him when he kissed her the second time. He would show her, prove to her, that he could do unpredictable. He could be less broomstick-in-the-behind, be less obsessive about his car and his possessions.

Who are you bluffing, O'Hannigan?

By August the first, he found it impossible to postpone any longer and called at Magdalen College early on Sunday afternoon. The weather-people had promised several hours of sunshine. Only a fool wouldn't grasp the opportunity in a country where hours of sunshine per week were often measured in single digits.

Connor waited at his usual spot. After five minutes, he wondered whether he had ever been reinstated to the realm of *persona grata*. He was ready to sound the retreat when Emilee appeared at the top of the stairs.

"Connor." She looked radiant, and she was smiling.

"Milady." He nodded and watched as color crept up her neck. "May I steal you away for a couple of hours? It's a mortal sin to be indoors on a day like this."

"It depends on your agenda, O'Hannigan." Emilee took her time down the stairs and glanced him over. She was fully aware of her flushing but refused to let the Irishman gloat at her expense. "I see you've made a smarter wardrobe choice." She grinned into his face. "Where are we going? Walking? Hiking? I'm not interested in racing down these narrow streets in your little sports car."

He laughed. "We can put the top down, then you'll experience the loveliness of the day."

She took a step back. "No thanks, no driving."

"All right, no driving. But we can do all of the other things. There's time."

"You don't have to leave in sixty minutes, before the carriage turns back into a pumpkin?"

"Not today, no." He coughed to hide his embarrassment. "I'm trying to pull the broomstick out a bit. Show some mercy."

She laughed, skipped past him, and took flight down a path. She turned to face him but continued walking, backward. "Have you ever been down the riverside, the Addison's riverside-walk?"

Connor shook his head as he caught up. "I didn't dare walk on these expansive grounds. The place is so grand. There must be several groundskeepers who could easily have taken a shot at me for trespassing—mistake me for a poacher."

Emilee smiled, "That's a lie. You know they would never do that. You're not afraid of anyone, least of all a simple groundskeeper." She touched his hand. "Did the strike go through?"

He turned his head away and mumbled. "No. They met our demands." It was clear that he was uncomfortable talking about the incident. She would have no problem telling him in detail about her days in class on campus, about the small battles she had to fight, every detail, every single day. He should be proud of such an accomplishment.

They were walking close to the river now, and she faced him. "How does it feel when you thwart them like that—pull a sock over their eyes?"

"A sock?"

"Don't play stupid with me, Connor. You put those white-coats in checkmate." She halted. "They—the owners, the employer, and the white-coat brigade—they couldn't have liked that?"

"It has nothing to do with 'like.' But it worked out quite fine. Don't concern yourself so much about my work-stuff. It's boring."

Emilee increased per pace. "*Nonsense.* I've lived such a sheltered life. It's fascinating to see how a shop steward, a single individual—and in this instance, *you*—can bring a gigantic factory floor to a grinding halt. That's powerful stuff." She noticed how his demeanor changed, how he stiffened up. She shrugged her shoulders and ran ahead, turning again. "You *truly* don't want to talk about work?"

He forced a smile. "You got *that.*"

"You wish to remain a man of mystery." She pulled a face. "Do you have any *other* secrets, O'Hannigan?"

"Of course not, Miss Stephens." He ran forward and grabbed her hand, which she allowed.

She swung his hand, glancing at him. "Why don't I believe you?"

"Perhaps because you expect the worst of people? Ones who dare to stand up to be counted."

"You're a pompous man."

Emilee chuckled and pulled her hand free, then clasped her hands behind her back as she continued walking.

He will have to prove himself in that regard. Trust must be earned.

They walked in silence for several hundred feet. Red squirrels darted from tree to tree, scurrying away as the two approached.

Emilee paused as soon as she spotted the small herd of roe deer clustered together. She pointed them out to Connor.

If he had any serious intentions with her, she added, he would have to learn, despite how painful and foreign it might be to him, that they have to be open with one another. They had to be honest—about life, about everything, about their individual lives—but also about life together as a couple.

"So, we're a couple now?"

She smirked. "I'm postulating, O'Hannigan. Don't assume *anything*." She took his hand. "Let's turn back. I'm thirsty. But I can't see us being a couple if we're going to have secrets from each other."

He laughed as he shook his head, mumbling, "Secrets are part of our lives, of being human."

She ran forward, pulling him along. "You'll have to choose. If you want part of me, there can be *no* secrets. Period."

They followed the path as it left the river and wound back toward the college. Only then did either of them speak.

"Connor." Her voice was soft, almost hesitant. "Tell me about your mother." She heard him draw in his breath, tensing as he walked. She squeezed his hand. Perhaps he would open one of his many secret trapdoors. She squeezed harder. "Please."

Avoiding eye contact, he looked down the path and followed the flight paths of dragonflies surrounding them. "Her name is Deirdre, *Deirdre* O'Hannigan."

He sketched a picture of a woman whom life had made much older than her sixty-five years. However, she still worked as a nurse, refusing to quit, like her husband, in his family practice all day long. Since the village was so small, his dad's practice served after hours as the village hospital.

"What's the place's name?"

"Annagassan."

"Anna Gassan?"

"*Annagassan*, with a population of less than two hundred at any given time. It sits on the shores of the Irish Sea, at the mouth of the Glyde River, forty-five miles north of Dublin."

It was more a glorified clinic than a hospital, he explained. The practice was attached to the side of the house, although his father had a specially equipped room, a mini-theatre, where he did small operations.

Like Father, Mother would *never* retire but continue serving the village people. They served their country, they believed, with their lives. Mother had become totally obsessed with working after his older brother had gotten killed a little over a year ago, a casualty of the Troubles of the North. Connor's voice broke at that point.

Emilee stepped from the path and pulled him along until they reached the protection of the trees. She tugged his arm until he sat down on a bench next to her. She pulled him closer. "The other day, you said you hadn't seen them in five years. You didn't go back even for your brother's funeral?"

He sounded tired, like an old man. "I went. I was there—but he, they, refused to see me, speak to me—I was dead, according to Father. I died the day I left when I made it clear I would not follow in his footsteps by becoming a doctor or fighting for the cause."

Emilee moved away on the bench to face him. "What's so terrible about becoming a doctor?"

His voice came from afar. "It's more than becoming a physician. It's about the lineage, the family tradition, our heritage, and about our duty toward our bloodline, of not breaking that. On a good day, Father could literally date it back—the family physician part—to the Battle of Boyne in 1690 during the days of King James II."

"*So?* That's part of history. It's got nothing to do with you. We live in the present, the twentieth century."

"Emilee, don't feel bad. Most people don't understand. It's complex. My father's sympathy, like his father, and his before him, and before him, were and will forever be for the aspirations of a united Ireland. Ulster has to become part of Eire again. To say he hates the British is a misnomer. It's deeper than that. The family has lent support to the resistance, over the years . . . over the centuries."

He became quiet for such a long time that Emilee thought he had drifted off into a deep sleep as his eyes remained closed and his breathing deepened. She touched his arm, startling him.

Connor grimaced and continued telling her how he'd grown up in Annagassan. He told her how he had eaten, drunk, tasted, and lived the Struggle all his life—how it had formed the core of the family. His sympathies, however, were different from his father's. Father couldn't comprehend that a son of his, an O'Hannigan, could dare to break the lineage.

Father had become intimately involved with the Troubles, yet he remained so naive, not realizing the British Police had planted spies in the village long ago to keep an eye on him. Connor had to get away, afraid of what it was doing to the family but also to himself.

So, as soon as he finished high school, as soon as he turned eighteen, he came across the Sea to England. The first few years he maintained contact, until his father one day simply told him not to visit again unless he was willing to follow in his footsteps.

He paused. "I have a cousin, Niall, who works with me at British Leyland. He returns every six months. His parents live down the road from mine in Annagassan. He fills me in." Connor was flustered now. "Niall secretly carries letters between my mom and me. I dare not mail it. Dad can't know. He'll destroy the letters. She knows when Niall visits, then goes over to his parent's place and reads the letters there."

Emilee leaned her head against his shoulder. Both went quiet. "Is he an angry man?"

"Father?"

"How much laughter was there in the house when you grew up, Connor?"

He sounded pained. "Life is serious, Emilee. He's a hard-working, stern man—a strict Catholic. He took care of his family and of the village."

"Did he hit . . . did he beat your brother and you?"

Connor pulled away. "Only when he drank."

"How often was that?"

Connor remained vague, willing to commit only to once a month, perhaps. "Father brewed his own liquor in his small cellar. Strong stuff." Connor had never developed a taste for the dark ale. Father would hit them, but only when he became really inebriated. That usually occurred on the last Saturday of the month, when he took his one weekend of the month off, when one of his colleagues from a neighboring town looked after the sick and the infirm.

The brothers soon learned to visit and stay with friends on those weekends.

"When your father was like that, did he ever raise his hand to your mother?" She whispered the question.

It was as if a viper had struck him. He jolted from the bench. "*Enough.* Leave my mother out of this!"

Emilee followed him, stepping closer, undeterred by his response. She challenged him to meet her eyes. "Has your father struck your mother? I'm serious. No secrets."

"Yes, he has."

"The words you used the other day when we were walking with Caroline and Douglas, about *spanking* a woman's bottom, teaching her a lesson. Were those the phrases your dad used against your mother?"

He held her gaze, his face grim. He gave a reluctant nod.

She took his hands and stepped back, seeking his eyes. "Connor O'Hannigan, will you *ever* hit or strike me again? Give me your word."

"*Never*," he whispered. He pulled her into his arms, crushed her breasts against his chest, kissed the top of her head, her eyes, her lips, then led her back to the path.

CHAPTER 19

A yellow kayak. August 1971

CAROLINE WASTED LITTLE time to analyze and interpret her friend's demeanor the moment they sat down at their usual table. She sensed the change. Her face was drawn as she took Emilee's hands.

"I thought you were *done* with the Irishman."

A soft rose crept into Emilee's face. She explained how she had avoided him for six full weeks, how she had refused to see him or meet with him. His red roses had ended up in the garbage and his letters remained unopened. She knew he was bad news— a bad apple, according to her friend.

"I met with him for the *first* time again last Sunday, but for several hours." She paused and glanced at her friend. "We talked a lot. I insisted that he keep no secrets from me." She leaned forward. "Did you know, Carrie, he's from an abusive family home? It explains so much."

"Shame, the poor boy." Caroline smirked. "Another reason why you should throw a wide berth around him. *You're* the one who'll be abused and assaulted, the one to be taught a lesson by him. He even *warned* you."

Emilee squeezed her friend's hands with so much force that Carrie cried out. Tears welled in Emilee's eyes. She wiped them and whispered, "He promised he would *never* lift a hand against me. He gave me his word."

"And you *believed* him." Caroline was now also crying.

She lamented the fact that nobody had been able to talk any sense into Emilee. It was as if her truest friends—Caroline, Douglas, Rachel, and Tracy—didn't exist, didn't matter, didn't have a clue about what they were talking about; they were a collection of nitwits who were out to spite their friend and rob her of a boyfriend.

Caroline reminded Emilee about what the chairwoman had said at the WLM meeting at Ruskin College over a year ago. Women had to take ownership of their own persons and bodies. They should stop being men's slaves, stop being their punch bags, their domestic servants, their baby machines, and their sexpots.

Emilee stared at her with wet eyes. "And I thought you hated the WLM."

"I never did. I just don't need to walk in a march at the capital to prove a point. Neither do I need an organization to help me tell right from wrong, and I hate to be told what to think, especially about myself and my body. I know when it's time to open my mouth and to speak up. As I'm doing *now*."

Emilee laughed. "Oh, Carrie, I *love* you—for being such a brave and honest friend. Don't worry. I'll give this O'Hannigan fellow lots of rope and time to see what he's *truly* up to. He'll be subjected to strenuous testing—be weighed and measured."

The next day, Sunday, Connor O'Hannigan showed up at Magdalen, again at two in the afternoon. He waited at the top of the stairs for Emilee, visibly excited. He explained how he had stumbled upon a unique gift for her, something small, as a token of his sincerity, since she clearly was not interested in red roses or handwritten letters. But, she had to come out to the car. The gift was a little bulky and wouldn't fit into her room either.

Emilee tripped along, bombarding the beaming Irishman with questions, but he refused to give her any more clues.

The moment they reached the street, it was impossible not to become aware of Mary Gabriella's presence, still in all her glossy glory but entirely dwarfed by the canary-yellow kayak tied to her roof.

Emilee came to an abrupt halt on the sidewalk, glancing from Connor to the kayak and back. "Something *small*?"

He chuckled. "What do you think? It's in excellent condition. I got it from an acquaintance. It comes with a splash cover, paddles, life jacket, the works." He continued when she said nothing. "I know you're into coxed eight rowing and kayaking is different, but it's perhaps something we can go do together *sometime*?"

She laughed and hugged him. "I'll learn. They have indoor training sessions in the warm pool for these little boats." She tiptoed and gave him a peck on the cheek, then stepped closer and stroked the yellow body, walking around the entire car.

"Are you certain you're all right, Connor O'Hannigan?" She glanced over the yellow body at him. "Tying a fiberglass boat to the vinyl top of your precious Mary Gabriella. Poor baby." She pouted her lips as she patted the car, taking care not to touch the blue body.

He coughed, embarrassed, and suggested they drive down to the Magdalen College boathouse and drop the kayak off in order to enjoy the rest of their afternoon. Emilee hesitated. She would need the rowing coach's permission, which she couldn't get since it was Sunday afternoon.

When he countered her with asking permission from the assistant coach, she groaned but still agreed to drive down with him to the boathouse since she did have a key. She was hopeful they would find an appropriate space for the tiny vessel, not wanting to bother her coaches unnecessarily on the day of rest.

The next day, Emilee arranged with her sweep-boat coach to store the kayak indefinitely in a discreet spot in the boathouse, away from the eyes of her teammates, for the remainder of her time at Magdalen. In exchange, she had to solemnly swear not to neglect her six-days-a-week sweep-boat rowing and practice even harder. She next bribed three training sessions off in the indoor warm pool. It had helped that she knew the kayaking coach.

By the third lesson, she had mastered the Eskimo roll and recovery of a capsized kayak in deep water, as well as how to reenter it. She was adamant to learn the techniques as quickly and efficiently as possible since fall was fast approaching. It would be unwise to attempt 360-degree rolls in near-freezing water outdoors.

Connor undertook to also practice and kayak on his own each week to get some of his form and breath back.

Connor had arranged to meet Emilee on the last Sunday in August at 7 a.m. a hundred yards downstream from the college boathouse in their respective kayaks.

The mist crawled unhurried and lazy around him. He had come much earlier to enjoy the silence of the early morning. The fog kept rolling in: bank after bank hovered then rolled on the water. He breathed the early morning flavors: the river, the sleeping town, the crispness of the waking day, the muskiness of the mist. Movement on the bank caught his eyes—a splash, then silence. A beaver?

The swash of paddles preceded his sighting of the yellow kayak as it glided closer. She called out, seeking affirmation in the poor visibility, and he immediately answered. Both of them sounded relieved and pleased. Their delighted voices became suspended in the swirling whiteness that folded in around them as if wrapped in cocoons.

The two kayaks drifted together and clinked like wine glasses. They embraced, giggling as they steadied their vessels and each other, bobbing up and down in the swell. Connor managed to steal a kiss before they drifted apart, laughing, and was immediately swallowed by the haze.

They would follow the Cherwell River north for an hour before turning back.

By the end of the first hour, the fog had thinned out as the friends turned their vessels around and headed south again. One could now smell the river water, a soft whiff of mire, reeds, birds, and morning fog. The town was waking up. Emilee, encouraged by the retreating mist, became bolder and performed several 360-degree rolls to loud cheering by her companion.

"Come on, Connor. *Your* turn for an Eskimo roll!" she called out, laughing.

"Sorry, Missy, but I've never had proper instruction in a heated indoor pool, unlike certain privileged people," he said as he paddled hard to get away from her sweeping paddle that was spraying water over him on purpose.

"Scary cat. I'll show you again. The most important thing is to *lean* back, *tuck* your paddle in sideways next to your body along the long axis of your kayak, like *this*, and *roll*."

Those were the last words Connor heard as Emilee disappeared under the surface to perform her roll. The remnants of a fog bank moved in and twirled around them.

What a glorious morning it had been.

He steadied himself with his paddle and peered at the spot where she had disappeared. *Strange. It usually takes her a single second to roll through the 360-degrees maneuver.* He stared as if hypnotized at the bottom of her yellow kayak, which started jerking.

Panic choked his throat as he ripped his splash cover free. "Oh my God, Emilee!" He pulled his legs out and toppled sideways, taking a breath as he dove down. His friend was hanging upside down in the water, her splash cover still in place, her face frantic, a few bubbles escaping her mouth. She gestured with her free arm. It seemed her lower arm, along with the paddle blade, were completely entangled in some water plant or reeds.

Connor shot to the surface, unclipped his floatation device, and took another deep breath. This time he ripped her splash cover free and started freeing her arm from the long, slimy, green tentacle-like vegetation. The plant wouldn't budge.

He kicked and pulled, in a frenzy now, until he freed her legs from the kayak. His lungs were bursting as he glanced at Emilee's face. Her eyes were closed and her mouth wide open. *Oh Lord, no!*

He popped to the surface again for air and hollered in cold blood. "*Help*! Somebody, help!" Then took another breath and dove down. The murky water didn't make his task easier. Emilee's body floated closer to the surface as he pulled with everything he had at her entangled arm.

Did he imagine it, or did her eyes open for a brief second as he pulled her paddle free from the water plant and then her arm? He grabbed her now-limp body and kicked with numb legs to get them back to the surface. He gasped and gulped for air, choking and coughing as he turned Emilee onto her back. *Thank God she has a life jacket on.*

He again yelled in alarm, this time louder, "Anybody, help!" *God, I'm so tired.* He pulled her lifeless body behind him, calling out, "Hold on, Em! Please hold on, sweetheart!" He was sobbing as he held her loose against his chest and swam a crab-like backstroke toward the closest shore. "I'm so sorry I bought you the blooming yellow boat."

He had no idea what had happened to their respective kayaks, their paddles, or his life jacket.

"Oh, damn the kayaks! And damn this fog!" he hollered as he struggled with the current and his friend's flaccid body. He was exhausted, his legs cramped, his heart pounded, and his arms felt like rubber. *O'Hannigan, you should have paid more attention to the lifeguard during water-rescue lessons in high school!*

He could feel some vegetation underfoot as he kicked toward shore. "Let go, you bloody plants!" he yelled through his tears and coughed, kicking harder. From time to time he hollered into the whiteness, smothering them. "Help! Somebody out there, help!"

The fog continued to lift and settle and roll around them. He kicked harder. *Was that the college boathouse?* The next moment the mist whited everything out again. *Dear Lord, it's been so long since I've prayed to you. Please let that be the boathouse, and whilst I'm begging, please let there be somebody who can help us.*

Several of Emilee's rowing mates were at the boathouse and heard Connor's intermittent cries for help. Three of them jumped into the river and pulled the exhausted, crying Connor and the lifeless body of their friend out onto the boathouse dock.

Fortunately, the rowing buddies had paid attention during life-saving class, so they set to work. One ran toward the college to phone for an ambulance.

Emilee was discharged from the hospital late that same afternoon, well, though still a bit shaken.

For the first time in eighteen months, since joining the team, she was exempted from sweep boat rowing on Monday, the next morning.

CHAPTER 20

Mr. O'Hannigan's apartment. October 1971.

WHETHER IT WAS her kayaking accident or being saved by Connor and her arising, deepening relationship with the Irishman, Emilee successfully applied for permission to modify her English and modern languages course. The faculty stipulated that she had to go abroad to the mainland to immerse herself in a foreign language for twelve months during her third year. She expressed her wish to drop the modern language part and rather expand her study of English, as well as medieval literature—and not leave the country.

Her friends, especially Caroline, reluctantly accepted her now-official boyfriend.

Emilee was ready to stand up for her man. "After all, friend," she told Caroline at their first eye-to-eye meeting following her near drowning, "He *was* weighed and measured. I tried so hard to find him wanting because he *has* issues. We know that. But he saved my *life*."

Even Caroline found it impossible to contradict such raw logic.

The yellow kayak, after being found later that Sunday morning by her rowing mates, was cleaned and stored in its special place in the boathouse and remained untouched.

Emilee only garnered the guts to try it out on the river early the following spring. She did, however, show up for coxed eight rowing on the Tuesday following her ordeal with the water plants. She felt safe enough being on the water provided she was not alone. She was at peace with the fact that she would never again perform a 360-degree roll in a river.

She would now see Connor every second evening during the week and for several hours on Saturdays and Sundays. They usually met up and spent the time in The Old Library. It required a juggling act on the part of Emilee to balance the rowing, the reading, and the tutorials while not neglecting her other friends—and now, Connor. One thing had to go, though: the swimming, late at night, with Rachel.

———

By the end of October, Connor had convinced Emilee to visit him at his apartment and study there at least once a week. It was much quieter than in the busy library. She would be able to accomplish so much more, he had said. He lived in Cowley, only minutes from the motor plant, and not too far from Magdalen. Mary Gabriella would be delighted to be of service.

Emilee rolled her eyes at his lukewarm argument, laughing out loud the first time he suggested it, but obliged weeks later. His arguments were relentless. After all, he had saved her life.

He picked her up with Mary G for the first visit on a Thursday afternoon at exactly five. She had to meet him outside the college gates. Emilee hugged herself in the much-too-thin-jersey-for-late-fall as she ran closer when he pulled to a stop. The skyline glowed crimson through the trees as he kissed her on the lips, then held the door, the white handkerchief in place, waiting an extra moment to check that she had removed her shoes before closing the door.

The apartment mirrored its owner. Connor waited on her to remove her shoes once inside the door. The place had a clean smell— not hospital disinfectant clean, but wood-oil, floor-polish clean.

For a moment, she shuddered at the thought of him seeing her dorm room. She believed in orderly disorder, or, as Caroline phrased it: controlled chaos. In her own defense though, she did clean up every weekend, and she knew, at any given time, where everything was, each apparently strewn-around item.

She followed him down the short hallway as he turned the lights on, into the mid-size hall that served as living and dining room.

It was clear Connor believed in minimalism and quality. Above the marble fireplace, a framed pen sketch of an unclad female figure filled half of the wall, the only picture in the room, with a tall, narrow window on each side; the velvet ceiling-to-floor curtains pulled far apart. Against the entire back wall was a built-in bookshelf in lavish dark wood. She was certain it was mahogany. It was filled to the brim with volumes. Two French lounge wing chairs and a leather chaise lounge sat on a Persian rug that covered the floor. Behind it, an imposing dark wood table with pedestal legs and six straight back chairs welcomed her.

Emilee approached the table with reverence. It reminded her of her grandmother's—the unique legs, not the size. She snapped her hand back at the last moment, remembering that her skin's oils may leave marks on the gleaming surface. She inhaled the subtle wood scent. Her eyes closed. She faced Connor. "Mahogany?"

He beamed. "Walnut."

Only then did he remember his place and took her shoulder bag with her study material, patting the backrest of the fabric-covered wing chair. "Please sit down. Where are my manners?" He chuckled as he moved through a second door opening and called over his shoulder, "I'm putting the water on for tea."

Emilee leaned back, savoring the soft welcome of the chair, only to jump up and scrutinize the drawing. A name was scribbled in the right-hand bottom corner. She leaned closer, on tiptoes: Deirdre O'Hannigan '68. She returned to the chair and closed her eyes. *Mother O'Hannigan: the diehard artistic nurse.*

Connor returned with a substantive tray. He had found room for a pot with tea, covered with a knitted cozy, two cups with saucers, proper tea spoons, sugar cubes and four scones, butter and jam, each in miniature bowls, milk in a petite jug, napkins, two plates, and two spreading knives. By the time he had placed the tray on the dining table, Emilee stood behind one of the upright chairs. She was famished.

"Do you mind?" he asked as he poured the tea through a strainer and handed it to her, then poured himself the second cup. Next, he passed her a plate with a scone, which she broke open and jabbed jam onto both halves.

Emilee placed her teacup on the coffee table, bit into the scone, and sunk back into the upholstered backrest. She inhaled deeply. The scone had been baked that morning. It was serene, having high tea with the royalty. She felt embarrassed. He must have baked the scones at the break of day. She didn't even have to close her eyes to be in grandmother's kitchen. Was there anything he couldn't do?

She smiled at him. "You baked it this morning?"

He nodded, then mumbled with a full mouth, "Couldn't sleep—was so excited about your visit."

"Was that when you polished the table, to impress me? No, it must have been your housekeeper."

Connor laughed, shaking his head. "You're looking at the housekeeper."

By the time she had finished a second scone and two cups of sweet tea, it was already past six. Connor had insisted on clearing the tray with its contents and left Emilee with her books at the dining table, but only after turning on another standing lamp which he had moved closer to the table for her. After he had cleaned up, he took a volume from the shelf and sat down in the leather wing chair.

Between her reading and making notes, she would chew on her pen and glance in his direction whenever she felt his eyes on her, which was often since he never opened the book. In spite of the table lamp next to him, it was impossible to see the aquamarine of his eyes. He glanced at her with his bored smile through hooded eyes. They appeared entirely black. The intensity of his gaze made it impossible to concentrate.

She remained unprepared for the sudden flood of emotion that would course through her. Since the accident, this would happen without warning. She cringed as the waves washed over her. She was underwater, hanging upside down in the kayak, jerking her entangled arm when she saw him dive in for the first time. How he fought to free her, each time going back to the surface for air—until it all went black.

As of late, she had become aware of so many foreign and unfamiliar sentiments. Connor scared her. He intrigued her. It ached so bad, right in the center of her chest, each time she looked at him. If it wasn't for him. *Dear, Lord. I love the man.*

By eight o'clock she gave up, packed her books, and dropped down in the wing chair across from him. "It's hopeless, Connor."

"Do you want me to retreat to my room?"

Where did he learn to speak like that?

She laughed, embarrassed. "No, that would feel odd. I'd prefer to have you around, nearby."

He got up and kneeled in front of her, took her hands, and kissed them. He took his time, teased each fingertip with a brush of his lips, peered into her eyes, as if searching for her soul, his eyes darker than usual. "Have I ever told you . . . you are *so* beautiful?"

She flushed but also laughed. "You have *forgotten*? You have brought shame on the house of the O'Hannigans."

"Only one way to rectify the transgression, ma'am." He laughed as he leaned forward, let go of her hands, kissed her on the mouth, took her shoulders, and pulled her toward him. He held her like this for a long time. She could feel his thumping heartbeat. When he leaned back, she opened her eyes to find him mocking her, daring her. His lips closed over hers with urgency, his hands cradling her neck. His mouth tasted of tea and of him.

Inside, she had come to life—glowing—from her lips down her neck through her entire body, down to her toes. This was what she had longed for. The realization remained a shock. Her nipples strained against the blouse, and the warm sensation traveled down to her belly button as Connor nibbled on her lips. His mouth moved to the tip of her nose and brushed over her closed eyelids. She moaned. His kisses traveled down her neck, then around to her earlobes and down to her collarbones. She whimpered. *Please don't stop.*

The glow had spread down to the valley between her thighs. She could feel the pulsing, the throbbing. She sighed as he pushed her back into the wing chair and kneeled between her legs, pushing them apart, inching closer, unbuttoning the top button of her blouse.

Closer, Connor, closer.

Her hands were in his hair, and she pulled his face against her chest as he unbuttoned a second button. His breathing came faster as he struggled with the third button and the next. When would he reach the last button? A quarter-inch at a time, he now pulled the blouse aside. Her pale skin was revealed, little by little. Parts of her breasts were exposed, the areolas dark from arousal. She shuddered when he blew on the nipples.

Her legs spasmed.

When his lips closed over a breast, she whimpered, arching her back.

As her pelvis throbbed, a sudden shock, as if electrocuted, pulsed through her. She cried out, uncomprehending, as if in pain, as if drowning upside down in the Cherwell River. She had no control over her reaction. She so longed his touch, his searching mouth, his velvet tongue.

So violent was her reaction that Connor stumbled backward and fell sideways as she sprung to her feet and clasped her blouse, crimson in the face. She stared at him, bewildered.

The disbelief and hurt in his eyes were unmistakable. "Why didn't you *stop* me?"

She sobbed as she grabbed her jersey and shoulder bag and made for the front door. "I don't know. I care so much for you, Connor. I'm confused. I'm not ready. Please take me back."

CHAPTER 21

Professor Thomas Hill. January 1972.

EMILEE DID NOT return to Connor's apartment for several weeks—not even to study— although they resumed their meetings in the library. But, she still had to see him every day, she claimed. The extent of physical contact between them was now limited to the holding of hands, sideway hugs, and peck-kisses— and only in public. That was the extent of intimacy she could handle at the time.

Connor—on the surface—accepted the state of affairs.

She had difficulty recalling when last, if ever, she had felt so unsettled. She was housing two persons in one body, it seemed. She was being transformed into a Jekyll-and-Hyde-like creature. Even the snow that fell on the first Sunday in the New Year could not lift her spirits. Looking at the virgin white cloak that covered her world only accentuated the darkness of her despair.

The more she thought about what was happening to her, the more she felt sick. Powerless. Helpless. She had taken to a daily ache, centered in her chest. She had turned into a stranger to herself.

To be with him was what she craved, and yet she was equally scared of being alone with the man. He intrigued her—had so

Danie Botha

from the moment they had met. He also infuriated her. He constantly forced her on the defensive. She could not dare lapse into complacency. It was a constant challenge, an intricate game which she cherished and dreaded—the incessant jostling.

What put her off though was the occasional ridicule, his biting sarcasm, which made her feel insecure, when, in reality, it was his insecurities and obsessions that invaded her calm and ordered world. That was what she had difficulty explaining when she lay alone in her bed in the early morning hours, listening to the sleeping town, to the bells and clock towers, wrestling with why she couldn't give up the boy from Annagassan.

Her close friends were the first to notice the waning of her effervescence, the dimming of her trailblazer-spirit. She appeared pale, they claimed—clearly unwell.

"When are you going to stop this madness, friend?" Caroline insisted.

"It's *nothing*—I'm fine. I swear."

"You've forgotten what fine looks like. You are *ill*."

"I'm in love."

Caroline snorted. "You *think* you're in love. You're confusing gratitude with smoldering affection."

Emilee would have none of it and fell back onto her latest crutch—tears. She had discovered she could cry at will. It solved nothing but diluted some of the pain and sometimes helped convince others to change their minds—give her some room—and others to back off. She now claimed they were only jealous that she had found happiness for the first time in her life.

"You call this *happiness*? You poor, poor, silly girl. You're the most miserable creature in all of England." They threw their arms

130

around each other and sobbed it out until all that remained was their deep-rooted trust, acceptance, forgiveness, and fathomless friendship.

Emilee had less trouble keeping up appearances with her rowing buddies. Winter had forced them indoors, and they had to row on dry land. It was easier to hide and escape into the brutal physicality of the repetitive action. They would simulate locking the blades in the water, all the while avoiding bum-shoving, keeping their backs straight and driving with their legs, repeating it over and over and over again.

Each time, Emilee attacked the rowing machine with so much force that the chain whined in protest until her perspiration pooled around her on the floor. The coach and assistant coach only shook their heads, not saying a word, but it was Rachel who, during unguarded moments, would give Emilee a knowing look: *You can't fool me, partner. It's that badass man from Annagassan I had warned you against.*

In the shower before class, Emilee would wash away the sweat and hurt and pain and longing that pulsed through her. For a few seconds, she would allow the water to spray over her breasts, conjuring a similar sensation to when Connor had blown on them before kissing the one and she had reacted so violently.

She was hoping, as she hoped every time now when she showered, turning the water to cold, that she could desensitize herself, if only slightly, and make them less hypersensitive, to lessen their longing.

When she finally turned off the water and grabbed her towel, she shivered uncontrollably. The water didn't help. Her bosom ached and begged for more. She was aware of a pulsing. She rubbed herself dry with haste, threw on her clothes, and scampered for a quick breakfast before running to her first tutorial.

—⚉—

It was more difficult to control her thoughts in class. The inactivity gave free range to her emotions, and her mind took off. Her pen-hand remained motionless on her notepad. All she heard was blabber. The man said nothing of importance.

Who was the stranger at the front anyway?

The English faculty had acquired the services of a new tutorial fellow: Professor Thomas Geoffrey Hill, early in January. He had received his doctorate the previous year and would be responsible for teaching the undergraduate students.

It did not take long for the word to spread, through even the third-year class, the very first day he appeared at the front. A visible murmur went through the group.

He used to row competitively, 1968 Olympics apparently, and, claimed Tracy Russell, he was only twenty-nine. "Can you *believe* it? Twenty-nine!"

Emilee broke her trance, pulled up her shoulders, and rolled her eyes. "And your point is?" she whispered. "Another young windbag—some kind of a linguistics *protégé*."

"*That* was high on the bitchiness scale," her friend whispered back. "Even for a woman's libber."

Emilee snickered and pondered why they'd never noticed the new Don around the university halls and grounds. It was impossible to have done so, claimed her friend, since he had been imported from Cambridge.

"So he was *bought* by Oxford."

"Stop being horrible. You should be impressed. He *rows*."

Emilee pulled up her shoulders. "So?"

"Shush . . . he's looking in our direction. Look how buff he is. You can tell, even with his winter jacket on."

"He must have bought his dissertation and doctorate on the black market. It's impossible to row at that level *and* find time for all the research *and* complete your thesis," Emilee mumbled.

"Bollocks. He's gifted."

Emilee immediately offered to ask the new professor for his home phone number. It was for her friend Tracy she would tell the professor. Her friend has fallen madly in love with him and was too embarrassed to ask.

Tracy jabbed her friend in the ribs, crimson-faced, hissing that she wouldn't dare.

Emilee's hand shot into the air. Tracy looked as if she was on the brink of an apoplectic attack and tried in vain to convince her friend to abandon her suicide mission.

"Yes, Miss?"

His shoulders are broad, Emilee realized when the man gave her his undivided attention. A bemused grin lingered on his face as he readjusted his tie and unbuttoned his jacket, slipped out of it, and draped it across the chair-back. His shirt stretched over his trim physique as he moved. Emilee swallowed.

"You had a question?" The man took a step in her direction, still grinning.

It was Emilee's turn to turn crimson. She stammered. "Y-yes, sir . . . My friend and I were wondering . . . should we take heart in the fact that it *is* possible to excel in academics and at the same time distinguish oneself in a sport? Or . . . are you an exception?"

A murmur went through the class. The professor laughed, looked away, and rubbed his chin before facing her again.

"Thank you for the compliment, Miss. But I thought that was what they teach you here in Oxford. What they encourage. Excellence in *every* aspect of life?"

Emilee sat down and mumbled, more to herself. "That was *so* arrogant."

Tracy sucked her breath.

The professor must have heard every word. "Are you perhaps confusing assertiveness with arrogance—and, heavens forbid, guilty yourself of the crime you accuse me of?"

The class applauded as Emilee held up her hands in defense. "Guilty as charged, sir. Please accept my apologies."

"Apologies accepted, Miss." Then he added, as he picked up a clipboard from the lectern, "Your name?"

"Emilee Stephens, sir."

"Miss Stephens—the humble one." He chuckled as he turned his attention to the rest of the class and continued with his lecture.

They were the last to file through the door when he called after them. "Excuse me, Miss Stephens?"

Emilee and Tracy turned back.

"Professor?"

"Only a housekeeping arrangement for the future. I'm new and I know I'm not twenty years your senior. I appreciate feedback and interaction in class, but I will not tolerate fraternizing with staff. Please don't cross the line of propriety, and don't try and embarrass me in class. You *will* lose the battle."

Emilee sucked in her breath, biting her tongue. *How dare he?* "*Professor.*"

He raised his brow. "That'll be all. You may go." He turned away. They were dismissed.

Emilee spun around with Tracy a short step behind, grabbed her friend's hand, pulled her through the doors, and hissed, "Such a pompous ass. He embarrassed *me*."

CHAPTER 22

A red Sunday. 30 January 1972.

As THE COLD trudged on through January—by the third week, snow blocked roads in Scotland, leaving the south shivering in its wake—Emilee agreed to visit with Connor at his apartment, but only for tea. There would be no studying or undoing of buttons.

Connor, grateful for the small victory, was the perfect gentleman and host. He even apologized for requesting her to remove her footwear, although now it made sense with all the slush and snow on the ground. Once inside the car, he offered her a small throw to cover her legs, which did not go unnoticed. She rewarded him with a glowing smile.

She felt the heat the moment she stepped through the front door. In her excitement to escape the cold, it became a brief struggle to free herself from her boots. She grabbed his arm and pulled him down the hallway.

The moment she saw the crackling fire she twirled him around. "You're a brave man, O'Hannigan. Leaving an unattended fire and vacating the premises to pick me up."

He smiled, a little embarrassed. "I couldn't let you walk into a freezing dungeon." He took her hand. "Come sit."

He had the two wing chairs turned around to face the fireplace. The tall curtains were drawn and the fire cast dancing waves over the glass covering the unclothed figure in the portrait. Connor handed her another woven throw for her legs.

"Don't move. Your only job is to warm up. I'll get the refreshments."

Once her legs had thawed, she was drawn toward the bookshelf. Connor poked his head around the door. "Sorry, the surprise item is reluctant to warm up. It's almost ready." His head disappeared again.

Emilee switched on the standing lamp and scrolled her fingers over the spines.

How she loved books. Hidden inside these covers were vast collections of stories, untold secrets, unshared truths, infinite knowledge, and real and imaginary worlds. Each volume ready to take its reader on a journey of possibilities.

Her fingers paused. She didn't know he read German. Another secret? She pulled out the thinnest volume—it was leather bound: *Manifest der Kommunistischen Partei*. The author: Karl Heinrich Marx. Was that *the* Karl Marx? Next to it were three large volumes. She leaned closer: *Das Kapital: vol. I, vol. II, vol. III*. They were also authored by K. H. Marx.

Connor called out in warning as he came through the door carrying a stacked tray. She slipped the book back. She will ask him about the book later. The cold had crept up her legs again, making it imperative to go stand right in front of the fireplace. Connor had pushed the two coffee tables together and placed the laden tray on it.

"*Apple pie*." Emilee leaned closer, enjoying the apple and cinnamon aroma.

Connor beamed as he cut a piece and handed it to her on a small plate.

"The truth, O'Hannigan. Don't tell me you baked *this*."

He laughed as he shook his head. "I have a confession. There's a small bakery where I sometimes buy my fresh-baked goods. I picked it up this afternoon."

"*Sometimes*. And the scones the other day?" Emilee furrowed her brow. "Don't lie."

He finished chewing. "Listen, I've baked hundreds of scones . . . it really isn't—"

"You *lied*."

He laughed as he poured her a cup of tea. "Well, I didn't technically bake them."

"Technically, you're a liar, O'Hannigan."

"It's a matter of semantics."

Emilee blew on her tea and took small sips, glaring at Connor with mock contempt. "We've established the fact you're not a truthful witness." She pointed at the bookshelf. "Have you read *all* those?"

He pulled up his shoulders. "Most of them."

She realized he was merely stating a fact. He wasn't boasting. His collection consisted of several hundred books. "Even the German ones?"

He chuckled. "You *did* study my collection. Yes, I try and obtain the English translation as well, to verify the accuracy of my understanding of the German tongue."

"Why do you have books about communism?"

He laughed. "I read many things. It's essential to become informed, to learn as much as possible about serious thinkers' viewpoints."

"But Marx was a communist."

"He was foremost an economist and a philosopher."

Emilee wouldn't buy the fact that Karl Marx should not be seen as one of the fathers of communism, not after penning *Manifest der Kommunistischen Partei.* She insisted on knowing whether Connor was a member of the British Communist Party.

He refused to answer, stating that owning books by one of the greatest thinkers of the nineteenth century didn't make him anything—only a bibliophile.

He continued to give her a biting dissertation on the multitude of flaws in the reigning capitalistic system: how it exploited labor, how it has made slaves of the workers and robbed them of their rights, how it made a handful of people staggeringly wealthy.

Emilee bit her tongue not to shoot back with the fact that the overseers of the communism machinery had positioned themselves to have access to unlimited power and wealth under the auspices of being the representatives of the state. She swallowed. "But I've heard most of the Union shop stewards are members of the CP." Her voice was small now, close to tears.

"Well, don't take everything you hear as the *gospel* truth!" He stood. "Come, it's dark and miserable outside. I should take you back."

Emilee cringed as she gathered the tea-stuff, wiping her eyes. She said nothing as she followed him into the kitchen and helped him put the soiled items in the sink. She was certain he didn't even notice how his words—or, rather, the way he spoke to her—stung, how much it hurt. The joy had deflated from her filled-with-wonder balloon.

—⚒—

Over the course of the next week, Emilee found it in her to forgive the hotheaded Irishman and resumed meeting with him every evening in the Old Library—until he didn't show up on Thursday evening, the twenty-seventh of January. He had given her no warning or indication that he had other plans.

Her first thought, when she realized that he wasn't coming, was that something bad had happened to him. She recalled his words when he had tracked her down to Magdalen College after she had told him that she resided in Ruskin College. "That's what I do, find people," and "I have contacts."

What could he have meant?

He had a telephone in his apartment, but she never before had the need to phone there. She had to search for his telephone number now, which was written on a small piece of paper but had disappeared in her dorm room among the mountains of papers and notes and textbooks that covered vast areas of the floor. She knew it was there. It wasn't lost, only misplaced.

Once she found the slip of paper, she used the phone next to the office. There was no answer at the apartment. She phoned with growing concern again on Friday and Saturday evening but had to be satisfied with listening to the endless ringing until she realized Connor's neighbors might become affronted.

It was Rachel who drew Emilee's attention to the urgent radio broadcast during the Sunday supper hour. The music program was interrupted—unprecedented—to make the announcement.

There had been a shooting in Londonderry, Ireland. Thirteen civil rights demonstrators were shot dead by the British Army with several more wounded. Emilee couldn't explain her sudden unease—she feared for Connor. The heaviness in her chest was unrelenting. They ran down to where other students had gathered in front of the television in the common room.

Raw footage was shown of the marchers throughout the day. There were thousands of them. Waves of people, mainly Catholic, ebbed through the Bog-side of Derry, waving placards and singing, defying the orders that the march was illegal. They refused to acknowledge the authority of the Northern Ireland government, who were mostly Protestant.

For the most part, the march remained peaceful as the protestors were forced to follow an alternative route due to barricaded streets.

Only later in the day did the emotions of the marchers boil over despite the bitter cold. The youth started pelting the soldiers with rocks and bricks until a water canon was sent in to disperse the unruly crowd. Rubber bullets were added to the armamentarium to subdue the crowd.

Then, in the late afternoon, sometime after four, British paratroopers were sent in to make arrests.

Apparently, enough was enough. The soldiers, however, began firing into the crowd, but this time with live bullets. People fled in horror as they saw their fellow marchers fall and bleed without getting up. Emilee gasped when she saw how the cameraman who operated the video camera had to run himself to keep up and stay out of harm's way as the shots rang out around him.

Chaos erupted.

It was live and real. People were falling, crawling away, shot in the back, dying. It was, after all, live ammunition. Stricken marchers were carrying a wounded young man, and a man in a black suit ran ahead of the group, waving a bloodstained white handkerchief as they tried to reach safety away from the murderous bullets.

Emilee sobbed and withdrew to her room.

Rachel ran after her to console her friend, but Emilee wouldn't let her into the room.

She went to rowing practice the next morning like an automaton and attended lectures as in a trance.

By noon on Monday, she found the *Guardian* newspaper in the common room. It stated: "The disaster in Londonderry last night dwarfs all that has gone before in Northern Ireland. . . . The march was illegal. Warning had been given of the danger implicit of continuing with it. Even so, the deaths stun the mind and must fill all reasonable people with horror."

Emilee put the paper down and walked over to the Old Library. She would find out for herself why this was taking place in Ireland. She had to learn more about Connor and the O'Hannigans and those who had come before them if she ever hoped to understand him and this land she was now living in and becoming a part of.

She forfeited her classes and tutorials for the rest of the day, only returning to her room when the librarians closed down for the night. It was close to eleven. She rubbed her red eyes as she stumbled to her dorm room; she had last eaten at breakfast.

It was a fitful slumber. She woke often through the night, seeing Connor's face in the place of the young man, whose bloodied body was carried by his friends with the priest running ahead, waving the red-stained white handkerchief. Each time she would wake and cry herself to sleep again.

—⟋⟍—

Connor had her called to the front door early Tuesday evening on the first of February. He seemed distant—a different Connor.

Only years later would she find the right words for his demeanor that evening: he seemed haggard and haunted. She hugged and kissed him and wouldn't let go. She literally clung to him.

He brushed her concerns off with nonchalance, claiming he had urgent Union business to attend to which had taken him to London. He swore he had never set foot in Londonderry. He even laughed at her outrageous suggestion. How would he have been able to travel that far in a day and a half? Even today she can still hear his laugh: "Preposterous," he had claimed.

CHAPTER 23

———— ⁓ ————

The lies we tell. Oxford 1972.

To HER ROWING and ten-books-a-month reading schedule, Emilee added studying the history of Ireland and the troubles surrounding it. She resumed meeting with Connor on alternating evenings, spending the other evenings in the library alone. She went back in time, all the way to the Anglo-Norman intervention on the island in the twelfth century. She had to know. She had to understand.

She now also read every newspaper she could lay her hands on and watched the BBC news. The world was outraged at the killing of the marchers. Bloody Sunday it was being called.

It was odd, Emilee thought, that Connor knew so much of what happened the day of the march and the shooting—the *small* details. He was quick to point out that there were only two reasons the people of Derry had gone ahead with the illegal march.

One was because of the British enforced internment of any terrorist suspects. When he noticed her blank face, he explained with great patience that internment meant detention without a trial. They could pick you off the street if they didn't like your face or attitude and claim you were a terrorist. The second reason was the claim that extensive electoral rigging had taken place, constantly favoring the pro-Protestant wards. The residents simply had had enough, so they marched, showing their contempt but also their solidarity.

Connor called the British government's official inquiry into the fatal Sunday shooting a sham, claiming the finding will be that the troops acted in self-defense.

"But there are reports that the IRA had snipers on the rooftops who fired first and that the paratroopers only returned fire," Emilee said.

"Into a crowd who had no firearms on their persons? Neither were there any reports of British troops who were killed by sniper headshots. Several of the demonstrators were shot in the back. They were running away, trying to escape the carnage!"

She had no answer to his logic.

His unflinching persistence of exactly what happened and how it differed from the renditions by the media and press was mere confirmation that the Union masters had not required his services in London during the previous weekend. He had been in Londonderry. He had marched along.

If he had been one of the organizers, it would make perfect sense. She found it lamentable that Connor had so little issue with being untruthful to her.

He assumed she was so naïve that she would swallow any fairytale.

In class, she maintained a low profile. She dared no witticism, although she paid extra attention to all the tutorials. She had sworn that fraternizing with staff was the last thing she would be guilty of. Not with arrogant bastards like Professor Thomas Hill, the Olympic rower, the magna cum laude PhD fellow on campus. She was amazed by the amount of bile she tasted every time she recalled their conversation, when Tracy was with her on the first day, when he'd called her back following his lecture.

Over the course of the following months, Emilee withdrew in part from the women's liberation movement by attending fewer of their meetings. Her complex relationship with Connor O'Hannigan and everything Irish and her already full academic plate made it troublesome to remain wholeheartedly in the game.

She had long since made peace with the supportive approach of the WLM toward all matters gay and lesbian, although she could not support the fierce drive by some to be anti-marriage and anti-male. She was dreaming of marrying one day and having children of her own.

What she had an issue with were the periodical attempts by radical groups within the WLM that pushed hard to promote militant communism ideologies sugarcoated in socialist attire. It was enough that she had to dance on eggshells when around Connor, with his open support of the "justifiable" struggle of the wronged workers' class, the proletariat, against the apparent wicked owners of the "means of production," the employers—the contemptible bourgeoisie.

—◦◦◦—

Toward the end of April, on a clear, cloudless day, Emilee summoned enough courage to pull the yellow kayak out. It needed a wash, but it also needed to be returned to its natural habitat: the river. It was covered with dust from months on the shelf. She had asked Rachel and Emma Davis, the assistant coach, to help her, to be around with her for her first time back after the accident.

Emma also had her own kayak and carried it out onto the dock.

Rachel acted as self-appointed MC and bossed her friend around. "Rower Stephens, prepare for pre-rowing checklist."

"Ready, ma'am." Emilee came to attention next to her kayak on the edge of the dock.

"Life jacket?"

"Life jacket—check," Emilee called out.

"Splash cover?"

"Splash cover—check."

"Intact paddle?"

Emilee raised her arms above her head, displaying the paddle.

"Bodyguard?" Rachel glanced in Emma's direction.

Emma laughed and hollered, "Bodyguard, check, ma'am!"

"Rowers, put your vessels in the water," Rachel called out as she helped Emilee get in and tuck her splash cover in place.

By the time the two kayaks returned three-quarters of an hour later, the butterflies in Emilee's mid-region had settled. She did not attempt another Eskimo roll, having solemnly taken the oath never to do it again, but she had found her rhythm. She glided half a length behind Emma as they raced toward the dock, where Rachel had stepped out of the shadows and awaited their arrival.

"Emma, did she make us proud?" Rachel shouted.

Before the assistant coach could answer, Emilee swept closer and performed an emergency stop, spraying the unsuspecting

Rachel with a wide bow of water from her sweeping paddle, yelling, "Yes, *exceedingly* proud!"

Rachel, soaked to the skin, screamed blue murder. She had to control her first impulse to dive into the water and capsize Emilee. Instead, she waited patiently on the dock until Emilee had loosened the splash cover before scooping up a handful of water and jetting it into Emilee's face.

"My felicitations, rower Stephens!" She laughed as she scampered away to avoid another arch of water coming from Emilee's paddle.

The three girls, giggling like teenagers, carried the two kayaks back to the boathouse, put everything back in its proper place, and hung the splash covers to dry. Emma was in a hurry and jogged ahead as they walked back toward the college.

Rachel turned to her friend, jutting her chest forward. "See what you did?"

Emilee lowered her eyes. The blouse had become transparent.

Rachel grabbed her crimson-in-the-face friend's hand and started running. "Don't worry," she laughed. "It'll dry. Let's catch up with Emma!"

Once they reached the rear entrance, Emma bid them farewell, and the two girls ran upstairs.

Rachel paused at her own room door, "Can I invite you to a late-night swim, partner?"

CHAPTER 24

Friends. 1972.

IT WAS CLOSE to eleven when the two girls slipped into the opaque pool. Despite the open blinds, the pool house remained in semi-darkness. Rachel suggested that they only do twenty laps, but Emilee insisted on completing the traditional forty.

Rachel waited on her friend at the deep end as Emilee completed her perfect forty and dragged herself out of the water. She rolled onto her back, wheezing and short of breath, sounding like a hundred-pack-year smoker.

Rachel swam closer, making clicking sounds. "I suggested we only do *twenty* laps, Miss Can't-Say-No-To-a-Challenge!"

Emilee rolled on her side, facing Rachel. "That will one day be my undoing."

By the time Emilee had regained her breath, Rachel had dropped her two-piece on the side. "*Come.* Time for our famous synchronized swimming routine."

Emilee slipped out of her bikini, readjusted her goggles, and dove in after her friend. Moonlight danced off the center of the pool. They soon were next to one another and completed perfect loops. The loops took them toward the deeper end where they made one big loop, chasing each other, in one fast circle.

It was a twirling of bare limbs and torsos, their bodies encased in moonlight-filled spheres of light, surfacing for a split second before disappearing into shafts of water toward the dim bottom of the pool. The girls went faster and faster, their hands touching fleetingly like doves in flight.

After half an hour, they had run out of breath. Rachel pulled her now-shivering friend out of the cool water. They slipped their bikinis back on and darted back to their rooms.

Once they reached the hallway, Rachel whispered, "Let's change in my room."

They toweled themselves before taking turns with fresh towels to rub each other's hair dry. They giggled and rattled helplessly as Rachel draped the damp towels over a chair. "You know the drill for hypothermia, partner. Body heat's required."

Rachel left the curtains closed and turned the glaring overhead light off. The room was dark save for the soft glow of a bed lamp behind them. Several minutes of skin-to-skin buddy-hugging were required for their shivering to subside.

Emilee turned around and faced her friend, their faces inches apart. She inhaled their warmth, startled by how calm she was. It was different from when she was with Connor. She craved to be with him yet never managed to relax. Tension always lurked beneath the surface. How she longed for him to hold her, cuddle her, until all the tension would drain away.

She hankered to be *touched*, but only by someone special, someone she trusted and loved. Connor was special—had he not saved her life? She was certain it would be different, so much grander and more memorable, than what she could achieve on her own. No angry and abusing hands should ever touch her again—not *there*, not anywhere.

She danced with butterfly fingers along Rachel's lashes and followed the arc of her nose, surprised by the number of freckles scattered across her friend's face. Her fingers moved, millimeter by millimeter, down to her lips. Rachel sighed and kissed her fingertips. Emilee imagined it was Connor's kisses. She shivered and sniffled.

"Keep your eyes closed now," she said as her fingers lingered on Rachel's lips.

Emilee was baffled by the surrender she felt. She had become weightless. It was as if she had risen off the bed, floating high above the ceiling—doing nothing but remitting. She found her emotions vexing. With Connor it was always a mix of yearning and anxiety. Now, it was only serenity.

She loved Caroline, and she loved Tracy, and even Douglas had a special place—that was a love distinct. The love she had developed for Connor was lucid, to the point that it distraught her. It held her captive and filled her with angst.

What she felt coursing through her now was foreign. Mother would have said: it *had* to be wrong.

There is awareness beyond classification or justification, even beyond condemnation.

She had always been baffled by how people could condemn in haste, strike out like a thunderbolt and consume with fire, without verifying facts or wearing another's shoes. She had learned the same people could be just as reluctant to grant mercy or offer forgiveness.

Condemnation comes easier.

If *this* could heal her aching soul—bring solace—could it be berated?

Emilee sobbed as her fingers traveled along her friend's chin and slipped around to her ears. She stroked the two golden studs before sliding down her svelte neck, coming to rest on the notch above her breastbone. She leaned closer and kissed Rachel's eyes, tasting her own salt tears as her hand traveled lower.

It was Rachel now who pushed Emilee onto her back before lowering herself on top, matching their bodies, limb for limb, breast touching breast. They were of equal height. Neither of them moved. Transfixed, Emilee shut her eyes as she realized they were both now hovering, suspended high above the town.

She peered at the city of dreaming spires, its centuries-old sandstone buildings obscured by trees, its hedges and cast-iron fences hiding the winding paths and roads and the network of waterways. Magdalen, with its deer park and endless grounds, beckoned in revered silence.

Rachel sat up and kneeled across her friend's abdomen. Emilee's eyes remained closed. She hovered above the fog-covered Thames as it coursed through the city, until she identified eight rowers on their sweep boat through a break in the mist. The rowers pushed hard as Rachel bent down and planted small kisses down her neck until her lips reached the valley on Emilee's chest, the foothills of the love mounts. Emilee shifted. She shook her head, grinning through her tears. She whimpered as she skimmed lower through the breaks in the fogbanks clinging to the river. She followed the rowers down to Iffley now, on the way to Southampton.

She could hear the coxswain's call, guiding her team to stick to the middle of the river.

"Time for something different," Rachel murmured as she rolled the yielding Emilee onto her stomach. Rachel jumped off the bed. "I'm getting some massage oil. It works wonders for burdened bodies."

With long, sweeping strokes, Rachel massaged Emilee's back, applying oil until her back gleamed as if burning. It required persistence for Emilee's body to remit before it relaxed and surrendered. Persistent hands pressed deeper into knotted muscles and hurts. Emilee was almost asleep now. Her entire body glowed.

Rachel's deft fingers marched in ever-widening circles, faster and slower, soothing and reassuring, faster and lower it went.

Emilee murmured. Her pelvis heaved.

"Time to roll back, Miss Stephens."

She pushed the now-flustered Emilee onto her back again, pulled the rolled towel out from under her hips, and applied oil to the front of her body, running from head to toes with butterfly fingers. Rachel kneeled forward, never ceasing the massage.

Emilee's eyes remained shut, but she started weeping again, shaking.

The river was wide open. The fog had lifted. It was only then that she noticed the second boat, which was half-a-boat length behind them. She called out again at the rowers—or was it at Rachel—they had to go faster, faster down the Thames.

Emilee shivered as waves built up in her core and shuddered through her as Rachel's deft fingers danced across her hills and valleys and secret places. Spasms shook her, seizure-like, again and again.

She willed herself that she was lying in Connor's arms, that he had brought about the elation and contentment within her.

When she woke an hour later, she was on her side, now under the covers, facing Rachel, who was sleeping. Emilee inhaled the fragrance of their bonding. A foreign awareness embraced her. It ached. *When have I last felt such happiness?*

She rolled onto her back and listened to the thumping in her chest and Rachel's quiet breathing. She squirmed, for a joy this vast could disappear as easily as the rowers with their sweep boats had.

Emilee wiped her eyes. She imagined Connor lying there, as he would have if he hadn't instilled so much conflict, so much fear, in her. She suppressed a sob. *Oh, Connor, what will become of us now?*

The east lighted up by the time sleep finally overtook her.

CHAPTER 25

Mr. O'Hannigan's therapy. July 1972.

Connor's prediction held true. The British government released a report in April exonerating the British troops from wrongdoing in the Bloody Sunday shooting. Those present at the march that day, as well as the video footage shot by journalists, had a different take on the facts. The resentment in Ireland multiplied on the heels of the report, especially when more British soldiers were sent to the island.

Connor was livid when news of the report broke but soon resorted to a sorrowful withdrawal.

Emilee found it challenging to lift his spirits. Little seemed to cheer him up. Even Mary G had lost her touch. They resumed meeting almost every day, alternating between the library and his apartment. The more she pressed him to get to the reason for his gloom, implying that it was his involvement in the troubles plaguing Ireland, the more he played it down.

Connor claimed the reason for his perpetual forlorn state was the games his union bosses played with them, the shop stewards. In public, they were the biggest of buddies, but in private, the union masters sided with the government and the employers, betraying the workers they officially represented.

By the end of May, Emilee had implemented part of her plan. She insisted on kayaking with him at least once a week, usually on a Sunday afternoon. On the other weekdays, she made him take a brisk walk with her for an hour. She believed it would lift his spirits and help him crawl out of the dark place he loved to withdraw to.

Initially, they only walked the Magdalen grounds. Emilee never tired of the deer park, fascinated by the lithe creatures with their moist noses and the abundance of birdsong. With her eyes closed, she always tried to identify the birds by their chatter and calls. There were the Jackdaws, miniature crows, with their black masks and gray mantels. The Starlings were easier to tell from afar, being so noisy and having shed their winter plumage. The Robins, often silent, stood out with their orange-red faces and white bellies. Their warbling "twiddle-doo" and "twiddle-dee" always brought a smile.

The groundskeepers had taken extra care that year to line the walking paths with rows of daffodils, blessing the eager hiker with their yellow splendour.

Soon, the duo crisscrossed all of Oxford on foot. On these walks, Emilee would do most of the talking and Connor had to do the listening.

She would tell him stories about Africa, about Katima Molilo and the Caprivi. She was no therapist, but in all her reading she had stumbled upon articles claiming the benefits of outdoor activities and discussion sessions to improve the health of individuals, especially those afflicted with bouts of depression.

She refused to take her study books along when visiting at his apartment, making it possible to keep those visits short, since she had to get back to her dorm room to study and read, she claimed. She allowed him to kiss her more passionately again, in private, even hug her, but she would not allow him to undo any buttons or unzip any clothing.

Although the frequent rain made the arrival of July less spectacular, Emilee was positive that she noticed a difference, an improvement in her Irishman's mood. Her modest plan was paying off.

It was time to implement the second part of her plan based on inspiration she had received while in the library. She was a firm believer of complete healing, and her Connor was doing so well.

In her expanded personal reading curriculum, she had come across the two books by Masters and Johnson. She was mortified at first. Stunned. Intrigued. Then elated. How could the researchers be so open about sexuality?

She remembered the weekend nights back home in Katima when she couldn't sleep, listening in the quiet house to her parents making love. Those old houses were never soundproof. She smiled. She wondered whether she should alter courses and change to psychology and psychiatry, or even to medicine. Then she would be able to really help Connor and people like him. She never shared with Connor that she was following a blueprint.

He was taken aback when she asked him how he felt about marriage. Whether he believed in it.

"I'm *Catholic*. How can I not believe in the institution of marriage?"

"That's not the same."

"Well, my parents are *married*." He laughed.

"I'm serious. Would you want to marry—marry your sweetheart?" Emilee couldn't explain why she had turned crimson.

"Are you proposing, Miss Stephens?" They were in his apartment, and he grabbed her around the waist and twirled her around. "You'll have to give me more time. This is a big decision to make."

Emilee pushed him away, but he laughed so much that he collapsed into the one wing chair. She sat down opposite him and waited for him to settle down. "I'm *not* proposing. *One* day, would you want to get married and have children? Only have one mate, one woman in your life?"

He was still grinning when he jumped off the chair and kneeled at her side. "Sure—*one* day. I'm not seeing anybody else at the moment."

She locked eyes with him. "What about making love? Wait with sex until you're married?"

"Emilee, do you *want* me to make love to you? Right now?" He leaned forward and kissed her.

She was bewildered by her own questions, pulling away, shaking her head. "No, Connor . . . I don't."

He sat back down on the carpet, laughing at her.

She stunned him a second time when she slipped off the chair, took his face in her hands, and kissed him with force, willing his lips open. "I *love* you, Connor O'Hannigan!"

He was lying on his back now as she leaned over him. She soon kissed his eyes, his dark brows, and his nose before seeking his mouth again. She was like a drowning woman reaching for a buoy. She couldn't care less. She would help Connor heal. It was even possible that this would help *her* heal.

Partially undressed, Emilee came to her senses when his lips closed over her jutting breast. She was sitting in his lap. She had allowed him to undo all the buttons of her blouse and pull her on top of him. She often chose not to wear a bra. The contact did not shock and revolt her like before, and she shuddered with anticipation, savoring the nudging, the yearning, the beckoning she felt.

She kissed him on the lips as she pulled free and sat back up, pushing him down on his back, before taking his hands and placing them on her breasts.

"I *love* you, sweet Connor." She leaned down and kissed him a second time. "One day, we'll . . . Come, I have to go."

She stood up and buttoned her blouse.

Connor's apartment became their meeting place of choice. Every evening she would bring her books and read and study after they had shared a light supper. Then they would talk, which oftentimes led to him kissing her, just before he had to take her back to Magdalen. Connor was a patient man. There was no need to rush.

By the third week on a late Wednesday evening, as soon as Emilee had put her books away and sat down across from him, Connor pulled her to her feet and kissed her hard and long. Then he took her hand and led her without a word down the second hallway toward the bedrooms.

She had never seen his room before. Her hand flew to her mouth. The room had its own fireplace, and near the bay window stood a baby grand piano. Above the fireplace hung a pen sketch of a faceless figure by the same artist.

"Do you play?" She pointed at the black piano.

"Sometimes."

"Another secret?"

"Another facet," he said as he kissed her, led her toward the bed, and made her sit next to him.

Connor seemed more preoccupied than usual. Throughout the evening, dark shadows kept appearing in his eyes, as if tormenting him, as if tempting to haul him back into his hole of despondency.

He walked over to the piano, opened it, and took position, then looked at her. He appeared deeply embarrassed.

"Emilee," he breathed, "I have a special gift for you—"

She bolted for the door. "I . . . I don't want you to make love to me, if that's your gift."

Connor started playing. The melody made her turn back. He continued playing and smiled at her. "Please, go sit on the bed. I was planning something different."

He got up and crossed the floor to fiddle with the fireplace. He turned his head as he kneeled in front of the hearth. "It's not that cold, but I thought this could be a substitute for candles." When the fire took, Connor pulled the curtains tight, closed the door without a sound, turned the light out, and returned to the piano.

Emilee sat down on the bed, her back straight, watching him; the only light in the room the glow of the fire.

He continued where he had left off. "Chopin—one of his nocturnes," he murmured.

Connor played with growing confidence. She tried to recall where she had last heard the piece. She closed her eyes and cocked her head. Her shoulders softened as his slim fingers danced across the keys.

"I'm not planning on making love to you, but I *do* want to give you a massage—a soothing massage, with proper massaging oil." He continued playing as he spoke. "It'll let you relax, then I'll take you back. You will sleep well tonight."

Emilee perked upright. "How are you going to do that with all my clothes on? The oils will stain—" She reddened in spite of the poor light. "Oh no, you don't!"

Connor tilted his head, the trademark grin in place. "Emilee, don't you trust me?"

"This isn't about trust, O'Hannigan!"

She refused to sit down and paced in front of the fire.

After playing for another five minutes, he succeeded in convincing her to return to the bed. He gave her his word that he would close his eyes, giving her the opportunity to undress at her leisure and get under the covers—not that the room was cold anymore—if that suited her better.

Emilee's back stiffened where she sat. Connor, saying nothing, continued playing with closed eyes.

When she finally jumped under the covers, her clothes folded in a neat stack on the foot of the bed, Connor stopped playing and walked over.

"May I?" He pulled the covers lower, completely unhurried. "If I may look just once, then I'll close my eyes. Promise."

She nodded.

He revealed her to the room, inch by imperceptible inch.

The soft glow from the fire caressed her body in warm colors and shadows, dancing over her smooth limbs, making him draw in his breath. Their eyes locked. He had seen her jutting breasts before, but everything seemed different now. She was more radiant than he had ever dreamed.

After picking up the oil and instructing her to turn onto her stomach, he closed his eyes as promised. "I'll start with your back."

He was a master it seemed, as he took his time, starting with her toes, anointing each one individually. Once he reached her mid-thigh, it was time to start with the other foot and toes. By the time he reached her shoulders and neck, Emilee was covered with copious amounts of oil.

She drifted off as he continued massaging.

More than an hour had passed.

He made her turn around and followed the same routine, but now on her front. She soon glowed. Her breasts and secret folds were left untouched. Being denied for so long, her pelvis took to rhythmic rocking, begging for attention.

His hands soon attended to her breasts. As he reached the outskirts of her core, she opened up and beckoned him closer. Even as she whimpered from minuscule spasms that now traversed her glowing limbs, Connor would not be rushed. The spasms increased in force, and she started sobbing softly. When she finally contracted around his hand, her cry of surrender shook the room.

It was after five in the morning when she woke up under the covers, still unclothed. Connor lay behind her. His hand rested on her breast. He was naked too. His breathing came regularly where he lay snuggled up against her back. She smiled as she extracted herself from his embrace. He'll have to be informed about his snoring.

When Connor dropped Emilee off outside the gates the Tom Tower chimed the sixth hour. She reached her dorm room on tiptoes.

CHAPTER 26

The second disappearance of Mr. O'Hannigan. 20 July 1972.

CONNOR DISAPPEARED FOR the second time in late July 1972.

In the south of England, it was a wet month, but in Scotland and Northern Ireland, it was the sunniest July since 1955.

For the past several months, the unwritten arrangement between Emilee and Connor had been to meet at five in the afternoon every other day. Once she implemented her plan of action to help Connor, by the end of May they saw each other every day, on her insistence. As July became increasingly wet, Connor would come and pick her up at the main gate with Mary Gabriella.

The afternoon following the night of ministrations in Connor's apartment, Emilee stood at the gate, armed with an umbrella, her shield against the miserable drizzle. There were many things the Irishman prided himself on, one of which was punctuality. Emilee refused to accept that he wouldn't show, not after her rapturous night. Something must have delayed him. Perhaps there was a mechanical problem with Mary G.

By 5:15 she had her first thought of doubt and immediately chastised herself for such disloyalty. The incessant rain did nothing to convince her otherwise. By 5:45 she had accepted the apparent truth and plodded back. She used the pay phone next to the admin office. There was no answer at his apartment.

She knew the tears were not far, but she was so upset that he had done it again. *He was not coming.* And she had thought, all these past weeks, that he was on his way toward getting better, getting his act together. What malicious effect could last night's session have had on his delicate spirit? *He* was the one who had initiated it. He had insisted on bestowing the gift—and she thought she had been the one affected most.

She wiped her eyes as she ran up the stairs to her room, where she cried for an hour. Then she changed into more practical outside clothes for the dreary weather. She was going to cycle to his place and confront him—demand an answer for his unacceptable behavior. She was nobody's plaything.

It was close to half-past seven when she took her bicycle from the storage room and jumped in the saddle. She still had almost an hour and a half of daylight at her disposal.

She arrived at the apartment partially soaked. The raincoat had been no match for the driving wind. The smell of fresh, moist earth during the rain was lost on her. She was increasingly aware of her own discomfort. She was cold and embarrassed as she stood at his front door, with no one responding to her knocking and hesitant calling.

When the neighbor across the hallway, an elderly gentleman, opened his door and peeked out, she realized the writing was on the wall. She had seen the old man before when she had visited.

"He left early this morning, honey. I don't think he'll be back tonight. He had a large and heavy backpack with him. He was in a hurry."

Emilee sucked her breath. *A backpack.* "Didn't he say *anything*, sir?"

"Not a word. He didn't even greet—not as he usually did. He left in haste."

Emilee thanked the old man and assured him she would be fine. She would wait a little longer if he didn't mind. She was certain he was mistaken. Connor would show up, any minute now. The old man gave her a pedantic smile before he closed his door.

Emilee dropped down on the doormat and leaned against the door, shivering uncontrollably. She felt and smelled like the wet kitten she resembled. She feared for Connor—the old man was probably right.

The cold made her hug herself and rub her arms and legs, trying unsuccessfully to instill some warmth into her damp limbs. It was after eight according to her wristwatch. *He will be here before nine. Have a little faith in your boyfriend, Emilee Stephens. Never mind the old guy. He's clearly off his rocker.*

By the time she had finally accepted defeat and returned to her bicycle, it was past nine and dark out. The rain held back until she reached the end of the street when the heavens opened. The beam from her handlebar-mounted headlight was swamped by the torrential-like downpour. Emilee's tears mixed with the driving rain as she bit her lip, leaning against the wind, and pedaled. There was no sense in turning back or seeking shelter. She was soaked to the bone.

Connor, how could you?

The only way to escape the deluge was to pedal harder and make it to the college. Her bicycle zigzagged along the edge of the paved surface, casting a feeble light ahead of her into the pouring darkness.

Whether she ignored the stop signal or didn't see it remains unclear, even until today. The blinding headlights that suddenly charged down upon her woke her from the trance she had been riding in, like someone possessed. Reflex made her swerve sideways, attempting to avoid imminent disaster.

The rain exploded into scattering lights, a car horn, screeching tires, the anxious hum of a large engine and blinding pain. This all mixed with her panicked cry, shattering the night.

The impact threw her and the bicycle into the air before she crashed into the shrubbery to the side of the now-drenched road.

Surprise preceded the burst of pain up her leg and arm until the mercy of blackness swallowed her.

Voices—faraway voices in the rain.

"*Miss*. Excuse me, Miss! Can you *hear* me?"

Oh Lord, what hurt so bad? Definitely a man's voice. Sounds familiar. And a second man's calling. What are they saying?

Rain pelted on canvas—or was it an umbrella?

"Please, *open* your eyes. Miss, can you hear me?"

Of course I can hear you, asshole. I'm not deaf—only wet and tired and hurting.

They were wondering out loud why she hadn't heeded the stop signal and had driven in front of oncoming traffic.

I was cycling in a cloudburst, you poor sod.

"She should be glad we didn't strike her head-on, Tom. Then she would have been a goner." It was the unfamiliar voice speaking.

Why did she have so much difficulty opening her eyes? Try as she could, it seemed impossible. Did the impact paralyze her eye muscles? Her brain, perhaps? The rain had subsided, but each man still held an umbrella over her prostrated form, where she lay next to her bicycle in the dirt, which was fast turning into mud.

The familiar-voiced man touched her shoulder, then squeezed it. "Miss, please *open* your eyes."

Emilee opened her eyes and sat up, causing both men to step back in surprise, but the one who touched her shoulder leaned close enough to keep the umbrella over her. The drizzle had started again. The car's headlights illuminated their drab group next to the road, like actors on a stage.

She glanced at her wrist and leg. Both throbbed. *They must be broken.* Her clothes, her jeans, everything, was soaked and caked with mud. Who were these men? Did they try to kill her—run her over? Why wasn't Connor there? Then she remembered. He had apparently left with the backpack.

Why wasn't Caroline or Douglas or Rachel or even Tracy there?

"What am I *doing* here?" Emilee squinted her eyes. "Did *you* knock me off my bicycle?"

The umbrella-holding man with the familiar voice gaped at her. "I'm sorry, but you *ignored* the stop sign and drove right in front of my car." Then he added, almost apologetically, "It rained hard, I know. You swerved away just before we hit you. It saved your life, but it was still an impact." He paused. "I can't believe you're not injured. Your bicycle's a wreck. Does it hurt anywhere?"

It was impossible not to notice the man's concern.

He closed his umbrella, handed it to his companion, and kneeled next to her.

With their faces now only six inches apart, she recognized him: Professor Thomas Hill, the anti-fraternizing tutorial fellow from their department, the new lecturer, the ex-Olympic rower.

She drew her breath and mumbled, "Professor Hill . . . good evening." She was probably in such a mess that the man couldn't recognize her. Just as well.

He leaned closer. "Do I know you?"

"No . . . you don't, sir. My wrist and leg . . . it hurts—just above the ankle."

Professor Hill leaned over and carefully pushed the wet sleeve higher to inspect her wrist. Emilee squirmed. He immediately apologized and then, with more caution, turned the bottom of her pants' leg up to have a look at her left ankle.

She was glad she had shaved her legs that morning. She gasped when she noticed the blood on her jeans and leg. Her once-white sock was pink from the blood that had been washed away by the rain. She was curious about the lack of pain she felt when she witnessed all the blood.

"Francois, give me a hand, will you? We need to get this young lady to a hospital."

Thomas Hill kneeled even closer to pick her up, putting out his arms, when Emilee scampered to stand on her own. She would not allow the arrogant fool to touch her. Her humiliation in the classroom was still fresh. Her left leg, however, would have none of it. It refused to carry her weight and gave way. She cried out as she careened forward.

Thomas Hill had lost his Olympic form but still rowed on a regular basis. He caught her and picked her up with little effort. For a moment, he grimaced as her soaked and mud-covered clothing made contact with his pristine jacket and pants.

Emilee protested as far as he carried her, but he was deaf to her pleas while instructing his assistant to hold the rear passenger door open.

After holding the door, Francois ran around, clambered in from the other side in the back and helped pull her in and make her comfortable. He grinned as if embarrassed as he slipped out of his jacket and draped it around Emilee.

Despite the rain and mud and her pain, it was impossible not to inhale Francois's warm, clean body as he stooped over her.

He smiled, inches from her face, his brows thick and heavy. "The name is Moolman, Francois Moolman."

"Emilee Stephens," she mumbled. Her eyes were drawn to his square jaw. There was something about its asymmetrical contour. He must have broken it long ago. Perhaps he was born that way. The poor man.

He grinned at her. The opposite of the arrogant English professor. Her face glowed, the cold in spite.

The professor had to repeat himself. "Francois? *Hello?* Let's go, *mon ami*."

The two men found room for the remains of her bicycle in the trunk of the car before getting into the front and setting off for the hospital.

At the hospital, Francois found her a wheelchair and helped her out from the backseat. This time he only held her elbow. He refused to take his jacket back. "You're soaked and you're cold." He smiled into her face. "I don't want your pneumonia on my conscience. I'll get it later."

Emilee whimpered, "Sorry for *ruining* your blazer."

He squeezed her shoulder and murmured, "*Nonsense*," as he pushed her faster down the hallway, forcing Thomas Hill to remain one step behind.

The x-rays showed a non-displaced fracture of her wrist but a complete fracture of her left fibula, mid-shaft. The doctors decided that surgery was not indicated and would treat her with two plaster casts and a set of crutches. Since it was close to mid-night and it had started raining again, she was admitted to the John Radcliffe for the night.

Emilee tossed in her unfamiliar hospital cot that night. The pain medication soothed the discomfort but clouded her mind. She cried herself to sleep in the early hours, when the moon cast its narrow bands of paleness into the room. The skies were clearing.

She cried for her parents in Katima, in Africa. She cried for Caroline and Douglas, whom she'd been neglecting the last six months. And she cried for Tracy and Rachel. She cried for Francois Moolman with his crooked jaw, wishing she had met him long ago. Then she wept for Connor, whom she was certain was now somewhere in Ireland with the bulky backpack. Crumpled in her hand was the sleeve of the mud-smeared, navy blue jacket of the man with the funny-sounding last name.

CHAPTER 27

— ᚗᚔᚗ —

A Friday unlike any other. 21 July 1972.

CAROLINE, RACHEL, AND Tracy insisted on coming along in the taxi. They were adamant to accompany Emilee from the hospital late that Friday morning. They giggled and snickered when they noticed the blazer. Emilee had managed to wipe the jacket free from most of the mud and dirt.

"You pitied the armor off your Prince Charming?" Rachel asked.

"He was only being nice." Emilee slanted her eyes.

"I understand there were *two* princes who came to your rescue," Rachel insisted.

"I said *enough*, Lloyd!" Emilee grabbed her pestering friend's hand and squeezed it until the latter squirmed. "Be *nice*," she pleaded.

When the four girls entered the foyer of Magdalen, they were met by a spontaneous chorus. Every student who was not in class at that hour was there to welcome Emilee back as if welcoming a war hero. She hobbled around on her crutches, astounded by the public display of affection. She waved at those present and touched hands with the girls in front. It wasn't long before she had to wipe her eyes, sniffling, as the throng made its way toward the common room.

Rachel took charge and brought some order to the looming stampede. "Thank you, girls. Thank you, ladies! This was kind of you all, but let's give poor Emilee a break. She's overwhelmed, as you can see. She *is* glad to be back, and love you all for it. But the doctor prescribed *rest*, so *scoot*."

The peace that had settled in the common room was short-lived.

Chaos broke out minutes after quarter past two that afternoon. The news spread like a forest fire.

The same girls now flocked to the TV to watch the news unfolding. The earlier jubilation about a friend returning from the hospital had turned into horror as they watched and listened, transfixed.

An explosion had rocked the Smithfield bus station in Belfast at 2:10 p.m. causing extensive damage to buildings. At 2:16 p.m., a second explosion had shaken the Brookville Hotel, also in Belfast.

Students who had relatives in Belfast ran to the admin office to find out what was happening. Those who were too late to get hold of the two coin-operated phones next to the office clustered together in consternation, their concerned voices echoing through the hallways, desperate to establish contact with someone, anyone, loved ones, on the other side.

When a third explosion rocked the LMS Railway station at 2:23 p.m., it became clear that this was no freak explosion due to some domestic misadventure but rather an orchestrated plan. Emilee sat galvanized, rigid, upright like a *meerkat*, listening. She realized the apparent goal was clear: to create fear, to destroy and to kill.

But why?

The girls held their breaths. Would there be another?

Emilee was oblivious that she had grabbed Caroline's hands in a death grip until the latter winced and extracted her hands. Emilee clutched her friend's hands again, more gently this time, as she sobbed softly. "Connor's over there, in Belfast. I'm certain."

She pointed at the screen. "*What* is he doing there?"

"You don't *know* that, Emilee. You only know what the old man told you—that he left with a backpack yesterday morning. Everything else is guesswork."

"No, Caroline. I can feel it *here*." She thumped her chest. "I'm going to be sick. He's *part* of the Resistance. That much I know now. It was bred, then fed, then beaten into him. It's woven into his marrow, entwined into his soul."

She stammered as she fought for control, pointing at the tube again. "Oh God . . . Connor saved my life, but *that*—what they're doing over there—is *not* resistance."

Tracy and Rachel squeezed in on the small couch next to the other two, desperate to see the small screen but also eager to console their friend. They kicked the crutches out of the way in their effort to place a reassuring hand on Emilee's shoulders. They all soothed now, echoing Caroline.

"You don't *know* he's part of the carnage, Emilee," Tracy offered. "Perhaps he again had to leave for London on union business."

Emilee laughed through her sobs. "Hah! He has so many secrets. Neither does he have any issues with lying. He wasn't in London the previous time and he isn't there *now*."

"For all you know, he might be in Annagassan visiting his parents," said Rachel.

Emilee drew her breath, facing Rachel, accepting the blade of a straw. "Do you think so?"

She dismissed it immediately, shaking her head. "Then he wouldn't have needed such a large bag. The old man showed me how enormous the thing was. Connor is strong. He struggled to carry it, the old man said." She staggered upright on her plastered leg and demonstrated with arms held wide.

All eyes returned to the reporter in Belfast. It was a little after 2:45 p.m. What they feared had happened. A fourth explosion, a car bomb, had just been detonated on Crumlin Road. A solemn silence had crept into the room. Voices became hushed; the generalized sobbing grew fainter.

Then the newsreader himself choked on emotions. "*Oh my God,*" he muttered. "*Not again.*" Number five—another car bomb—had gone off at the Oxford bus station. It happened at exactly 2:48 p.m.

Devastation was everywhere.

There were dead people now, mutilated bodies strewn on the streets—a bloodbath. Horror upon horror unfolded as the injured scampered to safety and searched for help.

The friends in front of the TV were hugging one another now, weeping. They prayed, like the rest of the country, for the wounded in Belfast.

Emilee became aware of an overwhelming sense of impotence while listening to the carnage that unfolded. *Oh dear, Lord. What's happening in the land? This is not a natural disaster causing that destruction—it has been planned. It has been masterminded by people with beating hearts. Fellow humans have meticulously devised it. Someone to make the bombs, someone to plant each one, conceal it, and someone to detonate them at a preordained time—detonate them among unexpected and unarmed civilians. The orchestrator was setting off the explosions like fireworks at a fair, with the same calculated indifference one would apply when slaughtering pigs.*

In the background of the newscast, they could hear the wailing of sirens and ambulances blaring in frantic efforts to tend to the injured and dying. It was merely the beginning.

Over the ensuing twenty-seven minutes, a total of fourteen more bombs were detonated. The last of the nineteen bombs was detonated at 3:15 p.m. at the Cavehill Road shopping center. It was another deadly car bomb that had killed two women, one a mother of seven, and a fourteen-year-old boy, as well as injuring bystanders.

Emilee sat squeezed in among her three friends, numbed like most everyone around, rocking herself back and forth, muttering, "Connor, I pray that you are *indeed* in Annagassan, with your parents. If you're in Belfast at this moment and in *any* way, shape or form, part of this, may God have mercy on your soul. And it will be the end of us."

Tracy murmured as she pulled her friends closer. "The *shame*. No flag can ever be large enough to cover such barbarity. They've killed . . . No . . . They've slaughtered *the innocent*."

Emilee remained huddled together with the three girls for a considerable time. She was recoiling, along with the nation, from the inflicted wound.

It was still Friday, a Friday unlike any other. Little would remain the same.

A different line had been drawn in the sand, this one drawn with more blood, its goal unclear. Perhaps to instill fear on a national and grander scale, or encourage giving up and stoking hatred.

Emilee pondered Tracy's comment and wondered: *Can any one of us claim to be truly innocent?*

CHAPTER 28

—⁓—

Visiting Annagassan. 25 July 1972.

WHEN CONNOR REMAINED unaccounted for by the end of the weekend—Emilee had phoned and cycled down to his apartment twice on Saturday and twice again on Sunday—she gave up her Monday morning classes without a second thought. She went straight to the faculty office and insisted on urgently meeting with the English department head. Refusing to back down, she remained standing in the outside office until the secretary gave in and granted her an opening.

Emilee requested a leave of absence with immediate effect, claiming compassionate leave, to visit the O'Hannigans in Annagassan. She was unable to shed the conviction that she would find Connor, if he were alive, in the hamlet where the Glyde River flowed into the Irish Sea. Her professor's initial reluctance ebbed away once she noticed the fire in her student's eyes, a determination that filled the room with its looming presence.

Emilee was relieved that it was mid-morning. All her close friends would be in class, making it easier for her to slip away. She was convinced that they (especially Caroline or Rachel) would try to stop her from going, claiming she was delusional or irrational. It was hard enough to do so on crutches.

Bloody rain. Bloody Thomas Hill. Bloody Connor. She used the pay phone in the foyer to book a taxi, then limped upstairs to her room to stuff a few pieces of clothing into a shoulder bag. Remembering about the weather, she grabbed her raincoat and a broad-rimmed hat.

The crutches slowed her down. As Emilee hobbled down the front stairs, Rachel swept around the corner.

"*Emilee.*"

"Hi, Rachel." A demure Emilee continued steaming toward the cast iron gates of the college, her bag bouncing against her side.

Her friend stepped in front of her with arms crossed, making Emilee bump into her.

"Careful!"

"*You* skipped rowing practice this morning . . . *Where* are you going in such a hurry anyway?"

"Annagassan. And you forgot about these . . . ." She held up her plastered forearm.

Rachel stepped even closer to her friend and smiled. "Silly me. I forgot. Yes, you can't row like that. But no, you're not going to Ireland." She stepped back and grasped Emilee's hands, resting on the crutch handgrips. "It's not *safe.*"

With their faces inches apart, their eyes whispered things their mouths dared not utter.

Emilee gave a sob, broke away, and hobbled toward the gate again. "It's not safe *anywhere.* I can't stay here. I'm *not* afraid of the bomb-makers. I *have* to find him."

Rachel ran alongside her now. "Then I'm coming *with* you! You're injured. How will you manage?"

"I'm not an invalid."

"You could easily have been. It's a miracle you're not dead."

"No. It's that arrogant bastard of a Professor Hill who's to blame. He shouldn't own a driver's license. He should have been more careful in the rain. He tried to kill me."

"Emilee . . . ."

They had reached the taxi.

"Allow me to *at least* come along."

Emilee shook her head as she hugged her friend then kissed her on the lips. "You can pray for me, but I have to do this on my own. I *have* to find Connor. I need answers."

"Do you have *money*?"

Emilee nodded as she hugged her friend again before tumbling into the taxi.

She had difficulty convincing the taxi driver to take her to the bank to draw money first. He mumbled about having had to wait for an hour for a bloody student, who, like all other students, wasted money like water and thought taxi drivers had all day to sit around. Only when she sniffled, wiped her eyes, and clanked the two crutches together did the driver back off, grumble once more, and turn the vehicle around to head for the bank.

Emilee took the first train to London and went on standby at Heathrow for a flight to Dublin. As she fidgeted for a comfortable position on the row of seats at the departure gate, she wondered how much the taxi would ask for the forty-five-mile drive from the Irish capital to the village of Annagassan. Probably the same as her plane ticket. She knew she could now kiss her planned visit to her parents back home in South West Africa goodbye. There would be little left of her savings.

It was already after six by the time she had purchased her air ticket. It seemed every man, woman, and child on the British Isle had planned on flying somewhere that night. There were no vacant seats on the three flights destined for Ireland. *Are these people all going to bloody Dublin?* Perhaps Rachel was right when she had tried to stop her.

Emilee bought an apple and drank her fill from the water fountains. Better turn every penny while they lasted. Heavens knows what awaited her once on Irish soil.

By midnight she had made peace with the fact that she would not be flying out that night. The official at the gate sounded optimistic that there would definitely be a bigger chance for a seat on the early morning flight, just before six.

After fitting her shoulder bag under her head as a pillow, Emilee wrapped her raincoat around her bare shoulders and looped the bag's strap several times around her arm. She had chosen a different row of seats, farther away from the departure gate. The apple didn't fill for long, and she returned to the fountain for a substantial drink to silence her stomach's rumbling.

The housekeeping staff's vacuum cleaner bumping against the chair legs woke her as the east lighted up. Sore-limbed, she hobbled to the washrooms to freshen up. It was almost five. *Nothing like cold water to revive the system*, she thought as she brushed her teeth, returning the stares she received from other travelers. *Bloody nosy people. What do they think, that I'm a vagrant or something?*

At least common sense had prevailed with the issuing of her plane ticket, Emilee realized, as she tried to find an agreeable position in her exit row seat. The crutches were shoved into the gap between the window and the seat. *Bless the kindhearted flight attendant.* The plane was only half full. Everyone who wanted to get to Ireland must have done so the previous night.

The airport in Dublin was equally deserted, making finding the taxi stand easier.

The taxi driver sensed her mood and didn't say a word the entire way up north. Emilee kept her eyes closed, leaned far back, and prepared what she was going to say after knocking on the O'Hannigans' door. Only when the taxi took the turnoff onto the R166 Southeast did Emilee glance at the sky, an ominous charcoal.

As they passed through Castlebellingham, a soft drizzle began, as if apologetic. Still, it was enough for the windshield wipers to be turned on. *Welcome to miserable Ireland, Miss Stephens,* the wipers screeched over the dirty windshield. She glanced at the somber heavens a second time. There would be no sun today, or the rest of the week for that matter.

The scrap piece of paper on which she had jotted down the address of Connor's parents was mushed up like a facial tissue, her own handwriting barely legible. When the driver turned around with, "The street address, Miss?" she spread it out on her lap for the hundredth time and then handed it to him.

Emilee noted the five arches of the ancient bridge as the driver slowed down to take the sharp turn as they approached the moss-covered, stone-walled structure. The stone and river and skies were of an identical hue—the color of infinite pale shadows. Down the first proper street they turned, and she stole glimpses at the Irish Sea as they rolled past the houses. The ocean offered its visitor the same morbid gray.

The rain, as if on cue, held back when Emilee stepped from the taxi. They had parked in the street in front of the last house, which stood apart from the rest of the residences higher up the street.

Nothing moved. Emilee wondered about the clinic Connor's dad apparently ran from their house. Where would all the patients then be? Attached to the side of the house, which reminded her of a medieval mansion, was a blackened stone wall, high, like the rest of the house, with a seven-foot solid wooden gate, much like a fortress. The only thing missing was a moat.

She checked the number on the piece of paper a second time and glanced up and down the quiet street. She paid the fare and made her way down the winding, cobbled path toward the house. It was impossible to do so quietly. As she leaned forward on the crutches for the door knocker, the door swung open, making her lose her balance.

"You must be *Emilee*."

CHAPTER 29

— ᴍ —

Meeting the O'Hannigans

EMILEE GASPED AS she stumbled forward, clinging to the crutches, fighting for balance.

He had warned me his mother was old before her time. This could be his grandmother.

A slim woman, her hair cut in a short bob, stood in the door opening, glancing down at Emilee. She was as tall as Connor. When she repeated her statement, Emilee noticed that mother and son shared the same nose.

Emilee took a step forward. "*Where* is he? Please tell me."

The woman didn't move, still unsmiling. She shrugged. "Oh, I thought you were Emilee. We've received word of a feisty young lady studying at Oxford. If you're looking for Dr. O'Hannigan, you'll have to take the hallway down to the clinic. That is, if he has an opening today." She stepped back and indicated with her right hand.

Emilee limped forward. "I *am* Emilee. I'm not a patient. I'm looking for Connor. Can you *please* tell him I'm here?"

The older woman smiled for the first time. She folded her arms across her slender chest. "What made you think you'll find him *here*, my dear?"

Emilee had progressed into the door opening. "Are you not Mrs. Deirdre O'Hannigan, Connor's mother?"

The woman stiffened and glanced behind her into the dark interior. "I am. *What* made you think you'll find him here?"

Is she going to keep repeating herself? Emilee felt the crimson creep up her neck, not from embarrassment but from frustration. She was being lied to. She was certain.

"I've known Connor for a while now . . . ." she stammered. "And this . . . this is the second time in a short few months he's just disappeared." She tapped her chest. "I can *feel* he's in this house . . . He *has* to be here . . . May I *please* come in?" Emilee propelled herself forward.

Mrs. O'Hannigan may have looked old, but she was swifter than Emilee. "Just a *moment!*" she called out before shoving Emilee back and closing the heavy door in her face. From behind the door, she called, "*Sorry*, my dear. Hope I didn't hurt you. I first need a moment!"

Emilee listened to the retreating footsteps. She hobbled around and faced the street, close to tears. *The witch. She could have made me break my other leg.* Her knuckles white on the crutches, she pondered her options. *Well, Miss Stephens, what did you expect? Certainly not a hero's welcome.* She wished Caroline or Rachel or Tracy, or even Douglas Harding, was there. They would know what to make of Mrs. O'Hannigan. She was now even more convinced her hunch was correct. *Why didn't I allow Rachel to come along?*

The door opened a second time, minutes later. It was a smiling Deirdre O'Hannigan who now ushered her in, apologizing as far as they went. Emilee, shaking her head, hopped behind her transformed host. *Was she going to take me to see Connor?* She only then noticed her host's emerald eyes.

The detailed furnishings—solid dark wood with copper trimmings—reaffirmed Emilee's belief that the O'Hannigan clan must have come into money centuries ago. Brass (or was it gold?) wall lanterns lit the wide hallway which led them into a majestic circular foyer, a vast space with a central fireplace.

The hearth's mouth, blackened from decades of use, cradled a lively fire—it cast reds and golds over Emilee and her host. Against the stone walls were Persian rugs and similar pen sketches that she had noticed in Connor's apartment.

There was no doubt in her mind who the artist was.

"Please sit down." It was not a request. Deidre O'Hannigan indicated a winged leather armchair, part of a small semicircle, one of many, to the one side of the fireplace. If packed, the room could probably seat fifty people with ease. It was not difficult to picture the throne hall of a king.

Her host clicked with her tongue, and the next moment two shadows joined them as if from nowhere. Emilee jolted backward, gasping, her crutches high in front of her in defense, as the Irish wolfhounds stopped inches from her face, sniffing her.

Mrs. O'Hannigan laughed. "Don't be afraid, child. They won't bite. They're trained. Meet Saint and Dublin. They'll keep you company." She clicked with her tongue again and pointed toward the fireplace, facing the hounds. "Stay."

Emilee plopped back into the chair, her heart racing as her host disappeared down one of seven dark hallways she now noticed led from the fireplace room. She glanced at the two dogs which had turned on their heels and slumped down in front of the fire.

There was no mistaking it: they kept their eyes trained on her. They must take their orders seriously. She shuddered, leaned back, and willed her eyes closed. *And I thought Connor was weird. His mother is stranger. This whole mansion seems odd. The dogs are to stop me from going to look for Connor?*

She must have dozed off a minute for she didn't hear them approaching, not until Mrs. O'Hannigan spoke.

"*Emilee.*"

She snapped out of her reverie and grasped the one crutch in front of her chest as she jerked upright. *The dogs!* A stout man with a silver ponytail towered next to Mrs. O'Hannigan. He glared at her, his arms across his chest.

"Emilee, meet my husband, Dr. O'Hannigan."

"Dr. O'Hannigan," Emilee murmured as she staggered upright and shook his outstretched hand. His eyes bored into her as his hand locked around her fingers.

The trace of a smile appeared. "We didn't know you were coming. We've heard a little about you, especially your involvement in the women's liberation struggles in London, but *this* is a surprise."

Connor's father indeed looked surprised.

Emilee swallowed several times, her glance shifting from the O'Hannigans to the two dogs and back. "I'm here to see him— your son." She cleared her throat and raised her voice. "I *must* see Connor. *Please.*"

"I believe my wife already told you that's impossible." He corrected himself. "He's not here. Why would he be *here*?"

Emilee recovered and, leaning on both crutches, inched closer to Dr. O'Hannigan. She looked up into his face, holding his glare. She whispered, "I know now he is part of the Resistance. I wasn't certain when he disappeared the first time at the end of January—with the march in Londonderry." She quickly wiped her eyes. "Then he disappeared twenty-four hours before the bombings last Friday, with a massive backpack."

Dr. O'Hannigan stepped forward.

Emilee didn't flinch. *The bastard, I didn't come here to be lied to.*

Connor's father's face was barely a foot from her own. "The backpack doesn't prove *anything*. We haven't seen him in over five years. Didn't he tell you?"

"He did. But it is one of his many lies—or, rather, half-truths. I believe he recently had a change of heart and joined the Irish effort . . . I think the two of you made peace again. *Please* let me see him." Emilee now turned toward Mrs. O'Hannigan. *Perhaps there was some mother's love left in her.*

She scowled at Emilee.

"If you believe he lied to you, *why* on earth did you go to all the trouble—the train, the plane—to come here?" His mother was now sneering at her.

Emilee stammered and swallowed several times, wiping her eyes once more. "Because . . . I *love* him." Tears were running down her cheeks. Her leg throbbed. She could not recall when last she had felt so undone.

An Unfamiliar Kindness

Dr. O'Hannigan's thunderous laugh filled the circular room, and the two hounds took that as their signal to jump up and bark, joining the melee. He gave a single signal to the dogs, which made them stop and curl down at the fire again. He faced Emilee.

"Love him? If I can give you *any* advice, Miss Emilee: do not fall for my son. He'll break your heart."

"But he saved my life . . . Yes, I know he has issues . . . Don't we all? But I *do* love him. May I *please* see him?"

Dr. O'Hannigan waved with his arms, dismissing her. "Sit down, child. You don't know what you're talking about. *Love.*" He snorted and recited in a hushed voice, as if to himself:

> *How far away the stars seem,*
> *and how far is our first kiss,*
> *and ah, how old my heart.*

He helped her back to the chair, avoiding her eyes. "Sit down, child. Please sit down. I will get Deirdre to bring you some soup and bread, but then you have to go. You *cannot* see him. He's anyway not here." He muttered under his breath. "*Resistance. Irish effort.* You know so little. You know *nothing.*"

Dr. O'Hannigan waited until she sat down. She clasped her shoulder bag, which she had never removed.

"I'll phone for a taxi to take you back. Did you come through Dublin?"

She nodded, numb, sniffing loud and wiped her nose with the back of her hand. *He might know Yeats, but he's no less a big, ponytailed bully.*

He spun around. "Deirdre, please give her some nourishment, but then she *has* to go."

Three or four strides took him from the room and he called over his shoulder, "Saint, come along, boy. Dublin, stay!" Then, as an afterthought, he hollered, "*Slán abhaile*, Miss Emilee!"

CHAPTER 30

Returning to Oxford

HALF AN HOUR later, Mrs. O'Hannigan's dispassionate figure was the last thing Emilee saw before the door slammed close behind her. She felt sick. Perhaps she shouldn't have finished the substantial bowl of soup and soda bread her host had put in front of her. But she had been so hungry. It didn't help that she had to gulp it down under the watchful eyes of Dublin, the wolfhound, and Mrs. O'Hannigan.

She wondered whether the taxi had ever left when she noticed the cab waiting on her, its engine running. This time the driver got out and held the door. He attempted a grin and tipped his cap. "Ma'am." It was the same man.

Emilee nodded before ambling inside. The driver had just turned the vehicle when she tapped on the glass partition between them.

"I'm awfully sorry, but I have to run down—" She glanced at her plastered leg. "Well, hop down to the beach and dip my fingers in the Irish Sea. Please. I *have* to."

The driver pulled up his shoulders. "Suit yourself. You'll be disappointed. It's not a nice sandy beach, Miss. There are only boulders."

"Please?" She tried to recall how many times she had used the word that morning. She wasn't used to so much pleading.

The man pulled the taxi to the side, jumped out, and held the back door. "Don't be long. The meter is running."

Emilee propelled herself toward the small path that led between the houses. The taxi driver hadn't exaggerated. Instead of proper sand, the beach was scattered with all kinds of boulders and rocks and stones, many the size of a man's head.

She was careful as she made her way toward the water and sat down on a solid rock close to the surf. She scooped a handful of fine stone and breathed the salted air. Shading her eyes against the midday sun, Emilee watched two gulls as they called to each other, dipped, then skimmed the gray-green waters.

She wondered what the locals called the mountains across the wide bay. Connor would know. She studied the clouds. It would be wonderful if they didn't have to drive back in the rain again. She shivered, struggling to shake the chill from her. She glanced across the bay a second time. During the short while she sat there, patches of blue appeared in the granite skies. The downpour would hold back a while longer. Perhaps one could learn to love this place.

Closing her eyes, she imagined a young Connor making his way along the pebbled beach with his friends, seeking adventure. It must have been grand, like young pirates on an eternal treasure hunt. Balancing herself with the crutches, she scaled the rock, standing high. The boulders made way to pale beaches on both sides, gray stretches of sand. *So the driver lied to me about there not being any sand. Too bad. If it weren't for this silly cast on my leg, I'd be wading in the Irish Sea.*

An Unfamiliar Kindness

At the airport, Emilee went on standby once more. It was close to nine and long dark out when the gate attendee beckoned her over. There was an opening if she was still interested.

How could I not be? I have not experienced much kindness here. How did the good doctor phrase it? I knew nothing about the Resistance or about love. Perhaps he was right. I am a fool. But it is hard to believe he is a maestro in matters of the heart.

Despite a thin jersey and her rain jacket pulled tightly around her shoulders, she struggled to warm up in her window seat. She kept rubbing her hands together and tucked the thin, complimentary travel blanket twice around her legs. She must have fallen asleep for she snapped upright when the craft veered to the side as they touched down in London. Her nose was pressed against the window as she watched the racing runway slow down when the brakes kicked in, pushing her forward in her seat. *Glorious. I'm home.*

She allowed herself reflection only once she was safe on board the London-Oxford bound—when she could relax. The clacking of the tracks and swaying coach always had that effect on her. She recalled what Connor had shared about his parents. And the way he had acted once he reappeared following Bloody Sunday, at the end of January. Then again, what was with his odd behavior the previous Wednesday night, before his latest disappearance, when she stayed the night at his place?

When I woke the next morning, he was naked too, embracing me. Did he lie? He had said he would only give me a massage. I must have fallen asleep as he played the harpsichord on my oiled body with his piano fingers.

She retraced her day, step-by-step, from the moment the front door of the O'Hannigan dwelling had opened earlier that morning. She chuckled. *What would Caroline call mother O'Hannigan? A she-wolf. Or perhaps a she-bear? Rachel would probably call her an anarchist, or, at worst, a feminist bitch with attitude. Poor Connor. How much love did he experience in that house? The Mrs. O'Hannigan I met seemed a far cry from the woman Connor had described to me.*

No wonder Connor had escaped their confines and had broken contact for so long. And when he left, it was more likely Dr. O'Hannigan who had severed all ties. Then again: Connor's mother—how can she be so cold-blooded? But living in that house, with that man of hers, must have deadened her heart as well.

What happens to one's soul when it is caught up in such an airtight enclave with little light or water or gaiety to grow in? With scant oxygen? Something has to perish. Dr. O'Hannigan must be one of those people whose entire mission is to rule over others, who sees it as his destiny, his birthright. A sacred entitlement—to rule his family, his clan, even the poor dogs—everybody and everything. And, God forbid, turn their hearts into stone, and perhaps use it to build an ever bigger mansion and a higher wall to keep strangers out.

Did they really think I was that stupid? It was so obvious when she slammed the door in my face the first time. She lied to me. They had both lied to me. He was a worse liar than his wife. Connor must be so scared of his father, perhaps of both his parents, that he didn't dare come out when I was there. Or, he was so badly injured that he wasn't even in Annagassan, but in Dublin, in the hospital.

Or—Emilee jolted upright in her seat—they had to restrain him and tie him down and gag him so he couldn't call out? Or, perhaps, and her eyes filled with tears, he had become so involved that he was the actual one to instruct his parents what to do, to lie to her, bettering even his own deceitful father?

When Connor had gone back home late last year, he must have reconciled with his dad, who then imposed certain conditions on him. Harsh conditions. Dr. O'Hannigan must have a formidable grip, an unprecedented influence, on his family, on the clan, to be able to control Connor from across the water like that. A true patriarchal figure with immeasurable reach.

No, that's not true at all. Dr. O'Hannigan's no fatherlike figure. He instills only fear. It's his weapon of choice. I was so aware of the total lack of love or affection in that house. There was a passion for the cause and an overwhelming sense of purpose, but no tenderness, no compassion, no affection.

They must have instilled the fear of the Lord in Connor. She was certain that Connor was now bound by a centuries-old blood bond that had followed the clan around on the island, bound by honor, tradition, fear, and a twisted sense of loyalty.

Emilee had the navy blue blazer belonging to Francois Moolman dry-cleaned and wrapped into a neat, brown package. She left it at the front desk of Magdalen College with a note.

When she was intercommed a few days later, she declined to go down. She did not trust her own heart. How could she become involved with another man, charming as he might be, and grateful as she was, if the first one was breaking her loyal heart, making her come undone?

The less ammunition she gave Professor Thomas Hill, which certainly would happen if she became involved with his friend, the less he could keep it against her during her year-end exams.

The note attached to the brown paper wrapping had to do.

CHAPTER 31

—ᴍ—

Surprises. September 1972.

"ARE YOU *CERTAIN*?" Caroline glanced around in spite of them sitting outside the library, off to the side; the trees could all have ears.

"It's been *eight* weeks. I'm *always* regular," Emilee whispered, smoothing her jeans, without meeting Caroline's eyes.

"Have you been to the campus clinic at least?"

Emilee shook her head. How does she tell her friend it wasn't necessary to visit the clinic, that she already knew? This morning, when she got dressed, she had noticed a change. Her nipples had felt different. They felt strange, as if she was aroused. And she wasn't. Her breasts were engorged. And for the second morning in a row she felt nauseated.

She had immediately stripped down and stood in front of her full-length mirror, inspecting her body, inch by inch, glancing at her reflection and silhouette from different angles. She had clasped her breasts, pushed and probed her lower abdomen. Her tummy was flat like before. She had laid her hand between her navel and pubis. There was nothing. But for how long?

"Do you want me to come *with* you?" Caroline pulled her friend upright. "Why don't we go *now*? The clinic shouldn't be too busy early on a Saturday morning."

197

"But I'm *certain*."

"What if you're wrong?"

Emilee, the brazen one, the sweep-boat rower, clung to Caroline for a moment. It was a foreign place, to bare one's soul, all masks removed—stripped naked. They would let her finish the year, her third. She would get her Bachelor of Arts, then what? She could be a teacher—perhaps.

She already knew what Tracy and Rachel would recommend. Get rid of it.

It.

They knew people who could help her. With discretion. No one needed to know. Or she could go to the hospital. Her friends would insist. It was one of the things the WLM had made clear from the beginning: women were to have control for a change over their bodies. They were no longer helpless baby factories. Women had choices now.

But was this a choice?

What if she wanted to keep the *it*?

You want to keep Connor's child? You want those strange O'Hannigans as grandparents? What if they found out and took the infant from you? Claiming you can't look after a baby without a job or a roof over your head. What kind of life would that be? Are you totally insane, Emilee Stephens? To even want to have it in the first place?

She would be able to hide her growing stomach to the end of the year. She shouldn't be too big by November during the exams.

Caroline reached for Emilee. "*Come*, I'll go with you."

Emilee allowed herself to be steered. The entire way she prayed she was wrong, that her certainty, for once, would be shaken.

—◁◇▷—

She hadn't told any of her friends about Connor, that he had returned from the dead, from the void, from the nameless place he kept going to when he disappeared. They would be incensed that he had the nerve to call on her again.

He did just that, two weeks ago. Showed up without any warning. It had been six weeks and no word. The silence, combined with his parents' response when she had visited Annagassan, was confirmation enough.

She didn't even think twice when the front desk buzzed her down. It had been the second day without her crutches, and she had to be mindful on the stairs. It forced her to go slower.

Unlike the first time she'd met him, he stood just outside the front doors, hidden from view. She only noticed her visitor once she was outside and he stepped from behind a column.

She spun toward the movement. "*Connor?*"

"Hello, Emilee." He put his hands out to touch her, but it made her step back.

He can't touch me. Not without an explanation.

He was as pristinely dressed as the first day they had met during the march in London. Everything matched: from his cap to his jacket to his pants. Those were new boots. She wished Tracy was with her now. She would be willing to hurt him.

"What do you *want* from me? It's been *six* weeks without tiding. I assumed you were dead!" She stomped down the stairs, not looking whether he followed her.

He caught up within a few strides. "I came *back*." He had stepped in front of her now, attempting again to take her hands.

She allowed it. "What do you *want* from me?" It was a raw whisper.

"I *need* you."

She yanked her hands free, eyes blazing. "Is that another one of your many lies, O'Hannigan?" She stifled a dry sob. "You don't need *anybody*!"

"You're not anybody . . . you're—"

"Stop your *bullshit*. I'm no longer the young girl you met in London." She wiped her eyes. "You think this doesn't affect me? After what happened that Wednesday night? Do you *really* think I'd have gone to your place if I didn't care?" She spun around, away from him, crossing her arms. Her breathing came fast.

Connor had to run around to face her again. "I'm really sorry . . . and I love—"

"*Stop*! Stop with the lies, Connor. You are *not* sorry. You don't *know* what love is, and I still don't know where you've been." She grabbed his wrists and willed him to look at her. "How about starting with *the truth*?" She squeezed harder. "*Where* were you?"

Color had crept up his neck. "Emilee . . . ."

"Why is the truth so foreign to you?"

"It's complicated."

"The truth can *never* be complicated." She sighed. "Why don't you *trust* me? I told you if there was *ever* to be something between us, there can be no secrets. You have so many secrets . . . so many lies . . . You can't distinguish truth from fiction anymore."

"I was in *Annagassan*."

Emilee gasped. "I *knew* it." She relaxed her grip and stroked his arm. "I was certain I would find you there . . . Tell me what happened." She took his hand and led him to a nearby bench, then pulled him down next to her. "*Annagassan* . . . That's a good place to start."

"I was recovering from a concussion when you visited my parents' house."

"Why did they both lie to me?"

"We can trust very few people . . . especially outsiders."

Emilee snapped to her feet. "So I'm an *outsider*. A moment ago you claimed you love me. This is beyond arrogance."

"Sit down, Emilee. Please. What I mean is, you're not Irish."

"*So what*? I'm a white African learning to become an English lady."

Connor choked as he laughed. "*English lady* . . . help us, dear Lord."

Emilee was back on her feet. "Such an insult deserves a slap!"

"*Apologies,* ma'am. You *are* a lady."

"How did you get the concussion?"

When he paused, she seized his hands, this time in a vice grip.

"There was an explosion."

Emilee tightened her hold on his hands. She forced him to look at her. "Were you in Belfast on *Friday*, the twenty-first of July?"

He nodded, the blush creeping higher. He didn't blink while holding her gaze.

She relaxed her grip as tears rolled down her cheeks.

—⟊⟊—

"*Emilee*." It was Caroline. They were at the front desk of the clinic. She handed Emilee a clipboard. "You have to complete this."

Once Emilee returned the clipboard, the nurse handed her a small plastic container and motioned with her head. Emilee followed.

Caroline took her friend's hand when she returned after having left the staff a urine sample, pulling her toward the exit. "Let's go sit outside. The nurse said it would take an hour."

Upon Caroline's insistence, Emilee told her about the visit to Annagassan. She started with the sulky taxi driver who whined when she first needed to go to the bank. She painted a picture of the moat-less, moss-covered stone mansion, of its mistress and master and of Dublin and Saint, the two wolfhounds.

"Tell me more about his mother."

Emilee retraced her steps from the moment she had leaned forward for the door knocker that morning and how the door had swung open.

After Emilee had finished talking, the friends sat quiet for a many minutes. Then Caroline leaned closer. "She must be a *she-wolf*, don't you think? *That* woman in Annagassan?"

They returned to the clinic more than an hour later. The nurse handed Emilee the result with a neutral face. Both girls went outside a second time and returned to the bench they had been seated at before. Emilee read the test result for the hundredth time.

Caroline remained silent.

When Emilee looked up, her eyes were filled with moisture. She refolded the sheet of paper to the size of a postage stamp.

A single word printed on paper that will change my life forever. Forever. Positive. Isn't it ironic to state the test result as positive when the implications can be so catastrophic—negative in the extreme?

Caroline moved closer and took Emilee's hands. She still didn't say a word, only pulled her friend closer in a sideways hug. She stroked her friend's hair with her left hand while continuing to hug her tightly with her right.

"Is it Connor?"

Emilee nodded. She told her friend about the Wednesday night she'd spent at Connor's place. Caroline tried to protest, but Emilee spared no detail. Once she was done, her friend leaned back, facing her.

"I would like to hear what Douglas and Tracy and Rachel think. I'm convinced you will be able to claim and prove beyond reasonable doubt that Mr. Connor O'Hannigan raped you on the night of July the nineteenth."

Emilee sucked her breath. "He never raped me."

"Well, did you give your *consent?*"

Emilee shrugged. "I agreed to a deep massage."

CHAPTER 32

— ᘯ —

Plans change. Oxford, Fall of 1972.

TRACY WASN'T HARD to get hold of. She had hoped to sleep in that Saturday morning, but she crawled out of bed when Caroline barged into the room with Emilee on her heels and stuffed the wrinkled page with the lab result in Tracy's hands.

Emilee, for once silent, plopped down on the foot of the bed, letting her friends do the talking. As of late, she preferred to do her trancelike floating escape, hovering over Oxford, looking down at the Thames. It was much easier to shield her eyes from the silver glare of the river's tributaries as they crisscrossed the town than to explain herself to her friends.

Tracy handed Emilee the lab paper. "Connor?"

How did they all guess?

"Does he know?"

Emilee shook her head as Tracy sat down next to her. "Are you going to tell him?"

Another shake of the head.

Tracy glanced at Caroline. "Just as well, then. The bastard doesn't *need* to know."

Tracy took Emilee's hands. "Are *you* okay?" She brought her friend's hands to her lips. "I can't *believe* you don't carry protection with you. What happened to the small packages with rubber sheaths that I gave you beginning of the year?"

Without waiting for an answer, she started changing into her day clothes, sending her sleeping garments flying. She turned around. "Don't tell me you've *used* them all?" She laughed. "You're a *foxy* lady."

Emilee hadn't moved from the foot of the bed, but her eyes were swimming. She shook her head again. "No . . . I still have them all . . . *This* wasn't planned . . . He only gave me a massage . . . He lied to me." She wiped her eyes. "What was I *thinking*?"

"You want to tell Tracy what he did after he massaged you?" Caroline had pulled the only chair in the room closer.

Color crept up Emilee's neck as she shared the detail of the night with her now-pacing friend. "There's not much more to tell . . . His hands worked miracles on me . . . I must have come several times that night and then fallen asleep, completely sated . . . I was not aware of us having inter—"

"Did he make you *drunk*?"

Emilee shook her head.

"Did he *drug* you?"

Now Emilee turned crimson. "Not with pills . . . Only his hands." She sighed.

Tracy turned to Caroline. "What does the almost-lawyer say? Didn't he rape her then? There was *no* consent."

Emilee waved as she snapped out of her daze. "Guys! Stop this . . . I gave him permission in a way. He bewitched me when he played the piano . . . He was so sweet . . . Then I consented to his intimate massages."

Both Tracy and Caroline shrugged their shoulders.

"What are your immediate plans then, Miss Stephens?" Tracy tried to sound like Professor Hill.

"Finish my year, sir. Obtain my BA." They all laughed now, despite the tears.

"And *then*?" Tracy switched to her normal voice. "You'll be five, six months. You'll begin to *show*."

Emilee plopped down again on the unmade bed, biting her lip. "I know."

"You're not *really* serious about keeping it, Emilee?" Caroline chimed in. "You *should* be able to teach next year, but if they see your tummy standing *there*, they won't give you a job. *Then* what? Our parents are in Africa. Who's going to look after the little one, even if you *do* find work?"

"I know people who can help you, if you don't want it done at the hospital." Tracy pulled her bed linen straight.

"No . . . I can't let them kill the child."

"It's not a child. It's a seven-week fetus. You won't manage to keep it *and* look after it. Abortions have been legal for many years. You only need two doctors to agree and then it's done."

Emilee mumbled. "It's an *eight*-week fetus. I know the Act . . . I've also been studying all things WLM. Two consenting physicians have to agree that the continuation of the pregnancy will be harmful to either the women's physical or mental health. There's *nothing* wrong with me physically . . . So I will have to get myself certified as a nutcase, or emotionally unstable. I won't do that."

"That's simply not true. It only means—"

Emilee made for the door. "I won't allow them to *kill* my baby. I can't do this!" The door slammed behind her.

"*Emilee.* Wait!"

The two friends followed the weeping Emilee, now racing, back to Magdalen College. It was impossible to keep up with the fleeing girl.

Once Emilee reached her room, she slammed and locked the door and wouldn't let them in. Their pleading had little effect.

Caroline was the first to come to her senses. "Let's back off for a while."

"Perhaps we've been too hard on her. She must be spooked. Let's give her a couple of hours. If she still refuses, I'll get Rachel. *She* may be able to talk some sense into the redhead."

Over the next several days, under Rachel's tutelage, the girls worked on Emilee to terminate her pregnancy.

She refused to listen to such talk.

But her friends persisted. They joined her in her room at Magdalen late every afternoon.

Rachel, Tracy, and Caroline took turns to state their cases.

Emilee was unemployed, they argued; therefore, she had no means to provide for the child. Her social network outside of the student body was limited. She had no family or parents in the country who could help look after the little one. She could suffer permanent psychological damage, and, most importantly, this was an unwanted pregnancy.

She had furthermore never consented to the physical union that had taken place. For all practical purposes, she had been raped.

They were not killing an unborn baby; they were saving a third-year English major student, Emilee Stephens, from certain ruin and destitution.

This was not infanticide. They were trying to save an adult's life.

By Friday, Emilee conceded.

By the next Tuesday afternoon, they had obtained the consent of two physicians, and the procedure was scheduled for 9 a.m. on the first Saturday in October at the John Radcliffe.

Connor called the front desk early Friday evening, the night before her scheduled curettage to remove the unwanted uterine contents. He waited inside the foyer this time, in clear view. He must have figured there was less to be secretive about. Emilee hadn't seen him in four weeks, not since the day he had confessed to having been in Belfast on Bloody Friday. She hadn't spent much time with him that day, being too upset. Crying, she had soon sent him packing.

Emilee was halfway down the stairs before she noticed him. She gasped and hesitated, but he had stepped forward and called her name, waiting for her at the bottom.

"Can we go for a walk?" He held out a hand. "We need to talk."

She pursed her lips, clasped her hands behind her back, and stomped after him. *He will not touch me. Why's he here? Someone must have told him about my condition.*

She followed him down to the river. "I told you I *never* wanted to see you again." She kept her hands behind her back. "Never means *never*."

"You didn't give me time to explain."

"There's *nothing* to explain. It was on television . . . in the papers . . . Your beloved IRA exploded twenty bombs, killing *nine* people and mutilating over a hundred. Only two of them were soldiers, Connor! The last bomb, the one at the shopping center, killed a mother of seven and a fourteen-year-old boy!" She dropped to her knees, crying out. "He was only *fourteen*."

Connor flopped down next to her, trying to comfort her.

She slapped his hands away and glared at him through her tears. "Didn't you watch? Didn't you see? Do you have *no* compassion? In this one street where the bomb went off . . . People were yelling and running, bleeding and . . . there was this body . . . well, only the torso . . . the rest was blown off." She bowed forward and hugged her stomach, rocking back and forth, the sobs shaking her shoulders.

Connor touched her shoulder.

She cried softer now. "You laughed the other day when you told me about your parents' distrust because I'm not Irish." She wiped her nose with the back of her hand and sniffed loudly. "I'm certain: every Irishman and woman today must be appalled at the horror that took place in Belfast."

"It's a war, Emilee."

"War is between soldiers . . . It was a massacre . . . Madness ... What were you and your compatriots hoping to achieve? What legacy do you want to leave behind for your children? Hate or hope?"

Sobs shook her slender frame now. She was inconsolable, trying to bury her head between her knees, hiding behind her arms as she curled into a fetal position.

Why did you come tonight, Connor? Do you know about our child? It is better not to be born than to know your father was complicit in a bloodbath.

Connor dropped down on the grass in front of her, hesitating before he took her hands. "I *need* to tell you . . . How . . . I got the concussion."

She refused to look at him. He gripped her hands and allowed her to cry some more.

"Emilee, after what happened in January in Londonderry, when thirteen of our marchers were killed, I was *so* psyched up for revenge, and Belfast would be it. But then . . . When I saw what happened that Friday afternoon—I think it was the fifth bomb that had exploded, the one at the bus station. The fifth bomb changed everything. We're not supposed to, but I went back—"

He paused, breathing deeply, wiping his eyes. "I've never seen so many injured, bleeding, screaming people and bodies strewn about . . . There was blood everywhere. I started crying. I took my jacket and wrapped it around an old man's leg—it was blown off below the knee. I couldn't stop the bleeding. So I ripped out my belt that held up my pants and made a tourniquet high up on his thigh to try and stop the bleeding. My hands were soaked with his blood."

Emilee was no longer crying and moved closer so she could cup his face with both hands, wiping away his tears with her thumbs.

"I think I lost it then . . . Once I was certain the old guy could make it, I ran to stop the next bomb from detonating. I raced to the next target, hoping I would be in time."

"Wouldn't they have shot you if they knew what you were trying to do?"

"Perhaps, but as I came running round the corner of the building we had placed the bomb in, it went off, sending me sprawling, apparently knocking me against a wall, knocking me out cold. When I came to, I was in my parent's house. I had a gash at the back of my head and on my arms and legs. My dad sewed me up. They told me I was unconscious for three days."

"The IRA didn't ask why you were *there,* so close to the explosion? Weren't you supposed to know *exactly* where the bombs were placed?"

"I had memory loss, remember?"

"What do they do to traitors?"

"Traitor? No . . . I believe in the cause, wholeheartedly. We still don't want to be part of the British Empire. But I'm no murderer."

"Did your father hide you in Annagassan?"

Connor chuckled as he pulled her against him, stroking her hair. "My dad's heart is not entirely made of stone. He fought them off. Many of the IRA members were disillusioned afterward anyway." He kissed the top of her head. "You are such a smart lass."

That night, Emilee stayed over at Connor's place for the second time. On her request, he played more of Chopin's etudes and nocturnes.

In was only early fall, without a chill in the air, but he built another fire for her in his bedroom.

He took his time as he oiled her lithe body. There was no rush. The kaleidoscope of colors dancing off her curves and contours surprised him. The darting flames cast golds and reds across her yielding limbs. This time she made sure they were both in an equal state of undress.

As soon as the first spasms rocked her body, she grew impatient. Not to have a repeat of that Wednesday night, she caressed him in return, teased him, kissed him, then guided him toward her core. She lost count how many times she came that night and only woke when the sun fell on the bed and on her arm that had slipped off the side.

Connor wasn't there.

She heard sounds coming from the kitchen. She rolled onto her stomach, halfway wrapped in a sheet, and watched as the minute arm of the wall clock approached twelve. It was close to eleven. She would tell him about the life growing inside her when he returned to the bedroom.

She prayed that Caroline, Tracy, and Rachel would overlook her betrayal.

CHAPTER 33

—ᜃ—

A wedding in Oxford. December 1972

As THE YEAR drew to a close, Emilee found it easier to hide the budding life in her lower abdomen. Winter jackets and coats tend to be more forgiving than human eyes—they were less biased. Caroline was the first of her closer friends to forgive her for making fools of them and everybody at the hospital for not showing up the Saturday at 9 a.m.

Emilee could never understand why it hit Tracy the hardest. Perhaps Tracy had taken it as a personal failure: that the Women's Liberation Movement had failed one of their own. The implications were, Tracy must have believed, that Tracy Russell was a fraud. If she was unable to prevent this from happening to one of her dearest and closest friends, what hope was there for the rest of the young girls out there?

Rachel, because of her predominantly philosophical outlook, couldn't care less. It was a free world, after all. Although, she openly pitied Emilee.

All three of the friends remained of one mind: the reason for Emilee's change of heart was clear and obvious. It even had a name: Connor O'Hannigan. And he was a man—not to be trusted, a man of secrets, a conniving and sneaky bastard, who deserved to be tarred, feathered, and banned if not lynched and neutered.

Not only was Emilee seeing him again, but she was also willing to carry his child. Heaven forbid, she started talking about marrying the man. Speak of falling under a man's spell. The cause of feminism had received a painful blow.

The trio nagged her to at least see the University psychologist. Rachel was convinced it was more serious and that the additional services of a psychiatrist were required.

Emilee nonchalantly brushed off their concerns. She remained unyielding, unruffled, and only smiled at their concerns. She indeed blossomed. A new purpose was shaping her life.

The biggest surprise was Connor.

When he returned that Saturday morning from the kitchen, he had placed the tray on the foot of the bed, barely giving her time to wrap a sheet around herself and move up against the pillows, before handing her the first course.

When she told him about her 9 a.m. appointment which she had not kept after he had cleared her plate, he didn't say a word but only took hold of her hands and looked at her with exuberant eyes. She could see how the news cascaded through him. His brow knotted and unknotted. His mouth alternated between a wide grin and pursed lips. His hands were unable to stop their fluttering.

No sooner had they finished breakfast than he had slipped off the bed and sat down at the piano. He played for an hour without looking at her. Only then did he speak. "You did right."

"You're not mad at me?"

He shook his head and played some more.

"For our child," he murmured.

He startled Emilee when he suddenly ceased playing and rushed over to the bed, kneeling at her side. "What shall we *call* her?"

"*Her?*"

"I'm convinced it'll be a little *girl*."

Emilee blinked, shaking her head. "*That* we don't know, Connor."

He leaned forward. "Can I look? Can I feel your . . . tummy?"

She turned rosy and laughed. "There's . . . nothing yet to see."

"Please?"

She lay back on the bed and inched the sheets down, allowing him to place his palm above her pale blond triangle. His hesitant touch startled them both. She gasped as Connor's hand lingered. His face glowed. She stumbled as she sat up and covered his hand with hers. "It's too early . . . It's so tiny still."

Connor leaned forward and placed his head, turned sideways, on her lower abdomen, making her lie back again, grasping her hips. When he looked up and kissed her navel, his eyes brimmed. Emilee laced her fingers in his hair. This was not the floor steward she had met two years ago.

Emilee stayed in Magdalen during the week and went to Connor's place on the weekends. On Friday afternoons, Mary Gabriella would wait with her master, an arm's length away from the main gate to the college.

On October 31, 1972, Connor O'Hannigan proposed to Emilee Stephens. She accepted, much to his joy, much to her friends' disbelief, and unbeknownst to her parents.

His parents, and especially his father, were considering reactivating the five-year banishment of their only surviving son, which had been terminated the previous year when Connor had joined the Effort, the Troubles. It would take immediate effect if Connor dared marry that "snooping-around-pretentious-red-head-missy-from-Oxford." As far as they were concerned, Emilee would always remain an outsider.

Since Christmas day was on a Monday, the wedding would take place on Saturday morning, December 23, with or without the presence or blessing of Dr. and Mrs. O'Hannigan from Annagassan.

From Emilee's parents, they received a telegraph with their best wishes but also regrets. It was unlikely that they would be able to attend the wedding. Emilee's grandmother had suffered a crippling stroke, and Emilee's mother had traveled by train to South Africa to look after her mother, who had been discharged from the hospital but required constant nursing.

The ceremony took place as planned two days before Christmas, without parental presence. When only two of Connor's friends attended, Emilee thought it wise not to probe. Perhaps shop stewards were supposed not to have many close friends. Caroline, Douglas, Tracy, and Rachel made out the witnesses on her side. It was a simple occasion. Emilee had agreed to let a priest marry them in an ancient chapel close to Connor's apartment.

They had agreed to wed Catholic but raise the child Protestant.

The entire week leading up to the ceremony, Emilee prayed for cold and miserable weather, preferably snow—it would grant her clemency. She could then bundle up legitimately and wear her long winter coat.

She had opted for a modest, beige dress—no veil, no train, neither hundreds of yards of fabric puffed in around her. She was only five months, but her slim figure made it impossible to hide her status entirely. The bride's radiant face made up for what the ceremony lacked in glamor.

Her few possessions from Magdalen College were moved to the Cowley apartment seven days prior to the wedding ceremony.

It was still dark out when Emilee woke after their wedding night. Outside, a winter storm raged. *Prayers do get answered.* She pulled the covers over her head and tried to ignore the racket. Sleet pelted the building. It wasn't the freezing rain that had ruined her sleep. Something had come loose. The banging continued, hitting the wall outside their window. *The bloody shutter. It'll be torn from its hinges.*

Connor didn't stir. His snores alternated with the rhythmic bashing outside.

She shivered as she crawled from the warmth behind his back. Even a jab in his ribs didn't rouse him. *The poor man.* She tiptoed past the smoldering fire and pulled her gown tighter, but it failed to stop her teeth from chattering. On her way back, she dropped a new log in the fireplace and blew the remaining embers to life.

Emilee pulled a blanket from the bed and dropped to her knees in front of the flames, where golden tongues twirled and danced, shooting high into the chimney. She hugged her knees and watched, listening to Connor's breathing and the wind that quieted down.

Mrs. Emilee O'Hannigan. What a strange ring it has to it.

CHAPTER 34

———⚊∿∿⚊———

A new baby and new troubles. 1973.

SINCE THE RIVER hadn't frozen over that January, Connor had to convince Emilee to quit rowing. Now she insisted on going for extensive walks.

She agreed to bid her paddles farewell, only because it became difficult to get in and out of the craft on the water. Her bulbous abdomen simply got in the way. She refused to back off from her plan to first walk with him to his work and then to her own every morning. And in the afternoon, she was there to meet him at the gate and walk with him back home. She never told him how far she went on her own, but she would go for miles, rain or snow, despite his concerns. Bundling up came easy for her.

They tried to save some money. It would come in handy once the baby was there and she couldn't work.

Emilee, always willing to learn new skills, including developing a thicker skin, convinced the principal of Magdalen College to allow her to continue working half-days in the student cafeteria, as she intermittently had as a student, despite her "condition."

The mockers regretted having said anything about her apparent stupidity of not terminating the pregnancy. Her resultant increase in girth and fuller bosom on full display implied she had squandered her future and her education. "Scandalous working there in front of other students in such a state," they claimed.

Stoic and unapologetic, she would cut them down with sharp reasoning and dark humor. To her, it was a life and death situation. She refused to be shamed. She was content with her choice and she needed the money. So, *to life* it would be!

When Emilee went into labor on the last day of April, she had not seen her in-laws since her infamous visit to Annagassan. They knew about everything Connor had reassured her. His father had not spoken to him, not since the wedding. "Principles are principles," the good doctor claimed.

Connor rushed with her to the hospital immediately after her water had broken, but he refused to use Mary Gabriella, claiming it unfit transportation for women in active labor.

Emilee panted. "It's only a *silly* car."

"The cab has a backseat where I can catch the baby if need be."

Emilee rolled her eyes at him. At least the taxi driver did not insist on her first removing her shoes and placing them in a black cloth bag before settling in for the ride.

However, the moment they reached the labor floor, Caroline and Rachel were there, waiting. They took over the moment the nurses turned their backs, banning Connor without much ceremony, claiming he would only upset his spouse and hence prolong the birthing process.

He shook his head at their nineteenth-century-midwife mentality and unyielding stance.

But as far as they were concerned, he would only be allowed back in when his wife was ready to push. Perhaps he'd rather find a newspaper to read, they recommended.

Emilee breezed through the introductory contractions, her cheering friends at her sides, with the nurses in the background checking in from time to time. The only sign she was in labor was a brief grimace when the contractions shuddered her body. Her eyes remained steadfast on the wall clock. She had decided it would help her remain focused if she knew what time it was. As the shorter hour arm crept past the three, the waves in her lower body increased in regularity and intensity.

At least the contractions warned her with some tightening before knotting her womb muscles and jabbing her in the side, doubling her over. She soon doubted the relevance of knowing the time at all. If only it would pass.

Rachel and Caroline took turns to help her pace her breathing. It seemed they had turned experts overnight. "Breathe, breathe, breathe, Emilee dear. There we go . . . slow, slow, slow now . . . and breathe, breathe, breathe."

If there were a rooster on the hospital grounds when the east lighted up, he would have announced the new day at the same instant Emilee felt the overwhelming urge to push. But the nurses wouldn't hear of it. "*No*, Mrs. O'Hannigan . . . You're not fully dilated . . . You can't push yet. That's my girl . . . Breathe, breathe, breathe . . . *No* pushing!"

"But I *have* to push! Connor? Where's Connor? Nurse? Caroline . . . Where's that bloody Irishman? I need him. Connor!"

"Mrs. O'Hannigan, not so loud. And slow your breathing. *No* pushing, I said!"

"I *have to* . . . It's too full. It's ripping me apart!"

Rachel dabbed the sweat from her forehead as Caroline dashed off to locate Connor. Rachel leaned in, wiped, soothed, and tried to hug the agonizing Emilee. "Don't push, sweet girl, don't push. You'll tear those lovely lower lips apart."

"I don't care," Emilee groaned. "They're not lovely anymore. Where's that Connor-man? He impregnated me. The bastard . . . Oh, it hurts really bad . . . and he did it while I was asleep . . . Oh dear, Lord . . . Help me . . . Oh shit . . . Oh, help me!"

Connor burst into the room, clearly uncertain what he had expected—a baby perhaps, but definitely not a cussing wife broadcasting to the world how she'd become impregnated. "Now, now . . . Emilee dear, settle down." He took over from Rachel and alternated dabbing her glistening brow and kissing her parched lips.

Emilee locked his hand in a death grip, making him recoil. "The nurse . . . wouldn't let me push . . . Connor O'Hannigan!" She gasped several times. "She was real nice all night . . . but now she's turning . . . Oh, dear Lord . . . into a real bitch!"

"Don't be mad at her. Slow those breaths, Sweetie Pie. Slow that breathing down."

She laughed for a moment before shuddering through the next contraction. "Don't Sweetie Pie me . . . You bloody Irishman. I love you. Hold me tighter . . . Oh, Connor! . . . It hurts so bad!"

"I love you, Princess . . . You're doing mighty fine. My sweet, white, African lady."

—m—

Caitlynn Aine O'Hannigan was born on May 1, 1973, nine hours and seventeen minutes after her mother and father had arrived at the John Radcliffe. At exactly four minutes after 8 a.m., she made her appearance. Her mother was still hollering blue murder, when the next moment the child slipped out, all slimy and coated with blood and muck, only to give her first hesitant cry, followed by another and another.

Emilee, who had quieted down, wept with abandon when they placed the wriggling, purple-and-pink-faced creature wrapped in white hospital linen on her heaving chest.

Connor, Rachel, Caroline, and the nurses all laughed and talked at once, congratulating and trying to hug and kiss her, but Emilee only had eyes for the little thing on her breast. She was horrified she may be dreaming, that it was all an illusion.

Her daughter was like the newborn puppies she had grown up with, the eyes all closed, grunting and moaning and sniffing, searching for a teat. Emilee pulled the child closer and kissed the wrinkled forehead and tiny, tiny nose. She beamed.

I love you, sweet child. You have a wiggly nose and the sweetest doggy-breath.

—ɱ—

Caitlynn was two months old when Emilee received a call from Connor's workplace supervisor. Her husband had been taken to the hospital. He'd apparently had a nervous breakdown that morning at work. Yes, he was fine—under the circumstances. No, he hadn't hurt himself or anybody at the plant. No, sorry, ma'am. I can't tell you anything more. No, I'm not a doctor, the man said. You'll have to ask the people at the hospital.

If she so preferred, a driver from the plant could pick her up in half an hour's time and take her to the hospital to see her husband since there was still ninety minutes left of the working day.

"But I have a *two-month-old* baby with me, sir. I can't just *leave* her here."

"Sorry, ma'am. Don't you have a carry cot? It's the only thing I can do. Mr. O'Hannigan is one of our best floor stewards. Our driver will be there in *exactly* thirty minutes. He'll get you downstairs at the front entrance. He will bring you back as well, but you can only visit for half an hour. Goodbye, Mrs. O'Hannigan."

Asshole of a man. No wonder poor Connor had a breakdown. Growing up with a tyrant and a she-wolf as parents, and now a pompous bastard for a boss, how on God's earth can one remain sane?

Her arms shook as she stuffed a few items into a bag and placed the sleeping child in the carry bag, petrified she may drop the baby due to her shaking. Just as well that she had gone for her walk earlier than usual. She couldn't walk Connor to work anymore but went on daily midmorning strolls.

She had managed to shed most of her pregnancy weight with her obsessive walking schedule. She always strapped the little thing in a special chest-pouch and simply walked and walked till the baby fell asleep. The two of them had just returned from a longer than usual walk, and she had barely finished breastfeeding when the man from the motor assembly plant had called.

Emilee willed herself to slow her breathing as she leaned far back in the speeding cab, her arms protective over the sleeping child.

Connor. How long have I lived in denial?

Rachel, Tracy, and Caroline would opine: from the beginning, from the very beginning, ma'am. The telltales were in London, they would say.

How did she miss the signs?

He had been odd, right out of the starting blocks. *But aren't we all a little odd?*

She should have known when she learned his car had a gender as well as a name, Mary Gabriella. And, having had to take off her shoes, weren't those all flashing, glaring, neon warning signals? And the ironed white handkerchief to use on the car's door handle?

Since Caitlynn's birth, he would get home on a Friday night long after she had gone to bed, when the clock tower chimed the single-digit morning hours. Reeking of liquor and smoke, he must have thought those scents masked the aroma of women clinging to him. It wafted toward her when he fumbled into bed in the dark, too lazy to first take a bath to at least hide his deceit. Her back was always turned to him, pretending to be asleep.

The tears in her birth canal had taken longer to heal than she had hoped. How she longed for his touch. How she had longed for his once passionate lovemaking. She would cry herself to sleep on Fridays, once he had rolled onto his side, away from her, and snored along in his drunken stupor.

She was planning on confronting him—someday soon.

It hurt even more when he didn't ask why she insisted that he wore a condom now.

She had thought little of it when he became obsessed with the baby the past several weeks, insisting on taking care of the child once he got home. But he was often disappointed that Caitlynn only wished to be fed and changed into a dry diaper before falling asleep again. It was futile to convince him she was too little yet to play.

The always pristinely kept apartment had since been transformed into a military-standard barracks—inspection ready any time of the day or night. Everything had its place, he would explain. There was no need to live in a pigsty.

Every day he would reiterate his requirements. *Everything. Had. Its. Exact. Place.* Soon, Emilee realized she and the child lived in a sterile, surgical theater. Connor would constantly wipe and shine the furniture expecting her to do likewise.

No longer was it sufficient for them to remove their shoes at the front door. There were cloths now that had to be walked on to keep the floors shiny. No longer did it suffice that the place was clean.

Dust had become the new enemy—any dust—on the floor, on the furniture, even particles in the air. The dangers were vast, he claimed. The unhurried twirl of dust specks caught in shafts of morning light, bursting into the rooms through the lace inner curtains, had always fascinated her. It used to take her as if on wings and make her join the sunrays outside, sweep her up, high, high above their apartment—make her float and dream.

Now it filled her with dread.

He had yelled twice at her the previous week after he'd gotten home and found dull spots on the hallway floor. The place wasn't shiny enough. It meant only one thing, he hollered—the place was *dirty*. Filthy. Which meant she was lazy. He made her scrub the whole place until two in the morning.

And each time, hours later, he'd apologize, himself in tears—only to repeat the scenario the following day, hollering at her, making her scrub the place, then apologizing in tears as if for the first time.

CHAPTER 35

——— ༄ ———

Becoming familiar with the new illness. 1973.

THE NURSE STEERED Emilee to Connor's private room, a small space to the side on the medical ward. Connor sat on the only chair, facing the window. Emilee remained standing next to the bed, the bag over her shoulder, with Caitlynn on the arm in the carry-bag. The nurse formed the rearguard.

. "*Hello*, Connor." She had to force gaiety into her voice.

He continued staring outside. "Hello, Emilee."

She would only later learn what blunt affect meant. Dismissing the nurse with a brave smile, she pulled a little bench closer to his chair, not letting go of the carry-bag. She had prayed the child would remain sleeping—now she wasn't certain. "You want to hold Caitlynn?" she asked anyway.

"If I must." He held out his arms, like a robot. "Thank you. Hello, Caitlynn." His voice remained monotonic.

She pulled the bench up close and kissed him on the cheek. "Do you remember what happened at work today? *Anything?*"

He stared at her, shook his head, and handed the sleeping baby back. "The nurse said I calmed down only after . . . they gave me an injection. I think the superintendent said I went bonkers. This injection . . . It made me kind of . . . I'm sorry . . . They say I'll have to sleep in the hospital tonight." He stood up, then sat down again. "Goodbye, Emilee. Goodbye, Caitlynn." He had turned back facing the window.

—ɯ—

Connor stayed in the hospital for two days. The doctors took a wait-and-see approach, working on the diagnosis they told her when she visited the next morning.

As soon as the driver had dropped Emilee off at the apartment after their first visit, she fed the child, changed her diaper, lulled her to sleep, searched for Mary G's keys, and went through to the living room where she crawled up on the sofa and had a good cry.

There was much to weep about.

Leaning over the sink afterward as she dabbed cold water on her face, she considered her options. Of her three closest friends, Tracy and Rachel would be the quickest to tell her, "Told you so, girlfriend."

They'd be right, but I don't need that now. Caroline will be kinder.

Connor didn't say, and she decided not to share her bold decision to use Mary G to get her and Caitie to and from the hospital. She realized the risk, trespassing on holy ground, but didn't have the stomach to deal with the assembly-plant driver or a taxi or the bus.

Caroline was sympathetic and didn't ask questions. She visited late the next afternoon and helped Emilee buff the place to a steady gleam. Connor would have to be impressed.

Life returned to near normal once Connor returned from the hospital. He didn't say a word about the shining apartment and went to work the next day. In fact, he didn't talk at all. For the next many weeks, the hallway-floor walking-cloths found no use as the master of the house adjusted to his new reality.

The doctors called it an isolated episode of mild psychosis. No further treatment was deemed necessary.

Her husband was not mad they claimed, not really—thank God.

—◦◦◦—

It was the same supervisor who called her—exactly one month after the first episode—at eleven in the morning. Emilee had strapped the little one into her body-pouch for their morning walk when the phone rang.

Connor had suffered a bigger meltdown this time, the supervisor explained. It had required four strong men to control him until the ambulance and the doctor had arrived and given him an injection. Yes, he had been taken to the hospital. She thanked the man—she found him almost compassionate this time—but declined his offer for transportation to the hospital. She would manage, she said.

Emilee packed a small backpack and took off with Caitlynn in the chest-pouch on their regular walk. There was little purpose for them in going to the hospital at that hour. Connor would be *unreachable* in his own medicated universe.

If he had acted out more violently than the first time, they must have sedated him with more and stronger drugs this second time. It would only upset her to see him like that, speaking to her like a robot. She'd walk to the university and see who of her friends she could find—one couldn't be picky in time of need. Nothing would happen if she paid Connor a visit only later that afternoon.

Connor remained in the hospital for an entire week following his second psychotic episode. Despite longing for his solid arms to hold her at night until she fell asleep, the reprieve, the relief, was greater of not having to spit and polish every inanimate object, never knowing if it would be good enough.

Emilee met Connor's psychiatrist, Dr. Peter Jones, on the third day of his second hospital stay. He sat her down and they had a thirty-minute talk. She wept almost as long.

Connor's disease had received a name: schizophrenia.

He would be placed on medication he'd have to take every day to help prevent a relapse. Perhaps lifelong.

Emilee was getting used to weeping in public places.

With Caroline's help the next day, they took Caitlynn along in Mary G and paid a visit to the assembly plant. Emilee had little trouble recalling the location and layout of the administration block adjacent to the factory floor, back from the time when she had paid Connor a visit with her bicycle. Mary Gabriela was parked in a shaded parking spot, its windows rolled down, where Caroline remained with the infant. Emilee, dressed in her Sunday best, went to meet with the plant manager.

Following her meeting with Dr. Jones, she had immediately phoned Connor's workplace and requested a meeting with his boss. Only after she had insisted and burst into tears over the phone did they agree to this meeting.

She left the boss's office twenty minutes later, proud that she had stood up to the man, this time without breaking down. The asshole. He'd only agreed once he realized she wasn't going to budge. She was given the assurance the Union would take care of Connor and his dependents. Management was considering giving him a month of sick leave.

The following week, a day after Connor had returned home, a social worker paid them a visit to verify they could manage with the new illness and the baby around. Connor only rolled his eyes at the plump, middle-aged lady. Ignorant people, he claimed. He did *not* have a split personality. The medication would keep him well, make him fire on all cylinders.

Emilee resumed taking Caitlynn on her daily walk. She needed it. The baby needed it, she believed.

At first, she invited Connor along on the walks, even pleaded with him, but he couldn't be bothered and preferred to stay home. He had books. He would read, he told her, every day she prepared to go out. She never gave up hope he would change his mind. In the end, stepping into the hallway, she would sigh, relieved to flee the confines of Connor's gloom. It was impossible to remain unscathed in his brooding presence.

The walk became her legitimate escape, her portal to an outside existence.

Eager to learn about Connor's illness, Emilee made it mandatory to visit the library on her daily walks. The librarians turned a blind eye (since she wasn't an official student anymore) as long as she allowed them to hold the now-blossoming Caitie, who would smile and laugh at the staff, grabbing their fingers and making instant friends.

Sometimes, when the place was quiet, the librarians fought over who got to walk with little Caitlynn, carrying her up and down the aisles, giving her mother freer access to the textbooks and journals.

As she read and studied for short periods at a time, Emilee thought about the O'Hannigans from Annagassan. Genetics played a role, the books said. How much of his present troubles did Connor inherit from those two hotheads? Did his mother neglect herself when she was pregnant with him, too scared to eat, hiding away from her bedeviled spouse?

Emilee wondered how long it would take Connor to discover that he may develop permanent tremors and involuntary movements due to the medications. Would he refuse to take the drugs if he knew? Then what? What would she and Caitlynn do if he had a meltdown at home?

Dear Lord, have mercy on us.

CHAPTER 36

—⚬—

The illness relapses. Oxford.
January 1974.

CAITLYNN AINE O'HANNIGAN was ten months old when she took her first steps in her parents' apartment. She completed the distance between the two winged armchairs pulled in front of the hearth without falling once.

Encouraged by Emilee and Connor's jubilation, her bravado doubled on the spot, and she let go of her mother's hand, having turned around on unsure feet, staggering with her diapered bottom, billowing sideways, toward her father's outstretched hands, attempting a repeat feat, muttering something that sounded like, "Walk . . . Walk."

Her foot caught on a slight fold in the carpet and she fell flat, face first, bawling. Emilee, laughing, scooped her daughter up, faster than the surprised dad could.

Connor remained in his chair as Emilee ambled around, searching for the child's soother, all the while patting her little back. "Now, now, Caitie. It's all right . . . Let's find your soother. You walked like a big girl. Mommy and Daddy are *so* proud of you. The silly carpet made you fall."

Where can the soother be? Caitie had it in her mouth a minute ago.

"Honey, please help me find her sooth—" Emilee, baby on the hip, turned around to face her spouse. Connor sat in the same position he had when Caitie had face-planted.

He brought his index finger to his pouting lips, mouthing "*Shuuut*."

He stood, raised his arms as if in benediction, and hollered, when Caitie took a breath before continuing her crying. "*Listen! Do you girls hear that? A marching band . . . They're coming this way.*" He gestured at the windows before marching on the spot, playing drums, then switching to playing trumpet.

Emilee laughed, certain he was joking. There was no music outside—only a forlorn January wind howled around the chimneys and shutters.

A few snowflakes had drifted down early that morning, prompting Connor to stoke a fire. She spotted the soother under the chair she had sat on, kneeled, grabbed the pacifier, put it first in her own mouth, rubbed it a few times on her sleeve, then slipped it into the still simpering child's mouth. She stepped in front of the fire, holding the now-comforted girl against her breast, grateful for the heat and the quiet.

Connor's howling, mixed with breaking glass, almost made her drop the child. She spun around. He stood behind the dining table, one of the straight-back chairs in his hands raised high like a weapon. The legs were inches from the ceiling. The turquoise vase he had given her as a Christmas present ten days ago lay in pieces against the bookshelf behind him.

Another howl escaped her husband as he glared at them, the chair raised higher. Caitlynn screamed hysterically. She had lost the soother again, and it had rolled against the foot of the fire-place screen.

Emilee scooped up the pacifier a second time, clung to her baby, glanced at Connor, and calculated her chances before bolting down the short hallway toward the bedrooms. She prayed the key was on the inside of their main bedroom door, where they usually kept it.

Connor, before he had become ill, had had a second phone installed in the bedroom a week after Caitie's birth.

"Where do you think you're going with my daughter, *woman*?"

Emilee, grateful for her persistent daily walks, completed the ten yards in record time. She slammed the door shut behind her, turning the key as Connor's full weight struck the closed door. The child had almost slipped from her grip when she'd spun around and grappled for the key. Caitlynn dangled from her arm.

She was sobbing as hard as Caitlynn as she pulled the baby against her chest, leaning into the door.

Did he stop taking his medications? I checked on him every day, but who knows? Perhaps he didn't swallow the pills I gave him?

He'd been complaining more and more the last couple of months about his persistent dry mouth and constipation. An O'Hannigan always has regular bowel movements, he insisted. Being constipated was a shameful condition to suffer from, apparently. Shameful.

And then he came across one of the articles about the side effects of psychotropic drugs a month ago, which she sometimes carried around with her, stating tremors and restlessness. Perhaps he had found an excuse to stop taking his drugs?

It had required concerted efforts from both her and Dr. Jones to convince him to resume his medication. They were busy deciding on an emergency plan—a crisis plan—for something like tonight but had never finalized it. Now this.

"*Emilee. Open* the door!" He thumped with both fists against the door, alternating it with kicks.

She could see the door vibrating under his onslaught. He was a strong man. The door was stronger. She scampered toward the bed, hyperventilating, clutching the screaming baby, and dialed the hospital. Her hands shook too much. She had to redial. *Please answer . . . Oh Lord, let them please answer the blooming phone.*

"John Radcliffe Hospital. How may I help you?"

Emilee explained, between sobs and a wailing child, that she needed an ambulance with a doctor and psychiatric nurses, immediately if possible. Her ill husband was breaking the place down.

No, this was not the first time, but the first time this has happened at home . . . Yes, if the switchboard could also phone the police. The police might be faster than the ambulance. Yes, at least four men, four police officers to restrain him.

"Your address, Mrs. O' Hannigan?"

She provided the information, pinching the handpiece between her ear and shoulder, and held Caitlynn on her left hip, having managed to slip the soother back into her mouth.

A powerful crash shook the door. It sounded like a chair had been shattered against it. She heard Connor's manic laugh from deeper in the apartment. Then silence. The baby settled down as she rocked back and forth, sitting on the edge of the bed, singing a lullaby, clutching her child.

She wasn't certain if she imagined hearing a siren in the distance. She tiptoed to the door after placing the now-sleeping child back in her crib next to the bed. Could she trust the silence? She knelt, took care to remove the key without a sound, and peeked through the keyhole. There was no movement in the hallway—empty. *Perhaps if she . . .*

A green eye appeared at the other end of the keyhole, followed by a thud against the door that made her yelp in terror, falling backward to the floor. She could smell his stale breath through the keyhole. Revolting.

Connor gave a manic laugh. "Emilee, why wouldn't you listen to the marching band? Why did you refuse to listen? It was only a stupid band for goodness' sake. I won't hurt you. The door . . . Open the door . . . I need to see my baby."

Emilee whimpered. "Connor . . . You need help . . . *then* you can hold her again."

Connor crashed once more with his full weight against the door. "Open the *fucking* door!"

The siren sounded closer. She leaned with her back against the wall. *The front door is locked. How are the police going to get in?*

She jumped when the phone rang. She picked up on the second ring. "*Yes?*"

"Mrs. O'Hannigan? Your front door is locked. How do you want us to get in? Can the officers use force—"

Connor must have picked up the second phone in the hallway. He hollered, "Don't you bastards *dare* break my door. Don't fuckin' dare!"

Emilee cried out, "Officer, break the door down. My baby girl and I have locked ourselves in the main bedroom in the back. *Please hurry!*"

"*Bastards!* Emilee!"

They had little trouble in kicking the door open, but it took four police officers and two paramedics to hold Connor down until the doctor could sedate him.

She refused to go to sleep in a hotel for the night. She phoned Caroline, who showed up half an hour after the paramedics had left with a subdued Connor. An armed policeman was stationed to stand guard in the living room for the night. It was after midnight by the time they had swept the shattered pieces of glass and stacked the broken pieces of furniture in a corner of the dining room.

Emilee, Caroline, and Caitlynn locked themselves in the main bedroom.

Emilee fell asleep in front of the fire in the old leather winged armchair, the child still on her breast. Caroline built a fire the minute they had locked the door. Sleet pelted the windows, rattled the shutters, and created sudden drafts up the chimney. It made the fire sputter, only to flame brighter, sending sprays of sparks up the shoot.

In the early hours, Caroline pulled the crib closer and transferred the baby from her mother's arms. After propping a pillow behind Emilee's head, Caroline pushed a footstool under Emilee's legs and covered her with a blanket. Pulling a second chair up against Emilee's, Caroline took another blanket and made herself comfortable. There would be little sleep tonight, but she didn't have the heart to wake her friend and move her to the bed.

—ɯɯ—

Connor's third involuntary admission to the hospital lasted all of four weeks.

The front door was fixed the following day. Caroline stayed with Emilee for the entire first week. Six of the original eight straight-back dining chairs had survived the carnage.

After repeated meetings between a now-docile Connor, Dr. Peter Jones, and Emilee, the decision was made to place Connor on an intramuscular depot injection of Chlorpromazine, also known as *Largactil*. They decided that if he refused his depot injection, he would immediately forfeit his right to live at home or go back to work.

Connor agreed.

—୰—

CHAPTER 37

Sharing a house with an unpredictable man. Oxford. Summer of 1974.

PEOPLE CAN RECOVER from psychosis. Some are fortunate and have a single episode. Those less fortuitous only recover but are not cured. Connor was no exception. He belonged to the unfortunates.

The intramuscular injections of Chlorpromazine had its desired effects: his psychotic episodes became nuanced.

He returned to work. Negotiations with the Union bosses made it possible for him to keep his position as shop steward and work fewer hours. Emilee, however, now commenced with two extended walks per day, taking the child and escaping the apartment, but only after she had polished every surface and object inside, creating miniature mirrors, which reflected all her furtive glances.

She found it impossible to believe the peace would last. Then she chastised herself for her lack of faith.

Thank God, Connor had good days.

They experienced happy days when the three of them would go for a picnic. Every week, following her first birthday, Caitlynn's legs became sturdier, her balance surer, and soon she took to running and some falling. Connor and Emilee were not finicky, whether it was Saturday or Sunday, if there were blue skies, or at least no rain, it was immediately declared a picnic day. Emilee would carry the blanket and basket while Caitie got a ride on her daddy's shoulders.

Feeding Caitlynn was a simple enough task. She had taken to eating solid foods but still preferred the breast. Emilee preferred the convenience and stuck to nursing her, much to her spouse's chagrin. Preposterous, he complained, that he had to share his wife's two precious attributes with a little wee girl.

Unlike his dad, Connor could be a perfect father, the perfect spouse on those outings—running with his daughter, twirling, holding her secure by the forearms. Around and around they spun, faster and faster. Caitlynn crooned, then even faster they went, until both collapsed on the grass, dizzy and laughing.

Seconds later the child would scamper to her feet with outstretched arms, "Daddy . . . Up!" She could never get enough.

And Connor obliged. Around and around they went again, always faster and faster, followed by more laughing and collapsing into hapless dizzy bundles. And toward her he would be the perfect gentleman, flirting even, making her laugh.

Emilee struggled to figure out what triggered his mood swings, the sudden erratic outbursts. When everything seemed perfect, the tiger would bare its fangs. It was the hardest on Caitie. Her luminous eyes would double in size when hell broke loose without warning. Her eyes then begged, *What's happening, Daddy?*

Following a meltdown, Emilee often wondered whether it had been worth the trouble of going for a picnic. It often started the moment they walked in the door, took off their outside shoes, and Caitie toddled down the hallway with Emilee a short step behind with the picnic basket and blanket.

The discovery of a speck of dirt could set him off—always something to do with innocent dust particles, suspended, twirling in the air.

They wouldn't even have reached the living room when he would remark, "Why is the place so *filthy*? *Emilee*, when was the last time that you cleaned the place?"

"Honey? This *morning* . . . Minutes before we left."

"You call this *clean*? Look at all this *shit*." He'd point at the shafts of light that fell in through the tall windows. Thousands of minuscule dust particles twirled and danced, ascending the light columns.

Caitie wobbled to behind the safety of her mother's legs and stared at her father, waiting.

They both had learned it was wiser to wait at a safe distance. It seldom took long before the fireworks started.

During those tirades, he often became vocal about her friends and her association with the women's liberation movement even though she was no longer a regular attendee.

"What is it with you and that tall girl? The one who rowed and swam with you—*Rachel*, isn't it? Is she gay?"

When Emilee gasped, he bellowed out a laugh. "I've seen how she looks at you. You think I'm blind? The way she touches you."

Emilee, now crying, would shake her head, by then only whispering, "How dare you say *anything*? She's a friend. Why do you think I insist on you wearing protection when we make love? You think I can't smell the women on you when you sneak in after a night out with the boys and who knows who else?"

Dear Lord, why do I even call it making love? It has become the copulation Douglas had referred to. Have we become animals?

This often made him back off a bit, blushing, mumbling, "It's an old childhood friend . . . She's been listening to my sorrows for years, and she provides some comfort. I've known her since I came to Oxford." Avoiding eye contact, he would adjust his clothing and iron out imaginary wrinkles. "It means *nothing* . . . You don't need to worry."

"What's her name?"

"Eileen . . . It's nothing serious . . . She's like an acquaintance."

"An acquaintance who has *sex* with you!"

That usually silenced him and made him leave the room with his tail between his legs.

Toward the end, Emilee recalled, their apartment became emptier. It looked barren and forsaken almost. He found little satisfaction in hurling the contents of the bookshelf around. Perhaps his books were the only things he still cared about. And she dared not try and pawn any of his precious volumes. Who knew how that would affect him? The furniture pieces and ornaments inconspicuously decreased in number every month, destroyed or damaged during his outbursts. Afterward, she would sweep it together, gather the broken pieces, and throw them out. There was no money to replace anything. Connor only worked half his usual hours, and Emilee had not returned to employment either.

According to the O'Hannigans from Annagassan, the three of them did not exist. They had lost their second son for a second time the day he'd married that redhead from Africa. All ties were severed. He'd have to fight his own battles—no support, no help, no contact. Neither did they have a granddaughter, they claimed. They had never laid eyes on the child.

When the fits took him, Connor no longer became psychotic but only upset and violent, to the point of cussing and shoving and slamming and breaking—enough to give the girls a good scare. Emilee couldn't dare retreat with Caitie to one of the bedrooms—it only fueled his rage. They became his captives. He demanded an audience.

Emilee scooped Caitlynn and settled on her winged chair, perched on the front, close to the fireplace. She pulled the child into her breast and murmured a lullaby close to her ear, rocking back and forth, her eyes not leaving her husband for a second. It was best there, on the chair.

Nothing she did or said at this point would help. The first time she had run to get her duster, broom, cleaning cloths, and floor polish he had yelled only louder. Caitlynn soon learned it was better not to cry. It only made Daddy more upset.

So they listened in silence, watching and waiting.

His tempests would die out like the flip of a switch. It seldom lasted more than two or three minutes. Without warning, he would deflate like a giant balloon—go *phiitt*—plop down where he was, pull himself into ball against the wall, and go mute. He would then sway back and forth like a rocking horse.

This was always the sign for Emilee and Caitlynn to flee to the bedroom.

He would come and apologize when he was ready. He always did. Sometimes he even cried, as if he meant it.

She pulled the curtains aside, pushed the windows open, and settled on the bed on her side, facing the breeze, which billowed the Dutch lace inner curtains. She had slipped out of her blouse and bra and nestled the child to her chest.

Despite her breastfeeding and Connor's complaints, her breasts had remained firm and small, although fuller. She thought they looked adorable, the areolas darker since the pregnancy. Both nipples were erect. By the time she switched breasts with Caitie, leaning onto her other side, hesitant steps had approached the bedroom.

Emilee glanced at the door, waiting for him to appear.

It was an elaborate tango for two.

Connor remained standing in the door, watching them, his shoulders stooped, an old man. He waited.

Caitlynn was on the brink of falling asleep, her little fists relaxed around her mother's breast, her eyelids fluttered but stayed trained on her mother.

Emilee smiled, kissed her brow, and stroked her cheek. She glanced at the door. He had not moved. She gestured for him to stop being such an idiot. She was still mad at him, the bastard—scaring them, insulting her, again and again.

He kneeled at the side of the bed and looked for her free hand, He brought it to his lips, kissing each finger. "I'm *so* sorry," he whispered. "Ashamed. What must Caitie think of me? That I'm a bastard father? Please forgive me."

How could I forgive you with the snap of a finger, Connor, as if you did nothing? Both Caitie and I are bleeding inside. It takes time to stop the hemorrhaging. I. Need. Time.

When she said nothing, he ambled over to the piano and sat down, opened the lid, and studied his hands so long she thought he had fallen asleep. Emilee was surprised. It had been months since the instrument had been touched. He pushed the damper pedal in and started.

He can be so considerate. That's why I still love him. But he remains a bastard. He's dangerous.

He played the piece he always did when he was in the pits: Beethoven's *Moonlight Sonata*.

The bloody Philistine. She had always loved it. He knew that. This was his peace offering. It had always worked.

He played the piece a second time, seeking Emilee's eyes. Forgiveness has to be earned, her eyes said. It can require the passage of months or years.

Connor, you always demand instant forgiveness. I can't do this anymore.

Caitlynn was asleep, her mouth agape.

Connor scooped the child up and laid her down in her little bed. "Don't cover up, Emilee." He sat on the side of the bed, watching her chest rise and fall. When a blush crawled up her neck, he laid down beside her and touched the one nipple that still oozed milk then licked it away.

Emilee shuddered and pulled him closer. "Just hold me."

She didn't crave intimacy. Her body didn't work that way. She wasn't a machine. *Who was Eileen? What did he think? Did he kiss her breasts? The bastard. What did she think? The bitch.*

He was only allowed to hold her now.

Perhaps later.

Early mornings always calmed her. Daybreaks. She may allow him to touch her then, when the promise of the new day lighted up the east, erasing the darkness of the past, washing away previous sins. And it had to be before Caitie woke.

Perhaps she would forgive him then.

In the morning.

Perhaps.

CHAPTER 38

Fooling people all the time is hard work. Oxford 1975

EMILEE DECLINED TO be serious when asked about her and Connor. They were in the midst of a cease-fire, she would tell her friends, laughing. *Life was good.* Her husband's illness was a thing of the past since the doctors had put him on the injections. They were able to be a happy family again. Couldn't they see how she flourished?

Few believed her—least of all, Tracy Russell.

She was the one who kept Emilee up to date with the progress made by the Select Committee on Violence in Marriage. This was made possible by the ceaseless work of the committee since the previous year—the fruition of their labor of love—all to better assist battered women, she informed her friend.

"I'm no *battered* woman," Emilee insisted.

"When will you stop the denial?" Tracy asked. "You don't have to walk around with *bruises* on your body to fit the description. You're a *prisoner* in your own house. You work like a slave. Your husband scares the hell out of you and your daughter on a daily basis. You live in constant fear, believing you don't have an option. He probably makes you believe it's *normal.*"

Tracy continued. "He sleeps with his old girlfriend once a week and tells you it's a platonic relationship . . . That you shouldn't worry too much."

"How can you *know* all that?" Emilee's bottom lip quivered.

"You *told* me parts of it." Tracy had Caitlynn on her hip and grabbed Emilee's hand. "The rest I'm only guessing. We *fear* for you, Em. You've *changed*." She squeezed so hard Emilee squirmed.

"He *always* apologizes afterwards, *doesn't* he?"

Emilee nodded and stammered. "That's why I find it in me to forgive him . . . He promises it will never happen—"

"That's what they *all* do—make false promises, only to repeat it over and over and over. He keeps you captive. I can *see* it in your—"

Caitlynn bubbled. "Mommy . . . See."

Emilee took the child and buried her face in her hair, glancing at Tracy, shaking her head. "Sweet Tracy . . . Say no more . . . This young girl understands *every* word."

They had visited Tracy at her office during her lunch hour. She worked full time for the Women's Liberation Movement at their branch office. They sat outside on a small patio. Emilee stood and held the now-squirming child.

"We'd better go." She pouted her lips. "Thank you for the concern . . . You are all so kind."

Tracy stepped closer and hugged mother and child. She wouldn't let go. She stepped back once she planted quick kisses on both their cheeks, then held onto Emilee's arm. "That's *exactly* why you have to listen to me, to us—for *her* sake—Caitlynn's. You're right—she understands everything. She did from her first month. But now she can tell you. Do it for Caitie, if not for your-self . . . You don't have to remain trapped—"

"I'm *not* trapped. I *love* him."

"Oh, Emilee."

"Goodbye, Tracy. I really must go. Connor is working a shorter day."

"Mommy . . . go," Caitlynn said.

The two women hugged a second time, and mother and daughter waved at her friend as she plodded back to her office's entrance. Tracy paused and looked back every few steps, doubt written on her face as she hesitated and raised her hand in a feeble wave.

—◦◦◦—

Emilee turned away, her face drawn. She pulled her shoulders back. It was time to meet Connor at the assembly plant. She had had to replace the body-pouch with a stroller, months ago. The Goodwill store's price was reasonable. The shop assistant's instant infatuation with Caitlynn had made the transaction less embar-rassing.

Until then, Emilee had never thought of herself as being in need. But her daughter had become too heavy to carry—not for the miles Emilee insisted on walking every day. Caitie must have taken after her. She now insisted on walking, by herself, on a daily basis. "Caitie . . . walk" was her new mantra.

They'd better rush, Emilee realized, looking up. The asphalt sky was pregnant with moisture, the air bursting with humidity.

It wouldn't be long now before the deluge. She should have cut her visit with Tracy shorter. Already the dress clung to her back. It was far easier to brave the elements than explain to Connor why she and Caitlynn couldn't make it in time. He expected them to wait on him, every day, at the end of his workday. They had to be at their exact post, at the boom, at the entrance to the plant—nowhere else and not a second late.

She gripped the stroller, clasped Caitie's wrist with the other hand, and ambled down the street. In her anxiety, it was easy to forget the age of the little hand clasped in hers.

An uneven spot on the sidewalk with a crack in the concrete made the toddler stumble, ripping her from Emilee's grip. Caitie screamed murder—both her knees were abraded. Emilee scooped her up, kissed the wailing child, kissed both *"auwies,"* then strapped her in and set off at a brisker pace.

"Sorry, Caitie. Mommy's so sorry that you slipped from my hand, but we have to hurry. Look at the sky—do you smell the rain? We're going to meet Daddy. Stop crying, sweetheart . . . Look at those clouds."

Caitlynn waved at the ominous clouds and muttered through her sobs, "Clouds . . . rain."

Emilee glanced at her wrist, the skies, and her child. She increased her pace. Perspiration now ran between her breasts. Her heart ached for the little girl bouncing in her carriage as they pounded down the uneven sidewalk. She was close to tears herself. They could not risk being late. Mary Gabriela was not available for her use, and they tried to save on bus tickets. They were late—all because Tracy wouldn't stop talking.

Tracy is so wrong. She knows nothing about me and Connor and Caitie. She knows shit. She's never been in love. Connor means it every time he apologizes after a meltdown. I love him, and he loves me. And that is good enough for me.

The first drops were the size of grapes and made plop-plop noises on the canvas sun-visor of the stroller, making Caitie laugh.

One hit Emilee on the nose, and she shielded her face with her hand. "Do you hear the raindrops, Caitie? They go plop, plop, plop."

"Plop," laughed Caitie. "Plop."

Emilee broke into a jog behind the stroller. *Bloody rain. Just hold off. We're almost there. Why does he have to get off at two? Such a silly hour.*

"Plop," crooned Caitlynn. "Caitie . . . bump."

"Sorry, Sweetie . . . We're late . . . Hold tight."

Emilee's breathing was labored as she maneuvered the stroller over the unkempt sidewalks, weighing her chances of crashing and being berated by her husband. She opted for the former. She could see the boom at the gate the moment they came flying around the corner. A glimpse at her wrist made her pray Connor's watch would be slow today.

It never was. He was always on time.

The rain stopped.

Thirty yards.

Connor stood next to the boom, to the side of the road.

Shit.

His arms were folded across his chest.

Ten yards. It was 2:03.

"*Daddy.*"

It was time for hugs and kisses for Daddy. He bent down, unclipped the child, and lifted her into his arms, covering her with kisses. Emilee received a scowl.

"Hello, Connor." Her breaths burned in her throat, her heart pounding.

He glanced at his wrist, then at Emilee, his face set.

"Caitie . . . auwie." The child touched both her scraped knees.

"Let Daddy see. My poor baby." They were outside hearing range from the gate when he turned toward Emilee. "Can't you take *care* of her? She might need to go to the hospital for a skin graft."

Emilee caught her breath. "She'll be fine . . . It happened on the way here. You know how she insists on walking and how bad the sidewalks are . . . I'll clean the scrapes and put on some Mercurochrome as soon as we get—"

"You just don't learn, woman, do you? Caitlynn could have broken her leg . . . You were careless and you're late . . . again."

"Connor, *please!*"

"We'll *have* to teach you a lesson. Nothing like discipline to get the message to sink in, is there, Mrs. O'Hannigan?" And he laughed for the first time, twirled with the girl in his arms, and strode ahead of Emilee.

He had never hit her save for the time he smacked her bottom during the walk with Caroline and Douglas. Thank God for that small blessing. When they get home, he'll insist she prepare him a meal but deny her any nourishment other than water. She would have to fast until morning—until Connor was satisfied the message got home.

She wondered if he would make her write the lesson out as he'd made her do before: *I should never be late. I should honor my husband. I should never be late. I should honor my husband.*

CHAPTER 39

An unexpected Christmas gift. 1975

When Connor mentioned his parents for the third time within a week three months before Christmas, Emilee paid attention. The one topic never discussed in the household on Morrell Avenue in Cowley, Oxford, was the O'Hannigans living in Annagassan.

Emilee bore them no ill will, other than indifference. Time lessens pain. They had chosen never to become part of Connor's, Caitlynn's, and her life—a loss all their own, in addition to denying her daughter the gift of grandparents.

Could it be?

She immediately prompted Connor for more news about his parents—when exactly had he last received word from them—but he became alarmed, realizing his slip, and turned into a sea anemone. For a brief moment, she had hoped. She was willing to forgive them, for Caitie's sake. He went all tight-lipped. Not another word escaped him about the couple living on the banks of the Glyde River on the Irish Sea.

As fall became a thing of the past and the nighttime temperatures inched lower, Emilee refused to back down with their daily walks. She had become good at adapting. With great care, she bundled them up. She would have trouble to forgive herself if Caitie ever fell ill due to her negligence. Not to mention what Connor would do.

She realized that it had become an obsession, the daily walk thing. She had to. Every. Single. Day. *If I don't do it, don't get out and walk, I'll lose my mind. I might become wild like him.*

Mother and daughter spent most of their hours away from the apartment in the library. Caitie's phlegmatic nature was a godsend. She occupied herself with sitting next to her mother, drawing and paging through picture books the librarians kept behind the counter for her. And she hadn't even turned three.

Each day, the staff would surprise the child with a different book with brighter and more colorful pictures than before, of animals, and birds, and wonderful places, and far, far away countries and people.

Emilee became a regular in the Old Library, just as she once had been. When she shared her dream with the head librarian of preparing for her honors degree in English Language and resuming her studies, she was offered a quiet side room, which made having Caitlynn with her easier. She had not given up on her dream of teaching, perhaps even lecturing at the University.

There was so much to do. So much to read, explore, rediscover, and unearth. Her hunger was fathomless. The extent of her literary famine revealed itself in time. How could she have forgotten the joy and liberation reading always brought? The power and privilege to muse over others' words and works, to dream up new and wonderful worlds beyond the ordinary, beyond the bleakness of her mediocre existence. The biggest solace was in nurturing a new secret, a secret she vowed to keep from Connor. The man had a suitcase filled with secrets. Here she could escape, together with her little girl, into a safe and secret place—a world of books and words and stories—where fairness, trust, and love were commonplace and unquestionable.

How could she ever tire of being surrounded by hundreds of thousands of loyal friends and companions, steadfast in their leather bound and hardcover bodies, that, when opened, always enticed her to come along on yet another journey? The respectful silence and hushed whispers allowed in the Old Library, mixed with the smell of leather and dust on printed page and the crispness of a brand new book never failed to calm her.

One small victory Emilee had accomplished before winter was convincing Connor to expect mother and daughter at the boom only at the end of his workday. No longer would they walk him to work in the mornings. It was too much for a two-and-a-half-year-old for goodness' sake.

He could not expect the child to brave the elements, not since the chestnuts and oaks had shed their leaves, preparing for another bleak winter. Many a morning now, a miserable wind howled around the corners, shaking the shutters, threatening to rip them from their wall mounts. When the first sleet fell, he required no further prompt.

Emilee had her plans made. She always gave her long-suffering husband a quarter of an hour following breakfast before she and the child, covered up with only their noses and eyes showing, took to the road—in the opposite direction than the shop steward.

She had to take her time now with the walking. Her compulsory fasting sessions had taken their toll. Its regularity had increased—three nights a week was no longer uncommon.

Drinking water to quiet the rumblings of her stomach only helped so much.

Emilee had always been a size six. Now she barely filled out a four. Although she craved the camaraderie, she was grateful that she saw less of Caroline and the clan. It was better this way. They would have dragged the social worker to the house and Connor to court. To what effect?

If Connor kept this up, she'd soon have to switch to preteen training bras—a disaster. Her breasts had always been her pride. What she was losing now, other than her soft curves, was muscle. She had not touched her kayak or a sweep boat or seen the inside of a gym since Caitie's arrival.

On the broken sidewalks, constant vigilance was required with the stroller. She could not afford to stumble and hurt the child or herself. In the library, she would insist on keeping her coat on, hoping the staff would not notice her dwindling frame.

Two Fridays before Christmas, Connor instructed her not to wait on him at the gate that afternoon. When she glanced at him in shock, to verify that she was not mistaken, he only laughed. He had to pick something up after work.

"I'll be taking Mary G."

Emilee stared at him. What wasn't he telling her? Has he finally decided to leave her for Eileen? Mary Gabriela was used on the rarest of occasions now. She decided to go only for a short walk with the child that morning. She couldn't risk the chance to be out when he got home. The repercussions were too vast. The vehicle would make it easy for him to be anywhere at any time.

There was a commotion early that afternoon at their front door. They could hear Connor grunt and heave. "Caitie, come see what Daddy has."

The child glanced at Emilee—uncertain, like her mother, about the change in the floor steward from Cowley. Out of place behaviors from her father never boded well. She knew that much at two-and-a-half.

Emilee smiled and edged her on, her eyes saying it was safe to go to Daddy.

He stood in the front door with a ten-foot evergreen. Caitlynn shrieked and ran toward him, clutched his legs, uncertain what to make of the tree her father had dragged in the door. Needles scattered everywhere. *Who will clean the mess Daddy made?* her eyes asked of her mother. *Will Daddy get mad at us, Mommy?*

Emilee shrugged her shoulders, and her eyes filled with moisture. She inhaled deeply. The aroma of conifer needles and cut bark filled the apartment and washed over her. She was in Africa—Mother, Father, and the brothers gathered around the tree, laughing, discussing which decoration should go where. She sighed, wiped her eyes, and took the child's hand.

Connor followed with the tree as far as the living room. When he saw her face, he said, "Don't worry, Honey. I have a special base, a pot, a large bowl-like container to keep the tree from falling over. You'll see." He laughed like the young man she had met years ago in London during the march.

Could it be? She only smelled the cut tree. There was no liquor or woman-smell on him. I haven't smelled Eileen on him for over a month now. This seemed the real thing.

"I also got some decorations. They're in the car." He ran down the hallway and slammed the door. Emilee noticed how the baffled child listened to the door shutting. Was she also thinking, *Daddy didn't slam the door because he was mad at us, Mommy. Daddy slammed it because he was happy?*

He returned minutes later, breathing heavily as he trudged down the hallway. In his arms was a wooden planter filled with medium-sized rocks. He paused to catch his breath, then asked her to help.

He didn't yell. He asked me. He touched me. When has he last brushed against my arm? Emilee held the tree upright while he first unpacked all the rocks, then placed them one by one, stacking them around the trunk, wedging them in tight. The tree wouldn't move.

"Don't worry about the mess, Em. I'll clean up once I'm finished."

Em. She tried to remember where she had put Dr. Jones's phone number. *How worried should I be? How long will this mood last? This isn't normal for us. He must have a fever. Perhaps a brain abscess. A tumor.*

Half an hour later, all the decorations were in place except for one. He hoisted Caitlynn on his shoulders and leaned in close. It was her task to place the angel at the top. Her little hands struggled to make the figurine's hook catch on the crown. It slipped from her hands and dropped to the floor—twice. Good thing it wasn't made of glass.

"Caitie, drop . . . little angel," the child lamented. She was close to tears, realizing her father's high expectations. In her life, there was the ever-present risk. A good mood, happiness, laughter, and peace were fleeting treasures, often apparitions, and could only last so long.

"Don't worry, Sweetie. Try again," Connor soothed.

Mother and daughter shared glances. Emilee beamed at her child. *Grasp each small mercy with both hands, my Sweet.*

Caitlynn stretched her arms a third time, holding the angel. Her hands trembled.

"Angel is happy," she declared when Connor slipped her off his shoulders and they stood back to appreciate their handiwork, clapping hands.

Emilee failed to remember when last she had felt such happiness.

—ᴍ—

Following supper, once Caitie was put to bed, Connor handed her a twenty-pound note. "My parents are coming for Christmas Day. They won't sleep over. They'll only be here for the day. Use this to buy a few small presents . . . and perhaps food and drink for the table that day."

Emilee burst into tears. His hand had brushed against hers, in affection, a second time that day. Until he had carried the tree into the apartment hours ago, he had not touched her in over six months. There had been no kisses, no hugs, no endearments. She had forgotten what it felt like to be held. He had not made love to her since after Easter—even with a sheath.

Her shoulders shook now as the sorrow of years broke free. So unaccustomed to release had she become, the heartaches washed out of her burdened soul one at a time. This was no simple thing. Each heartache required many tears. The weeping wouldn't stop. She turned away from Connor, who stood watching her, uncertain about his next move. He had not scripted this. Being angry was easier.

He knelt beside her but hesitated to touch her. His hand hovered. When he touched her shoulder, at first it sent a shock through them both. He tried again. His hand stayed. "Now, now, Em . . . I'm so sorry . . . Perhaps twenty pounds is not enough?"

She laughed through her tears, wiped her nose, and put out her arms. "Silly man. Just hold me."

When they retired to the bedroom, Connor clambered onto the bed and pulled her against his side. That only opened the floodgates wider. Shaking his head, he swung both legs onto the bed and pulled her into his lap. Different tactics were required. He rocked her back and forth now, uncertain how to make her stop other than yelling at or ridiculing her. Her sobbing slowed down only once his hands found their way, stroking her back, and after long minutes of unfamiliarity, trailing down the bend of her arms.

He had forgotten that it could feel so good. She was so soft. Perhaps he had forgotten to feel. Be human.

What has become of us? It wasn't only my illness. My wife is skin and bone—my beautiful redhead from Africa. Connor O'Hannigan, you're a bloody, bloody bastard. A rotten coward. You've screwed up so bad.

She allowed him to kiss her.

He kissed first her hair. Then her ears. It took longer to kiss away her tears. They would not cease. Then he kissed her fingers.

One at a time. He kissed her lips. Her neck. Her toes. He kissed her entire body. Her back. Then her front. Her breasts. By the time he entered her, two hours later, he was also weeping. They shuddered together, their cries of release hollered in unison.

That is how they fell asleep—on their sides, spooned together, his left hand on her left breast. As they had the first time.

CHAPTER 40

Grandparents for Christmas.
Oxford 1975

"Do you have a picture of them? Of your parents?" Emilee rolled out of Connor's embrace the next morning.

"What for?"

"I want to show Caitie. It will be easier for her to understand. She has never met them."

When evening fell, Caitlynn O'Hannigan could say "*Opa*" and "*Oma*." She now had many questions. "*Opa* comes Christmas, Mommy? And *Oma*?"

"Yes, Honey." Emilee scooped her up and hugged her until she squirmed. "That's what Daddy says."

Connor had unearthed a postcard-size framed image of his parents. It was placed on the mantelpiece, below the pen sketch by grandma Deirdre. Caitlynn paused in front of the photo every time she entered the room. If Emilee were around, she would point at the picture. "Look, Mommy, Opa. Look, Mommy, Oma."

———※———

Christmas Eve was a quiet affair. The fragile peace between the three occupants of the apartment on Morrell Avenue had survived another day—it continued to last. Presents would be opened only once the grandparents arrived Connor had decided, which meant they were in bed by an unfamiliar, early hour.

In the early morning hours, a blow shook the entire bedroom. Another whack followed. The window and its entire frame sounded as if ready to crash into the room. Again, it slammed. *Wham!* Emilee jerked upright, listening to the night. The new day was reluctant to enter the room. Next to her, Connor's regular breaths were that of the just, deaf to the jangle outside. She turned her head—not a sound came from Caitie's room. *It's that stupid clip. How many times have I asked him to fix the bloody shutter? They're too big and too heavy.* The wind must have picked up. She could forget about sleep.

As she tiptoed to Caitie's room, the early light silhouetted her fleeting form, the diaphanous nightgown unable to hide her svelte bareness underneath. The child had the blankets pulled up to below her chin. Emilee shuddered and smiled.

My sweetest, sweetest child. I will never grow tired of the wonder of having you, your kind face, watching you breathe. We have tasted such unforeseen happiness these last many days.

She kissed her daughter's forehead and peeped through the lace curtains. She sucked her breath and pressed her nose against the pane.

Another present, a miracle: snow in London on Christmas Day. It will be in the papers—in human history, they will say. For who knew how long the white powder would last? She poked her head through the curtains a second time, wiped her breath from the window to create a looking hole, and peeked outside. Pity there was not enough snow to build a snowman. She would wake

Caitlynn as soon as it was properly light outside. Some miracles are short-lived.

She rushed back to their bedroom. The shutter needed to be fastened. It might wake everyone in the building, for goodness' sake, if it didn't tear from its hinges before she got to it. She had to be quick. If only she could let her little one sleep a while longer. Who knew what the grandparents' visit would bring? The day was still concealed. Nothing was certain.

The window, stuck from snow and ice, required much heaving and the occasional cussing to push it up and open.

When it gave, she tumbled halfway through the created opening, gasping and grasping, until she was hit in the face by sleet. *Thank God for a curtain to hang on to.* She must have cried blue murder without realizing it. The surrounding apartments' lights went on.

"*Emilee!*"

By the time Connor reached her, she had regained her balance, the curtain in a death grip in her one hand, her other hand clawed around the window frame.

Connor clutched her around the waist anyway and moved her aside with care. It required great dexterity to make the shutter-clip catch from inside the bedroom. Twice almost, Connor lost his footing. When he snapped back into the room, he shoved the window closed and disentangled her from the drapes.

Emilee let go as he crushed her against him. They both shivered now, wiping snow from their faces. He wouldn't let go—not until the warmth of their bodies merged. His hands soon discovered her nakedness underneath the thin nightgown.

She leaned into him as his hands wandered.

He nuzzled her neck, cupped her breasts, and whispered, "Why the racket, woman? Did you try and *jump* out the window?"

She shook her head and pulled him closer. "It's that stupid shutter."

His lips were on her ear. "We'll get it fixed. *Come back to bed.*"

"It's snowing."

"I know. Merry Christmas."

He swooped her into his arms and carried her to their bed. He kissed her, starting with her toes, as the day crept into the room.

—⁓—

Emilee noticed the taxi first. It was their second time outside that morning. It had been impossible to keep Caitlynn indoors, not since she had tasted and played with the snowdrifts after breakfast. They had even built a lopsided snowman then, more the size of a garden gnome, which had all but thawed away.

The three of them had struggled to scoop enough snow together, only able to form weird, little snowballs. Miracles fade away so fast. Only in the shady spots could they find clumps and scant amounts of powder.

She froze as the taxi's doors opened and first Dr. O'Hannigan, and then Mrs. Deirdre O'Hannigan, stepped out. The timing was perfect. Emilee was struck by two snowballs—one from Caitlynn and one from Connor. They howled as she shrieked with indignation, glancing into the faces of her in-laws.

Emilee recovered fast. "Look, Caitie! Here's Oma and Opa!" She brushed the snow from her coat and waved her daughter closer.

Caitlynn required no further instructions. She ambled toward the cab. The driver had taken a single case from the trunk and handed it to the man with the silver ponytail. Emilee took her daughter's hand as the vehicle pulled away.

"Opa! Oma!" Caitlynn pulled her hand free, ran the few yards, stopped in front of the giant from Annagassan, and stretched her arms outward. She expected one thing of this big man.

Dr. O'Hannigan glanced, first at his spouse, then at Connor, at Emilee, and then down at the little girl. He dropped the case on the snow-covered gravel and went down on his haunches. His solid arms met hers, and, carefully, as if taking hold of a butterfly, he picked her up. "You must be Caitlynn?"

She fizzled over, shaking her head. "No, Opa. I'm Caitie."

Connor kissed his mother on the cheeks, picked up the case, and shook his father's hand, who had moved Caitlynn to his left arm.

Deirdre O'Hannigan gave Emilee a nod before she spun around and tripped alongside her son.

Dr. O'Hannigan got hold of Emilee's hand and squashed the bones from it. He gestured her to go ahead of him and the little girl.

Caitie's cup ran over as she rode on her grandfather's arm.

When the O'Hannigans from Annagassan left five hours later, Emilee received a peck on each cheek from her mother-in-law and a smothering bear hug from her father-in-law. "Handshakes are for strangers," he had mumbled. Up to this day, it is uncertain how big an effect the bottle of Dún Léire had played in all of that. Connor had twice called her "my love" in front of his parents.

As they held the door of the taxi and helped him in, Dr. O'Hannigan's steady baritone rang out:

Although our love is waning, let us stand
by the long border of the lake once more.
Together in that hour of gentleness,
when the poor tired child, Passion, falls asleep.

Despite the fading light, Emilee's cheeks glowed with a healthy rose. Caitlynn O'Hannigan went to bed that night the happiest child in all of England, Scotland, and Wales—and most certainly, of Ireland.

CHAPTER 41

When illness strikes. January 1976.

IT IS OUR ignorance and indifference that declare miracles a rarity. But miracles often are short-lived—fleeting, like dew at daybreak, like transient morning mist.

The howling was unmistakable—the thrashing, followed by silence, then another crash. Another chair shattered. That left four of an original eight. Connor's voice, unintelligible in the January night, echoed from beyond the dining room. New Year's Eve had come and gone. So had the peace.

Their private miracle had lost its luster.

Emilee listened, uncertain as to why it reminded her of a story she had heard long ago: the story as recorded in the Gospel of Matthew about the possessed men of Gadarah. *Did Connor sound like them?* From the dining room came the sounds of a possessed, or at least a wounded soul—her husband in this case. He was not from Gadarah but Cowley, a little farther down the road.

On tiptoes, she snuck to Caitie's room. The darkness granted her clemency. She scooped the child, hand on her mouth, eyes pleading, and retreated to their bedroom. She had mastered the art of locking a door without a sound, months ago. Shaking, hunched on the floor next to the bed, her eyes fixed on Caitlynn, she dialed.

The hospital's receptionist put her through to the psychiatric wing without delay. Must be because she had become a regular caller. Perhaps they knew her voice by now. She repeated—whispered—her plea for help. Only once the siren cut through the night did she join Caitlynn on the bed. Mother and daughter clung together, two castaways holding fast to a buoy, adrift in a sea of uncertainty.

Connor was to remain in the hospital for seven days this time, another involuntary hospitalization. Emilee met with Dr. Jones on day two. The doctor had a different plan: increase the medication dosage.

"Will he *ever* get better?"

"We don't know." The doctor drew doodles on his writing pad, watching her.

"I *need* to know. I fear for our daughter."

"People can and *do* recover, Mrs. O'Hannigan. . . . We'll just have to work *harder* on relapse prevention."

Emilee shrugged her shoulders. *So Caitie and I have to be more accommodating? Be more forgiving? Can't you see I'm already skin and bone? How haggard do you want us to become? You bastard.* She was tired of hearing the doctors' eloquent phrases, hollow words strung together offering little comfort and scant solution. Their words were merely underwear pegged to a washing line billowing in the breeze.

And yet, her hope for healing had been rekindled.

Didn't the doctor say people do *recover?*

She shared their Christmas miracle with the good doctor: how, until two days ago, they had been blessed with three weeks of normal—twenty-one miraculous days of having a husband, a lover, a friend, and a father who was present, who listened, who laughed again at silly things, and who showered them with love, kisses, tumbling, and playing hide-and-seek. She was surprised at her happiness. She had misgivings that it could last.

"And look what has happened now. It must be my lack of faith."

Dr. Jones laughed. He dismissed her argument as utter nonsense. Lack of faith it was not. Didn't she understand? It was due to insufficient antipsychotic medication. It was a pharmacological derangement. Adjustment of the dosage would fix the problem. She'd see.

They all saw soon enough.

—⧜—

A taxi brought Connor home on the afternoon of the seventh day.

Earlier that same morning, Emilee had received a phone call from the hospital psychiatry ward, preparing her for his arrival. By noon she found it impossible to sit and wait any longer. Her excitement overcame her fear, and she bundled the two of them into Mary G and took off for the supermarket. A celebration meal was called for. She allowed Caitlynn to help her push the wire cart, and, later, assist with preparing every dish—handpicked courses she knew Connor loved.

Dr. Jones had promised her husband would be more than fine. So his return was as good as settled then: a surprise supper for a transformed man.

They both heard the vehicle on the gravel outside, a door slamming, and then singing. The food was ready; the table laid.

Caitlynn stood on a stool next to Emilee to reach the counter. Caitlynn's brow knotted. "Daddy sings, Mommy?"

Emilee nodded, scooped up her daughter, and rushed to the front door. Her hand on the doorknob was shaking. She willed her hand to settle while they waited. She had become good at waiting, at anticipating the lashings of words and bracing for the jabs, the hurt.

She could not recall hearing Connor sing. Ever. Not even when he took a bath. He played the piano like a master, but he didn't sing. His off-key singing preceded his stomping up the stairs:

> *Now Eileen O'Grady, the real Irish lady,*
> *I'm longing to call her my own.*
> *I'll not be contented until she has consented,*
> *to be Mistress Barney Malone.*

With the child clasped in her arms, she lurched back as he brushed past them, reeking of ale. Connor made a half-salute in their direction and staggered down the hallway, a bottle clutched in his left hand. Forgotten, his own rule of first taking off outside shoes.

"Ladish . . . ladiesh . . . *Where* is Miss Barney Malone?" He burped.

She closed the front door, pulled the shivering Caitlynn against her, and followed Connor.

He stood in the living room at a loss until he noticed the dinner table. "Fancy supper . . . *How nice* . . . but I'm not hungry." He gulped two mouthfuls, belched, wiped his mouth, and stomped toward the table. With a single swipe, half the plates, dishes, and glasses crashed to the floor. Connor gave a boisterous laugh.

Emilee gasped, stumbled backward, lost her hold on the child—then caught her again. Caitlynn's nails dug into her mother, sobbing silently into her mother's neck. Who knows what Daddy will do if he heard her cry?

Connor took another mouthful and kicked a chair out of the way. "There will be *no* party here tonight! Not *tonight!* What were you thinking, woman?" He stomped toward the bathroom, oblivious to the world. "I need to pee."

The door banged closed behind him. It was impossible not to hear his dissonant serenade continue:

> *. . . I met this fair treasure while walking for pleasure.*
> *She looked up at me then she cried . . .*

Emilee dashed for their bedroom, Caitie still in her arms, snatched her purse from the floor, and darted back for the hallway—an art to perform, carrying a child on tiptoes without a sound.

Connor fiddled and sang in the lavatory. Good. *So much for thank you for a lovely meal, Honey. I see you helped your mommy, did you now, Caitie?* None of that.

Their winter coats hung on hooks behind the front door. She ripped them down, put Caitlynn down outside the door, and pulled the front door closed behind them with great care. She dared not leave a trail or a sound. She thought she heard the bathroom door fly open.

With the purse swinging from her elbow, she snatched Caitie in one arm, held their coats in the other, and raced for the stairs. They'd put the coats on once outside.

We're not staying here another night. I'm not hiding behind a locked door again, phone in hand, waiting. Waiting for what exactly, Emilee O'Hannigan? For him to change? The good doctor knows shit! What was he thinking? What was Connor thinking? Largactil and booze? It'll kill him if he doesn't kill us first.

As they lurched down the stairs three steps at a time, Emilee grasped the side rails with the arm that also had the winter jackets perched over it. Two steps from the bottom, as they pummeled toward the little foyer, glass exploded a floor above them.

Did he just smash the bottle?

Connor's curses and yelling echoed down the hallways. *"Emilee? Caitlynn?!"*

She panicked and missed the last step. *Oh Lord, my ankle.* As they crashed to the floor, she jerked the jackets in front of them to soften their fall, turning sideways in an attempt to let the child fall on top of her. Emilee's head smacked into the carpeted floor.

There was no time to think or see what was injured. They could hear Connor stomping closer. He was gaining on them. Emilee scrambled to her feet, slipped the child's arms into her little coat's sleeves, pulled her own jacket on—the buttons had to wait—grasped the purse again, snatched the girl by her arm, and lunged for the front door. She could hear Connor at the top of the stairs above them. He was so close now.

"Emilee!"

As they burst from the building, large white flakes sifted down in no apparent hurry. Mother and daughter gasped at the sudden contrast and paused at the unexpected serenity. They caught their breaths as the snow settled upon them.

By the time the flurries had reached the pavement, only wetness remained—iced remnants they would soon discover. The flurries had pulled a fog blanket over the town. It was impossible to see the other side of the street. Pale halos of light danced atop lampposts, pointing the way in an eerie fashion.

Going down the final three steps toward the street, Emilee lost her footing a second time as she tried to spare her right ankle. She ended up on her back with Caitlynn on top of her. At least this time they had their jackets on. They stared, transfixed at the fluff that had settled on their hair and jackets and faces. Mother and daughter opened their mouths wide to taste the white flakes, which melted on their tongues like communion wafers.

The doors to their apartment building crashed open and spewed out a cursing, hollering bundle of a man. He exited so quickly that he lost his footing, cussing all the way as he went down. The thud as he crashed into the low flowerbed wall was enough to silence him.

Mother and daughter burst out laughing, relieved that their pursuer had failed to catch up. They took comfort that he had knocked his head hard enough to be quiet, if only for a minute.

Theirs was a laughter of disbelief for the brazenness of being outside on a night like this, a night of white splendor and domestic horror, of serenity and madness, of a reminder: perhaps there *was* another world outside of the apartment on Morrell Avenue.

CHAPTER 42

An unfamiliar kindness.

EMILEE GLANCED AT Connor's unmoving bundle on the top landing outside the apartment building. Before doing up her own, she kneeled and buttoned up her daughter's jacket. She scooped the girl into her arms, ignored her throbbing ankle, and set off at a steady, limping pace, following the halos of light down the street.

A final glance at the entrance confirmed the huddled figure had started to move. She increased her strides. With each lamppost they could reach, their escape, their disappearance into the white nothingness, became more certain.

She had not given any thought about where to go, as long as it was away. She heard the vehicle approach long before its headlights sliced two blinding ivory columns ahead of it into the white darkness. *I have to wave it down.* Switching the child to her other arm, she stepped down the curb and waved with her now-free left arm. It was too late. The night had already swallowed the car, lights and all.

She was aware of how unwise it was to be walking in the street that night, alone, shrouded in fog, not even fifteen feet of visibility, with a child in her arms.

"Emilee?!"

It was impossible to see him. *He sounded so close.* Who knew fog could become an ally?

Another vehicle approached. *This one's not getting away. Connor might pound on us anytime soon.* She held the child securely, took one step farther into the street, and waved with all her might as the unseen engine roared down on them, blinding with its bouncing shafts of light.

Emilee stood firm.

Caitlynn found her voice the moment Emilee realized her mistake.

"Mommy, jump!" In her terror, the child pulled with all her might toward the sidewalk, willing her mother to respond.

Emilee flung herself and the child out of the relentless path of screeching brakes, booming engine, and blazing lights.

The driver had noticed them, but too late.

This time, Caitlynn was flung from her arms.

Emilee crawled on all fours on the icy sidewalk toward her child. Her knees stung. They were probably bleeding. Both of them were crying now, as mother huddled the child in her arms, kissing her tear-streaked face, wiping the incessant flakes from their faces.

The vehicle had come to a standstill and was immediately shrouded in whiteness. A voice called out. A car door slammed. The voice approached.

"Hello . . . Is there anyone out here?" It was the voice of a man fearing what he would find. Perhaps he was certain he hadn't hit anything, but one could not be certain, not in this indomitable mist.

"Hello?" Softer now. Pleading.

Emilee scurried upright with her daughter. "Over here," she whimpered as she hobbled toward the vehicle.

The voice belonged to a body. A tall body. She wiped the flurries from her face and shielded her eyes against the flakes. Recognition made her draw her breath: Dr. Thomas Geoffrey Hill, professor in the Department of English and ex-Olympic rower. She had last seen him at the end of '72, during her English literature final paper.

"I couldn't see you walking . . . the fog . . . I'm sorry. Not until I was right on top of you . . . Are you hurt? There's *two* of you? . . . A *child*?!"

Emilee repositioned her grip on Caitlynn and inched toward the vehicle. "Please, sir . . . You *have* to help us—"

Connor's voice drifted toward them from the twirling nebulas. "*Emilee! Caitlynn!*"

Emilee realized the professor must have drawn his own conclusions. His brow raised high: their disheveled appearance, both her knees' skin grazed off, her hair a mess, outside this time of the night, in this weather, with a young child in her arms. She must look as questionable and horrible as she felt.

"*Quick*, sir. Don't let him find us . . . I'll explain inside." She pattered next to the car's back door, her eyes pleading, her hand on the door handle.

"*Emilee!*" Connor was so close now. Any second and they'll see the owner of the brusque voice.

"Jump in then," Thomas Hill instructed and steered them inside the car, then slammed the door.

The car took off, tires screeching, and veered once or twice until the driver found control. He met her eyes in the rearview mirror. "Do you need to go to the hospital . . . for the child?"

She shook her head.

"Do you want me to take you to friends?"

Emilee shook her head a second time, burying her face in her daughter's hair. "He'll find us there."

The new leather smell of the car's interior was reassuring. She relaxed into the soft backrest. She was certain Caitlynn and she reeked of angst, sweat, and damp hair, like wet cats.

He turned around, still driving, but slower. "Do I *know* you, ma'am?"

Emilee chuckled, embarrassed. Thank God he couldn't see her face turn crimson. "English literature—class of seventy-two, Professor."

He pumped the brakes, "The cheeky redhead . . . Miss Emilee . . . Stephens?" Then he eased off the pedal before slamming them again, making them all jerk forward. "You drove your *bicycle* in front of my car years ago . . . during the rainstorm, *didn't* you?"

"I'm afraid so . . . I'm now Emilee O'Hannigan."

"Yes . . . Of course . . . You're married." He gestured, first at Caitlynn, then at the road behind them. "The man back there . . . your *husband*?"

Emilee's eyes brimmed with moisture. Not trusting her voice, she nodded. She prayed for the earth to swallow her. *He must think I'm an idiot to have ended up with a jerk like that. And I am. Where will we go? I can't go and jump on Caroline and Tracy's backs. It may not be safe there. Connor will find us.*

Five blocks farther he pulled to the side of the street, turned off the engine, and turned to face her. A muscle in his jaw twitched. "Shall I then take you to the police station?"

"Please, no . . . I've been there before . . . They won't believe me."

"Well . . . I can't leave you here . . . Then I'll take you to my place. Until we've decided on the best plan of action?"

Emilee wiped her eyes and sniffled loudly. "Yes . . . Thank you."

She was certain she had read in his eyes what he didn't ask. *Were you so desperate that you'd have jumped into the first stranger's car? Anything, to get away from that man? Wasn't it a terrible risk— a new gamble? Where's your pride? Do you have no shame?*

She held his gaze.

Her eyes countered: *I'm desperate, not broken. There's a difference. This is not about pride or shame or risk. I'm calling on you as a decent human being, as one human to another, not as woman to a man. Will you help me and my child? At least for the sake of the child?*

He turned back and watched her in the mirror.

Emilee challenged him to look away first, surprised by the sudden anger welling up within her. *What is it with men?*

He lowered his eyes. His jaw had stopped twitching, she noticed. Lips pursed, he nodded and turned the key.

CHAPTER 43

—ᘺ—

A safer place to stay. Oxford. January 1976.

ONLY WHEN THEY turned onto Banbury Road heading north did Emilee relax. The fog and flurries lifted and closed back in, enough to read street names. She closed her eyes and her hold on the child softened. She savored the comfort, the warmth, the protection. It was impossible to shake the cold. She unbuttoned her coat and nestled the child inside, covering them both with the tail ends.

The wipers labored across the iced windshield. She found the screeching reassuring. Perhaps it was the assertiveness of how it dealt with flakes and flurries and ice in its path—without hesitation, without flinching. It did what it was designed for, created for.

Why had she never noticed how synchronized the two blades worked? Two partners. Two soulmates. There was a method and a rhythm. Had she never paid attention? The right-hand blade completed only 150 degrees, flush with the end of the windshield, synchronizing with its left-hand mate, allowing it a full 180 degrees, over and over and over, never missing a beat, never out of sync, never backing down.

Isn't this what Connor had overseen: the putting together of motor vehicles on the factory floor, like giant "mechano-sets"?

Her Connor. Her wonderful, enticing, charming, lovable, horrible, frightening, intimidating, abusive Connor.

The flurries increased as they turned onto Five Mile Drive. The roofs of the detached houses were now shrouded in lacelike veils, alternating in whites and yellows as the headlights skirted by and lampposts cast their steady halos outward.

Emilee could not recall having been on this street before. She did not recognize any of the houses. Perhaps because it was too grand for her. The professor slowed down and turned in at a detached double-story, then inched through an entrance with meter-high stone walls and trimmed hedges on top. When the car traveled twenty feet down a real driveway and stopped in front of a freestanding, flat-roofed, single garage with a narrow walking passage separating it from the house, she thought, *He must be doing well.* Most of the houses only had open parking spots out front or on the sidewalk—if you were lucky.

Caitlynn was asleep. When he turned off the engine, his eyes met Emilee's in the rearview mirror. *This is it*, his dark eyes said. *My humble abode*, the eyes mocked.

Thomas Hill held the door for her as she clambered out, pulling the half-awake child along. His outstretched arms offered to take the child from her once he closed the rear door.

Emilee forced a smile and shook her head. "I'll manage."

A nearby tower chimed eight times.

Three brick chimneys towered above them as she followed him around the car to the front door. She did her best to hide her limp. *Grand place. Tudor finish on the outside. He's in the money, but in a classic way.*

Their savior stepped back to grant them access through the door, a heavy mahogany contraption. Emilee strode into pristine warmth and saw oil paintings, tapestries, and Persians on the floor. She thought of the stone mansion in Annagassan and the place she'd shared with Connor in Cowley. This house had a lightness about it, an effervescence that was foreign but lured her in nevertheless.

The foyer brightened up as its owner flipped several switches, forcing the visitors' eyes higher, up, up, to explore the vaulted ceiling twenty-five feet above.

Emilee stole a glance at the carved staircase and spun around, facing her benefactor. He had turned the key in the front door.

"Thank you . . . for doing this, Professor," she stammered, shifting the sleeping child in her arms.

"It's my pleasure, Mrs. O'Hannigan."

"I'm so *embarrassed* . . . for forcing . . . for inconveniencing you." She could not shake her blush.

"No one is forcing me . . . The name is Thomas." He stepped forward. "Please. Let me take the child." This time it was not a request.

Their hands brushed as they exchanged the sleeping girl, their faces inches apart. It was impossible not to inhale his clean warm smell. She gasped, stepped back, then followed him into the living room where he laid Caitlynn down on a couch, close to the fireplace. He slipped the child's shoes off and placed them side by side in front of the couch. He smiled into Emilee's face, who cast her eyes down.

Then he became all business. Once the fire was lit, he dragged a winged armchair closer and motioned her to sit down before scurrying from the room with a promise of blankets.

Emilee jumped back up and kneeled next to the sleeping girl. She placed feather-light kisses on the child's closed eyes when the professor swept into the room, arms laden with blankets.

"Let's get you guys out of those *wet* clothes—"

When he saw Emilee's face, he added, "Your wet *coats* . . . just use the blankets. We'll warm you up, feed you . . . Get you upstairs to the bedrooms." He pointed to the ceiling.

Emilee slipped the damp coats from the child and from her own slender frame and handed them to Thomas, who stood watching her, eyes brooding, a mere yard apart.

"*What?*" She met his eyes.

"You're *beautiful* . . . I noticed it that first day we met in class . . . but you've lost so much weight. That man's an asshole. An idiot—"

She shrugged her shoulders. "He's ill."

"He's *dangerous.*"

Emilee lurched forward, her face inches away from his. "Just because you have a PhD doesn't make you an expert in psychiatry and social services, Professor Hill. You know *nothing* about us—about *him!*"

Thomas Hill staggered backward as if struck on the chin. "You're right—I know very little. I'm sorry. But to be *so* desperate to barge into a winter storm with a young child, fleeing in front of my car. How can you *defend* him?"

"He's her father."

"The more reason not to terrify you, make you flee into a night like this. Only a madman—"

"He's *not* mad! He's *sick*!" Emilee cried as she grasped the professor by his jacket sleeve.

Thomas Hill spun around, took her hands, and pulled her against him.

For a moment she relaxed and leaned against him, gave a sob, inhaled him, and felt his warmth before shoving him away. "How *dare* you? You know I've been terrified . . . We fled into the night, into the cold, fearing for my child . . . for our lives."

"I did *nothing* except show some kindness." He turned away. "*You* waved me down, remember? After almost getting yourself killed."

"But still—"

He held up his hands and marched to the door. "I'll *leave*."

"Please . . . *Don't* go!" Emilee slumped onto the chair, her shoulders shaking. She sobbed almost silently.

Thomas Hill gave three steps and remained standing next to her chair. This forced her to look up at him. His eyes were black now, unreadable, the jaw twitching, the lips pursed. He crouched and held onto the armrest. He met her eyes. "*What* would have happened if Mr. O'Hannigan had caught up with you tonight out there?"

She shook her head. Her lips spelled *I don't know.*

"You're a brilliant and competent young woman. When I found the two of you tonight, you were hysterical, terrified, desperate . . . and he's not *dangerous*?" He shook his head. This wasn't about logic.

Emilee clasped his hand as he rose, making him crouch again.

This time their noses touched, making her gasp. She jerked her head as if stung.

His hand had found the nape of her neck. "Emilee . . . ." He leaned closer—she smelled the mint in his breath.

"Thomas . . . ." She staggered upright but didn't let go of his hand as she wiped her nose with the back of her free hand. She smiled through her tears. "I'm too messed up right now . . . I need a moment."

When he stepped back, she grabbed one of the blankets he had brought and busied herself with tucking it around her daughter before wrapping one around herself. She moved away, closer to the fireplace, then turned to face him. A shiver ran through her as she hugged her shoulders, studying him.

Her benefactor stepped closer again, then paused. There was no art in catching a bird with a broken wing. He closed his mouth.

"Thomas?"

"No, it's nothing." His eyes mocked hers. "It's good to have you here." He coughed as if embarrassed, pointing at the room. "This place needs people."

"There's no Mrs. Hill?"

He laughed, pulling up his shoulders. "No. Too much trouble."

He crouched and stoked the fire to hide his own discomfort. Satisfied, he turned to her. "Have you guys had anything to eat—any supper?"

Emilee's eyes brimmed with tears as she recalled the loving care Caitie and she had taken to prepare a surprise supper for

Daddy—and how it had ended up on the floor, desecrated. She wiped her eyes and shook her head.

"Will she eat soup?" He gave another easy laugh. "Soup will take a few minutes though. Let's get you something to drink first. Where are my manners? Coffee, whiskey? Hot chocolate for the little one?"

"We'll *both* like hot chocolate." Laughing came easily to her host. She liked that.

When he returned with a tray, Caitlynn was sitting on her mother's lap in the armchair next to the fire. She cowered into her mother as the stranger placed the tray on a nearby coffee table. She whispered into Emilee's ear while glancing at the man.

"Caitie, this kind man is my friend, Uncle Thomas."

"Hello, Caitie." Again, the friendly laugh. "Here's some hot chocolate for you, and it's not too hot."

"Hello," Caitie whispered as she and her mother got up and came to the coffee table. The girl glanced at Thomas Hill through hooded eyes, attempting to hide behind her mother's leg. "Thank you . . . Uncle," she murmured, then took her half-filled mug with both hands and sipped, her cautious eyes not leaving their host. It was easier to stand and drink than to sit when one was almost three years old.

CHAPTER 44

—————— ·w· ——————

Rescuers and friends. 1976.

EMILEE BOLTED UPRIGHT the moment her cup was empty. *I forgot about Connor. How long have we been here? Thirty minutes?* Enough time for him to harm others or himself—even freeze to death. He could have knocked his head again.

Why do I still feel sorry for the man?

The crackling fire, the sanctuary, and Thomas Hill's oozing persona had clouded her common sense. She had to phone the hospital.

They can track him down.

The telephone was in the kitchen.

Caitlynn refused to be left alone, despite a blanket tucked around her shoulders, nestled in front of the fire. Neither would she walk. She only clung to her mother's arms.

Thomas placed a pot on the front burner while she dialed.

"No, I don't know where Mr. O'Hannigan is. He left the apartment thirty minutes ago . . . Yes . . . I'm safe . . . as well as the child . . . I'm with friends . . . No . . . I won't be staying at our apartment tonight."

She cupped the receiver and glanced at Thomas Hill who busied himself with the soup.

"They want a contact number . . . May I give them yours?" She turned crimson as she repeated the number he said out loud to her.

He faced her once she replaced the receiver. "Friends?"

She stammered. "I couldn't say . . . ."

"That you have found safe haven in the house of the unmarried English professor?"

"Thomas."

"You couldn't tell the hospital this Hill-guy has actually saved your hide a second time." He chuckled. "At least I got to carry you the first time when you tried to commit suicide—"

"That's a *lie*. It wasn't attempted suicide!" She pulled out a chair at the kitchen table and slumped down with Caitlynn on her lap. "I didn't realize you kept track of the times you had to *rescue* me." Her crimson color was no longer due to embarrassment. She jumped upright, knocking the chair over, and repositioned the child in her arms. Her eyes bore down at him.

Thomas kept stirring the soup, not looking up. "I never kept track . . . I just find it curious that both times when you ended up in front of my vehicle, it was when you tried to get away from that man."

"*That man* happens to be—"

"Your child's father. He's also your husband. And you're a loyal spouse. He's smart. He doesn't leave any physical marks on you but nevertheless abuses you. He makes you live like a prisoner and works you like a slave—all to shine the silly apartment. He's a shop steward, a big shot at the Cowley assembly plant. He's a closet communist and is suspect of having been involved in both Bloody Sunday as well as Bloody Friday in seventy-two."

Now ashen, Emilee gasped, plopped right down again, and drew the child against her chest. She shivered uncontrollably. She kissed Caitie's head and peered at the professor through slanted eyes. "How do you know all that? . . . How did you figure—"

He had dished the soup into smaller bowls and placed two in front of her and the child. A third one he placed across from them and handed her a small and a large spoon, as well as napkins.

"Forgive me. I didn't lay the table properly." He met her eyes and smiled.

Her eyes never left his face. Her face remained pallid. "How do you know that much about us? About *him*?"

He took a spoonful and grinned.

She whispered now. "Who *are* you?"

"Emilee." He reached across the table and placed his hand on hers.

She didn't pull away and struggled to control the shivers that rocked her body.

"I have many interests . . . I don't only lecture English literature and row to stay fit. I'm fascinated by international politics. I've studied the Troubles."

"That doesn't explain how you could *know* about—"

Her host laughed and pulled up his shoulders. He took a mouthful and said, "Come eat, before it gets cold."

She inhaled the heady vegetable broth. She was ravenous.

"Thomas?"

He touched her hand again. "Emilee, how do I phrase this without making you blow your top? You've become blind. Being with him for so long . . . all the abuse."

"He's never *hit* me."

He squeezed her hand. "As I said. He's slick—clever and well-read. Why do you even *defend* him?"

She mumbled. "I told you: he's ill. He can't help it." She bit her lip. "There's Caitlynn. I love him."

"Yes, there's always a child. Love? You love what he once was . . . In the beginning, perhaps. I'm no doctor, and yes, he can't help for the schizophrenia, and there are many forms of abuse."

Emilee jerked her hand away. She still had not touched her soup. "You now sound like Caroline, my one girlfriend."

"Perhaps you should introduce us . . . She must be a wise woman."

Emilee gave a bitter laugh. "I would *never* do that. No woman is safe around you . . . She's married anyway."

He looked at Emilee and gave Caitlynn a big grin. "I believe the two of you are safe here, don't you think?"

It was now Emilee who reached across and touched his hand. "I'm so sorry . . . I'm talking without thinking." She wiped her face, exhausted and embarrassed. "Thank you for having us. Yes, I'm certain we're safe here. This has never happened before. We have never had to run away like we did tonight."

Connor became a hospital inpatient, his future discharge date shrouded in mystery. The current plan was to wait and see.

Dr. Peter Jones would not commit to any predictions about the long-term mental health of his patient. He had been proven wrong so many times now. Even a seasoned psychiatrist had his limits. He resorted to vague generalities as he had in the past.

Emilee found it even more deplorable this time. She vowed to uncover the uncomfortable truth. How else could she adapt and build new or better plans?

Caitie and Emilee visited Connor every day during the first two weeks. None of the visits lasted long. He sat and stared out the window, oblivious to their presence. It was hard for her and the girl to do all the talking. The medication was heavy. It made him walk and talk like an automaton. By the end of the first month, her visits dropped to twice a week. By the third month, she went once a week. By then she had the candor to drop Caitie off for the half-hour at the library and race with Mary G to perform the perfunctory visit.

He only had eyes for the window.

The social worker received word and paid them a visit to reassess the situation at the Morrell Avenue apartment. Emilee rolled her eyes. Had she not learned how to handle almost any situation now? Actually, Caitie and she. What would she have done if not for her little angel, always ready with words of wisdom, the sunshine seldom leaving those luminous eyes? Why the official concern all of a sudden after more than two years of indifference?

She shared her dreams with the worker about teaching English at the university level. She wasn't certain but thought she noticed the social worker roll her eyes, probably thinking, *Yeah, right. That's what they all say. All the mothers claim to go out there and change the world only to remain at home, feet in slippers, curlers in the hair, cigarette drooping from the mouth, remaining on welfare forever.*

Emilee thought, *I'll show you bastards. It'll be more than a dream.*

Every day, Caitlynn and she resumed their trip to the Old Library. They usually went by foot (with the stroller as a backup), and, if the weather was miserable, they took Mary G. Connor wouldn't be the wiser, which was best. There was much catching up to do in the world of literature.

The motor industry union kept their word. Emilee received a check in the mail every two weeks. They wouldn't commit to how long this would continue. It seemed the new motto was, "Wait and see." What was becoming of their world?

Emilee refused to wait and see.

The biggest surprise was when Caroline and Douglas showed up at her doorstep one evening in early March. They had great news. No, she wasn't pregnant. They had decided to move back from Southampton. Caroline had never felt at home in the harbor city. She had passed the bar exams and had taken up a junior position at a firm in town.

The greatest news was that Douglas had quit his association with her Royal Majesty's Ocean Liners. He had left employment on the *Windsor Castle*. Being the printing officer for the last two years had taught him what he needed to learn. It was time to step away. He was opening his own printing shop in Oxford to publish books. He believed there was a void in town which had to be filled.

Emilee refused to let them leave that evening.

She remained brave in front of Caitlynn, but as soon as the child fell asleep in her lap, the floodgates opened. She told her friends about life in the Morrell apartment for the three of them, about Annagassan, and about the importance of a dust-free establishment.

She cried because her last girlfriend-to-girlfriend talk with Carrie had taken place outside the clinic when she'd found out she was pregnant with Caitlynn. She was hungry for company, for the love of friends.

"*Please* stay." She clung to Caroline's hand.

"Emilee, you don't have a spare bed—"

Emilee would put them up for the night in Caitie's room. The girl was sleeping in her bed now anyway since "Daddy is sick and at the hospital."

They were huddled in the dining room at the table, sitting on the three remaining mahogany chairs, the only ones that had survived Connor's meltdowns over the years. The union checks only went so far.

What mattered now was that her friends, who had been as good as dead, had returned. The good Lord had answered one of her prayers.

All her talking had made the fire die. It no longer cast dancing colors over the room's occupants. Only glowing embers remained—enough to still heat the room.

Emilee wouldn't accept no. Her cheeks were wet. She sniffed and wiped her nose with the back of her hand. "I am *so* glad you're back, Carrie."

She kissed her friend's fingers before grabbing Douglas's hands. "And thank you, Douglas Harding, for putting up with us. I knew the day we ran you over in the Windsor Castle with your silly pamphlets you were trouble—"

He laughed. "You're indomitable . . . The same BS as back then. I just never had the nerve to tell you."

"You liked us too much, Mr. Harding."

She grinned, sniffing loudly, then faced Caroline. "Your husband is *insulting* me, but I still want you to stay the night."

CHAPTER 45

Old and new friends. 1976

THOMAS HILL'S VISITS to Emilee and Caitlynn became more frequent than the arrival of the union checks. At first, he dropped in at random. It took weeks for him to realize how determined Emilee was—how adamant she was with her walking schedule and studying. To him, it seemed she was always at the library. Mother and daughter were away for the best part of the day. And when he found them at home, Emilee was the one who cut his visits short. It was always Caitlynn she claimed who had to be put to bed.

Soon she filled a size-six dress again—no more training bras. Thomas's eyes confirmed he had noticed it too. There were no more dizzy spells or stumbling over sidewalks—all small wins, little mercies that appeared weekly.

Perhaps it was his doctoral-fellow background that made him study the movements of the female inhabitants of the Morrell Avenue apartment in more depth.

He didn't become a smart man by chance.

On Thursday afternoons, he noted, she left the child with the librarians and escaped to a coffee shop for an hour.

Thomas decided to surprise her and bring an old acquaintance along.

Francois Moolman was on his second visit to Oxford as a visiting lecturer, this time as a doctoral fellow. Thomas was convinced his presence would make Emilee more receptive. He recalled how blatantly his colleague had made a pass at the injured student en route to the hospital on the night of the storm when she had ridden her bicycle in front of his car. There was also Emilee's blunt rebuttal by way of the note attached to the dry-cleaned jacket. He needn't worry. The PhD-fellow would serve as a watertight decoy.

They found her alone at a table at the back of the coffee shop.

"Emilee." Thomas coughed in his hand.

"Oh, hi, Thomas." She shrieked when she noticed his companion and knocked her chair over as she scrambled to her feet. "*Francois!*" Her arms were around the visitor's neck for a prolonged hug before he could utter a word or step aside.

"Miss Stephens." He rubbed the dent in his jaw as he freed himself and righted her chair. His eyes danced over her blushing effervescence. His eyes spoke louder than his lips dared utter.

"It's *Emilee.*"

Thomas Hill stepped between them and steered her back to her chair. "But *you* have to address him now as *doctor.*"

Emilee plopped down, ignoring Thomas, and turned toward Francois, reaching for his hand. "I'm *so* glad for you, *Doctor Moolman.*" She studied him, head askance, rolling the title on her tongue. "Have you joined the staff here at Ox?"

His mouth opened but Thomas was quicker. "The Dons wouldn't listen to me—kept dragging their feet. Now Cambridge has *bought* him. He starts there next year."

Her eyes shot fire at the ex-Olympic rower who basked in his arrogance.

The server stepped closer and addressed Thomas. She must have witnessed the power play. "Excuse me, sir. Is your table ready to order?" Her sweet voice matched her petite stature, but it was her vivacious bust line that caught Thomas's attention—two perfect globes displayed at eye level.

Emilee snorted and turned back to the visiting professor.

Francois smiled. "I never got the chance to thank you in person, for dry cleaning the jacket."

Emilee struggled to get rid of her blush. "I was such a fool . . . I didn't have the guts." She shrugged. "That's why I left it at the front desk with a note."

He noticed her wedding band as she played with the rings to hide her discomfort.

"I didn't know," Francois murmured, his eyes on her hands.

Her eyes pleaded with him. "It's *complicated*."

Thomas jumped to his feet and took their order from the server, relieved for the distraction and another opportunity to ogle her chest.

Emilee's eyes bored at Thomas until he dropped his gaze from her bottom when the server walked away.

"*What?*"

"She's barely eighteen."

"She's *perfect*." He whistled softly.

"Wolf."

Thomas Hill laughed and turned his attention to his colleague.

Emilee leaned back, hands clasped around her coffee cup, her glance shifting between the two English professors, listening to their banter.

I should have removed the wedding bands. It's over between me and Connor.

Francois broke the spell when he pushed his chair back. "You'll have to excuse me, Emilee. I'm leaving at daybreak—on a visit to Windhoek. I'm glad we've met again, but I have to get back to my room." He put out his hand in greeting, but his eyes said he'd prefer to stay. "I start in January at Cambridge." He gave a half-salute in Thomas's direction. "So long, Thomas."

Emilee, frozen for a moment, took to her feet and darted after the new Don from Cambridge. She grabbed his arm as he reached the exit. "Francois, wait—"

Francois Moolman spun around, a slow smile appearing as he cocked his brows.

"I'm *so* glad I've seen you," she whispered, then hugged him. "Thank you for coming along with your friend, with Thomas."

He shrugged as he stepped back. "My pleasure."

Emilee's hand lingered on his arm. It was impossible not to breathe his fresh, masculine smell. "I would like to meet with you for coffee after your return from Africa. *Without* your friend." Her gaze dropped to her wedding bands. "It's over with the Irishman. My daughter and I are not safe with him anymore. I'm tired of living in fear." She met his eyes, unflinching. "I'll explain *then*."

Francois pulled free. He rubbed his chin. "*Goodbye*, Emilee."

CHAPTER 46

The games we play. 1976.

THOMAS THOUGHT HE had it all worked out when he showed up at Emilee's door on a Friday evening in late March with a bushel of roses, a bottle of wine, and a wicker basket.

"*Surprise.* May I?"

Emilee shrugged her shoulders and stepped back, Caitlynn at her side, beaming, to let him in the door.

"Uncle bring roses," Caitie said, insisting on Thomas lowering his hand so she could smell the individual flowers.

"*And* he brought some wine and food," Thomas said.

"Caitie doesn't drink wine. Caitie drinks milk."

Thomas laughed, put his gifts down, scooped her up, and twirled her around. First, he went slow, then increased the turning to a dizzying speed. He then ran in ever-changing circles with the little girl in his arms. They yelled and danced like Indians in a war party. The child shrieked her enjoyment and egged him on. They went faster and wilder until both collapsed on the rug in front of the fireplace, exhausted.

There was so much laughter. Her child sounded happy again.

"Mommy, Uncle Tom is funny."

Emilee smiled at her and watched them without a word, her eyes cautious. Thomas was so much like Connor—when he'd had his good days.

Thomas packed a fire in the living room when Caitlynn toppled over after their picnic supper on the Persian carpet in the living room. Connor would have had a heart attack—one did not eat sandwiches on a handwoven Arabian rug. When inside a house, one sat at a table to eat, not on a carpet on the floor.

She then allowed him to carry the child to her bed. She showed him where the bottle opener was kept, as well as the glasses.

Thomas pushed the two winged armchairs out of the way and pulled the large carpet closer to the fire, threw a couple of cushions down, and handed her a filled glass.

Emilee watched him over the rim of her glass. "Are you taking over the place, Professor Hill?"

He dropped down next to her, clinking her glass. "I thought you loved that—strong men."

"Are you confusing strong with domineering?"

"Touché." He clinked her glass a second time and added wood to the fire.

Their thighs touched in passing. She did not move away. Neither of them said a word as they watched the flames flicker and leap, throwing colors and shadows across them and across the room.

By the time their glasses were empty, he'd gotten up and built the fire up high a second time. They were lying on their sides now, facing one another, each with a pillow under the head. His long fingers traced her arm, stroked its length, and lingered in the fold of her elbow.

She found it hard not to smile.

His hand traveled to her chin, then her lips.

She kissed his fingertips.

He leaned in closer. She inhaled his mint breath. Clean. Fresh. It was good. She shivered as his hand found the nape of her neck and pulled her closer. She closed her eyes and allowed him to kiss her.

Her lips parted.

Each kiss became more urgent.

She rolled onto her back, and he followed with one swift move of his leg and hooked in at her thigh.

Emilee gasped when he raised himself, now almost on top of her. She squirmed and rolled away from under him and sat up, crossing her legs in front of her.

"Time out." She held up her hands in front of her chest.

"*Why?*" He mimicked her sitting position and took hold of her hands.

"What do you want with me?"

"I'm happy with kissing." His hands had other plans though, as he pulled her closer and stroked her upper arms. His fingers soon found the buttons of her blouse.

She gasped but didn't pull away.

He chuckled. "No brassiere."

She held his gaze.

Once all the buttons were undone, he pulled the front open, millimeter by painstaking millimeter. His eyes never left hers. He was in no hurry.

She sighed.

Only once he had pulled her shirt completely apart in front did he glance down. The flickering golds and reds from the fire caressed her bared breasts—bathed them with abundance, the nipples puckered erect.

Thomas smiled at her. "They are more beautiful than I had ever imagined—"

Emilee sucked her breath. She had been so lonely. She craved to be held.

His arms had dropped to his sides. He watched her like an artist who couldn't decide which part of her to paint first.

She gazed at him.

Surrender often takes us by surprise.

He sat back and studied her more—the light playing over her face and chest, rising and falling. Both nipples stood firm and unflinching.

She lay down on her back, her eyes never leaving him.

He knelt at her side and kissed her fingers, then moved up her arm, past her elbow, brushing with his lips. He leaned ever closer and kissed her lips, then each breast in turn.

Emilee gasped a second time.

She lay farther back and put her hands behind her head, arching her back. "You never told me. How do you know that much about us . . . especially about Connor?"

He laughed as he took most of her left breast in his mouth. She moaned.

He took a breath. "I told you . . . I have many interests . . . I did some research."

"That explains *nothing*. The things you mentioned, no one knew about except for—"

He smiled at her as he cupped both firm globes, making her shudder. "You know how it is . . . Friends talk."

Emilee sucked her breath as she shoved him away from her. "*You bastard*!" She lurched to her knees, her blouse pulled forward to cover her chest, her face glowing—but not from arousal.

"What the hell?" her visitor called as he righted himself.

Emilee scampered to her feet, buttoning her blouse. "'Friends talk,' you said." She stepped closer to the still dazed man, their faces inches apart. "*Which* friend?"

Thomas stepped back and chuckled, rubbing his chin, shrugging his shoulders.

Emilee stormed at him a second time then grasped his forearms. She paused and stepped back, drawing her breath. *Impossible*. Her eyes filled with moisture.

She turned away from him, facing the fire and hugging herself. Her shoulders shook. "No, no, no. How *could* you?" She spun back.

Thomas raised his hands in defense.

"Rachel?" Emilee's eyes were wide.

"How did you work *that* out?" He was the first to lower his eyes.

She addressed the room now, perhaps even the fire. She sounded like Connor minutes after he had received his tranquilizers. "You should leave . . . Go." She faced him one more time, betrayal written over her entire frame. She didn't realize she stooped forward now, like Connor on a bad day, looking ninety.

"You must have slept with her . . . You dined her, wined her, made love to her—no, copulated with her . . . and got her to talk."

"Emilee . . . Let me *explain*."

"You have to *leave*."

—⚡—

CHAPTER 47

A child needs grandparents. Caitlynn visits Annagassan. April 1976

EMILEE RECEIVED A call from Dr. Peter Jones on April 5. He requested that she meet him at the hospital that same afternoon. He would like to share his plan with her in person. Her husband had been under Dr. Jones's constant care for the past several months and had met discharge criteria. He was ready to be sent out.

Don't be alarmed, he reassured her. The hospital team was not considering sending him back to her and Caitlynn and the apartment in Cowley—at least not for the time being. Here the good doctor coughed, as if embarrassed. He explained. The hospital had acquired the services of a new occupational therapist who recommended that Mr. O'Hannigan be sent for convalescence, away from his regular surroundings.

He would stay with his parents—who had agreed—in Annagassan. Dr. Jones coughed again. The hospital had given considerable thought to the logistics. Connor's father, Dr. O'Hannigan, along with his mother, would accompany Connor the entire way. His parents were arriving early the next morning and would bring him by taxi to the apartment for the bag. They would then immediately leave for the station, catch a train to London, and fly from Heathrow.

If she could have a bag packed for Connor, ready for the next morning, for his parents to pick up?

Emilee agreed.

—⟋⟍—

The O'Hannigans arrived by taxi three minutes before ten the next morning. Emilee and Caitlynn met the trio outside the apartment. They had found it impossible to remain cooped up any longer. Once Emilee had told Caitie who was coming, she was at the front door every time a vehicle crunched the gravel outside.

Emilee had figured her in-laws wouldn't get there before nine, so she took off with Caitie an hour earlier for their first walk of the day.

When the taxi pulled away, having dropped off its passengers, it was Caitlynn who darted forward. "Daddy!"

Connor smiled and picked her up with a demure "Hello, Caitie," then planted a kiss on her head. No hollering and twirling and kissing took place.

Emilee received the shadow of a hug and a peck on the lips. His hooded eyes were empty.

From her mother-in-law, Emilee received a kiss on each cheek and the now-famous polar bear hug from Dr. O'Hannigan.

Grandfather O'Hannigan made up for his son's apathy and twirled his granddaughter several times as they turned around to go in.

Earlier that morning, on their way back from the walk, Emilee had picked up fresh scones. She made Connor's favorite tea and prepared everything exactly as he had done that first day she had visited him at the apartment: teapot, cozy, doilies, little plates, jam, softened butter, fresh whipped cream—the works. She added two cups for his parents and a small glass of cold milk for Caitie.

Emilee insisted on serving, bidding everyone to sit down. Her in-laws didn't let on that they found it peculiar there were only three long-backed dining room chairs adorning the majestic ball-clawed table.

As she held the tray for Connor, he smiled for the first time. There was the hint of a sparkle in his eyes. He murmured, "You remembered, Em. Thank you."

She almost dropped the tray when he tried to kiss her. She dabbed the milk that had spilled with a napkin, her cheeks flushed. It had been so long. *Yes, I still love him.*

Caitlynn shrieked, "Daddy kiss Mommy!"

Even Deirdre O'Hannigan found it impossible not to chuckle.

Dr. O'Hannigan's thunderous laugh filled the room as he patted his son on the back—only a pat, but still firm enough to buckle the blushing Connor's knees.

Emilee wondered what they had fed him at the hospital. He had put on weight, but it wasn't muscle—he was weaker, almost flaccid.

After first inquiring whether Emilee would mind, Mother O'Hannigan insisted on helping Connor pack. Deirdre O'Hannigan knew best what the weather was out in Annagassan. She used to do it for him when he was younger.

Emilee didn't mind. It was clear that Deirdre O'Hannigan knew what was best for her son.

Caitlynn and Emilee took it on themselves to rather entertain Connor's father, who had, according to his son, a heart made not entirely out of stone. They were willing to test that theory.

When they bade the trio farewell an hour later, Emilee had to hold Caitie firmly to prevent her from bolting from her arms and running after the departing taxi.

The child sobbed. "Why Daddy go, Mommy? Why Opa and Oma leave?"

Emilee nestled her face in her daughter's curls, hiding her own tears. She could still feel the touch of Connor's lips from across the laden tray. For an hour, the sun had returned to his eyes.

—m—

Two weeks later, Emilee received a letter from Ireland, written by Dr. O'Hannigan and addressed to "Dear Emilee and Caitie." It was accompanied by a check made out to her for airfare, taxi, and the train. Would they be interested in visiting Annagassan—perhaps for a week?

Mother and daughter were welcome to come straight away, as soon as Emilee could secure a flight. She only had to let them know when to expect the two of them at the front door. The phone number in Annagassan was also provided. Dr. O'Hannigan furthermore offered and promised to keep the two wolfhounds, Saint and Dublin, out of the house and out of their way.

Emilee found seats for Caitie and her on the Thursday morning flight out of Heathrow two days later. Their trip promised to be considerably easier since Caitie didn't require diapers anymore. She was a big girl now.

Emilee dropped by the library to inform the staff about her absence since she had become a regular, although still unofficial, student. It was the least she could do.

And, she had to visit Caroline and Douglas. She had to share the news—the possible good news—with somebody. Tracy was too tied up with the WLM issues as of late. Rachel and Thomas she didn't want to see, which left not many good friends standing. She pondered whether to tell Carrie about Rachel's betrayal, then decided against it. Caroline, since the beginning, had always only tolerated Rachel, never really warming up to her. She didn't need another "I told you so."

Emilee and Caitlynn were blessed with patches of blue sky when the taxi dropped them off at the stone house next to the Irish Sea. There was no rain in sight—not a single gray cloud to spoil the azure heavens.

When the heavy door swung open, Emilee took a surprised step backward, expecting a brimming Grandma Deirdre.

They were met by a grim-faced mistress of the house. No "Welcome Emilee and Caitlynn."

Caitlynn Aine O'Hannigan ignored her grandmother's foul mood, shrieked, threw her arms wide open, and dashed through the door. She was ten days short of her third birthday when she came close to running Mrs. Deirdre O'Hannigan off her legs inside her front door.

CHAPTER 48

Caitlynn Aine O'Hannigan turns three. 1 May 1976.

DESPITE THE CHILLED atmosphere, Dr. O'Hannigan kept his word: both Saint and Dublin were kept in a fenced-in kennel at the back of the stone mansion. Only at night did their frustrated howling remind the visitors of their banishment.

Connor avoided Emilee's eyes as she searched for an answer for the icy reception she had received from his mother. She was convinced that had she come without the child, the front door would have been slammed shut in her face a second time.

Caitlynn refused to surrender her effervescent spirit to the sulking moods of her father or grandmother. The grandfather was less cantankerous. He was the one who soon shooed the trio outside, to go show the child the sea.

The little girl needed only one walk along the pebble and rock-strewn beach that first afternoon to fall helplessly in love with the bay, with the rocks, the sand, the pebbles, the broken shells—with the entire village.

There would be no more late-mornings after that, not for the entire week of their visit.

At daybreak, the child stood on Emilee's side of the bed. She would whisper, "Mommy, Caitie go walk."

Groaning, Emilee grumbled, "It's still dark out, honey. We'll go later. Go back to sleep."

"No, Mommy. Caitie see sun. We walk on sand. We go to sea. Caitie loves the sea," her whisper-voice no longer a whisper.

Soon, Connor and Emilee trailed behind their daughter, rubbing the sleep from their eyes, as the toddler scampered across the wet sand to play catch with the foam as the surf rolled out on the beach. She shrieked as she noticed the imprints her feet left behind. Then she paused, fascinated by everything she encountered: a wet leaf, a buried shell, a colorful oval rock, the dried and hollowed-out front leg of a crab, fragments of wood, and an abundance of seaweed. Every item had to be inspected, touched, picked up, smelled and—heaven forbid—tasted.

"Look, Mommy, tree." Caitie held a dripping piece of seaweed, an almost-black, ancient, miniature tree, slime and moss-covered, complete with pungent aroma to match. She brought it to her lips.

Emilee squealed and pulled a sour face as she wrestled the sea grass from the child's hand, wiped her hands dry, scooped the child up, and ran with her through the shallow surf. "Let's see if we can find Oma some shells, sweetheart. Oma loves shells."

"Caitie find Oma shells," the child murmured.

Emilee called over her shoulder, "Keep up, Connor!"

She put her daughter down and sprinted ahead, creating two arcs of foam and water as she went. The child laughed as she pitter-pattered behind her mother, then turned around and hollered, "We find shells, Daddy. Mommy says, *come!*"

—m—

On the morning of the fourth day, during their sunrise beach walk with Caitie, Emilee garnered enough courage to face Connor. "I don't understand. Your father *invited* us. He sent me a generous check to cover the expenses. But it's crystal clear that *they*—well, *you* and your *mother*—don't *want* us here!"

"Mother is in one of her moods . . . It must be her menopause."

"I'm not stupid. She's years beyond that age, Connor." She turned and scooped the child up, pulling her tightly against her chest. "Perhaps the two of us should go back . . . back to Oxford."

"*No,* Mommy, Caitie *stay!*"

Emilee kissed her daughter's cheeks until she squirmed away.

Connor fell silent and hastened his pace, forcing Emilee to stretch her legs to keep up on the wet sand while carrying her daughter.

"It was my *father's* idea."

"So you *didn't* want us to come!"

He sighed as he slowed his walking.

"I'm going to pack our bags after breakfast."

"Please don't . . . It gets lonely . . . Mother doesn't like going for walks anymore. She has stopped talking to me."

"There's your dad."

Connor squinted and pointed at the sun, tapping his wristwatch. They turned around. Mother O'Hannigan hated to wait on guests at her breakfast table—not even on her son.

"Dad's in the clinic all day."

Emilee raised her brows and said nothing. What kind of research did Dr. Peter Jones and his occupational therapist do?

Caitlynn leaned across the gap between her parents and touched her father's arm. "Caitie stay with Daddy."

Emilee searched her husband's eyes. His lips were tight, his face empty.

Dear Lord. When did his soul slip away from us?

She buried her face in Caitie's hair as she hastened to keep up with the child's father, who had now chosen to move away from the wet sand, heading to between the boulders, ever increasing his pace.

—⁓—

The evening before Emilee and Caitie's return, Connor breached the taboo subject. Years later, Emilee realized how good he was at setting explosives—at priming things that could be detonated.

"My parents and I were wondering if you would mind leaving Caitlynn behind for the weekend—"

She gasped and clutched her hand over her mouth. "But it's her *birthday* on Monday!"

Why does he refuse to call her Caitie?

Connor held up his hands. "It's *only* for the weekend, *two* days extra . . . I'll have her back in Oxford by Sunday evening."

Emilee's eyes grew larger. "Will you be okay to fly . . . *with* her?"

Connor chuckled. "I've been here almost four weeks . . . Annagassan has been good to me." Glances were exchanged between parents and son. "I'm much better. We'll manage—Caitlynn and I. Trust me."

She turned to Caitie, her eyes brimming.

"Caitie stay with Daddy and Opa and Oma, Mommy!" The child, unable to contain herself, scampered to her feet on her chair.

Emilee made her sit again. "My sweet . . . I don't know . . . I'll miss you so *much*." She sniffled and blew her nose in the paper napkin, then took her daughter in her arms.

"Don't cry, Mommy."

"Emilee . . . *please*." A shadow of Connor's lazy smile had returned.

Grandfather and Grandmother O'Hannigan said nothing, but their eyes pleaded along with their son.

Connor kept his word—that once.

The doorbell of the Morrell Avenue apartment rang at exactly 6:15 on Sunday evening, May 2.

Connor must have decided not to use his key but waited on Emilee to open.

"*Mommy!*"

"*Caitie!*"

She swooped the child off the floor and smothered her with hugs and kisses until the girl shrieked in surrender. She took Connor's hand and pulled him through the front door. "Thank you for keeping your word."

He knotted his brows and pulled up his shoulders—the smile had reappeared.

Before breakfast on Caitlynn Aine O'Hannigan's third birthday, her father kept pestering her mother not to return too late from the library with her that afternoon. He promised to prepare a surprise early supper for the three of them. He further claimed he had to make up for a supper he had destroyed so unceremoniously many months ago during one of his outbursts, which was true enough. Mother and daughter thought it was an excellent idea.

Connor kept his word. He treated mother and daughter to an elaborate three-course meal, the likes of which they had last seen when his parents had visited at Christmas. Refusing any help, he cleaned up and did the dishes.

A soft drizzle had settled over the town from early afternoon.

"I have one more surprise, ladies," Connor announced, as he slipped out of his apron and folded it into a neat square as the clock tower chimed the sixth hour.

Emilee looked at him with expectation. He remained a man of mystery.

"It's a special birthday cake I have to pick up, at that bakery where I always get our freshly baked goods from. I had them make a few changes to the decorations. They promised to have it ready after six."

Caitlynn danced around her father. "Caitie goes with Daddy?"

"Yes, my sweet."

Emilee followed them to the front door until she remembered the inclement weather. "Let's just get your jacket on, Caitie."

"Caitie not wear red jacket, Mommy."

Emilee laughed as she pulled the child's arms through the red sleeves. "It's raining outside my darling. You always loved this jacket."

She scooped the child and smacked a kiss on her lips. "I *love* you, Caitlynn." A shudder shook Emilee's shoulders, and she buried her head for a moment in her child's hair.

"I *love* you, Mommy."

Connor grinned at her. "We shouldn't be too long."

Emilee leaned through the door and waved after the two as they walked down the pale hallway.

"*Bye-bye*, Caitie!"

Her daughter's laughter bristled through the long narrow space as she turned, clinging to Connor's hand. She waved. "Bye-bye, Mommy!"

CHAPTER 49

The search. May 1976.

WHEN THE BELL tower chimed seven individual hours, Emilee jumped to her feet and paced the apartment. It was impossible to sit any longer. She returned to Caitlynn's bedroom for the hundredth time, pulled the inner curtain aside and studied the gravel path behind their building: no sign of Mary Gabriella.

Odd. The bakery couldn't have kept them more than fifteen minutes.

Could Connor?

She brushed the possibility of another meltdown from her mind and started for the front door—she'd polish the floor. Perhaps Connor would notice, appreciate it even. She willed herself not the think and waxed harder.

She grasped her chest when eight hours chimed across the silent town. She bolted to the window in Caitie's room. The road was still empty, the single lamppost now casting an anemic glow in the early evening over the gravel path, the low brick wall, and the trimmed hedges.

Then I'll walk to the bakery—see for myself. Only then will I phone the police.

The bakery was locked up when Emilee reached it twenty minutes later. Her breathing came fast as her nose pressed flat against the glass of the front door. Inside, the only light was from narrow neon tubes in the now-empty display cabinets. She scrutinized the hand-painted board with hours of operation a second time: it still said *Monday to Thursday 6 a.m. till 7 p.m.* Only on Friday evening were they open till nine.

She wiped her tears with the back of her hands, hurling her purse farther back over her shoulder, alternating walking with running, only to walk briskly again. Faster and faster she went as she neared the apartment on Morley Street.

She had to dial twice, her fingers shook so much.

The constable took down her particulars between her sobs and gasping. He remained calm and soothing, reassured her not to get too distraught, not yet, since it was only nine in the evening.

The policeman chuckled as if embarrassed. "Didn't your husband simply drop in for a pint of ale or two and forgot about the hour, ma'am?"

Emilee sucked her breath. She had to bite her tongue not to yell at the man. "Visit a pub with a three-year-old?"

The man chortled again. "It's known to have happened."

"To be in a pub with a three-year-old *and* a birthday cake?"

The constable agreed that such a combination was indeed odd, especially when Emilee reminded him it was only Monday evening—not Friday, when the men often went a-drinking.

Again, the man agreed but remained reluctant to open a missing person's folder. Not just yet. Would she call the station again by midnight if her husband and daughter had not shown up?

Emilee seethed as she tried Caroline's number. *The ineptitude of the police force. Their glaring indifference.* There was also no answer at Tracy's. Rachel and Thomas were out of the question. Francois? Cambridge was too far away to be of help.

She again dialed the first number. *Pick up, Caroline. Please pick up.*

Douglas answered. Yes, Caroline was there, but what was the matter?

It was impossible to keep the angst from her voice, and the floodgates opened, even before Douglas handed the mouthpiece to Carrie.

They promised to be at Emilee's place within half an hour.

She tried Tracy Russell again. Thank God she answered.

"Do you think, Connor . . . ?" Tracy offered.

Emilee sucked one of several deep breaths. "I refuse to think *anything*, Trace. My baby is gone. That's all I know. Connor is better, but he's still ill. *Anything* is possible." She broke down, unable to continue.

Tracy promised to come over right away. Yes, with a flashlight. But why a flashlight, she wanted to know.

"Just bring your bloody flashlight, darling. Will you?" Emilee pleaded.

Emilee opened the front door to Tracy, whom she wouldn't let go of for a solid two minutes, hugging her breathless, then dragged her to the living room to one of the wing chairs, only to run back to open the door for Douglas and Caroline.

To keep her hands occupied, Emilee insisted on brewing a strong pot of tea for her friends.

Noticing her trembling hands, Douglas gently pushed her aside and took over the pouring.

The telephone rang at seven minutes to ten. Although the phone was in the short hallway, halfway to the bedrooms, Emilee picked up on the second ring. She could move fast if need be. It was the sergeant this time.

"Did you *find* them, sir?"

"Negative," the man said. "However, one of my men has discovered the abandoned vehicle that belongs to your husband."

The man informed her this had prompted them to open a missing person's folder.

"You found Mary Gabriella?"

"I understand your daughter's name is Caitlynn O'Hannigan?"

Emilee plopped down on the floor, hanging onto the handpiece, silent for a moment, catching her breath. Connor would never abandon his car. Her and Caitlynn perhaps—but not Mary G. Never. She staggered upright, clasping her chest, leaning forward to will her pounding heart slower.

"Yes, sir. My daughter is Caitlynn. No, the car is Mary Gabriella. Thank you, sir. . . . I'm okay now."

She swallowed several times, then laughed through her tears. "He would never abandon his car—not Connor. What could it mean?"

The policeman insisted that she come to the station. There was much more to explain. Yes, immediately.

Emilee plodded back to the room where her three friends sat waiting. None had touched their tea. They studied her face.

"They found Connor's car—deserted—doors ajar. No sign. No sign . . . of him or my *baby*."

Douglas snapped forward as Emilee collapsed.

As soon as the three friends had revived Emilee by making her drink two sweet cups of tea, they bundled her up, and the four of them set off in Douglas and Caroline's sedan for the police station.

Mary G was found a little after nine, explained the sergeant, with doors wide open, halfway up the sidewalk, close to the Castle Mill stream. A destroyed cake was found on its side next to the vehicle, and a bloodstained shoe, probably belonging to Connor, had been lodged between the gas and brake pedals. There were also blood smears on the driver's seat.

Nothing else.

The sergeant asked her many more questions. Why, why, why, he wanted to know.

Officers were sent to the train station to look for leads.

Police patrol boats soon scanned the rivers and canals.

The four friends refused to be let out of the search. They worked in twos, each with a flashlight. Working from east to west, they combed the streets. Not until the east lit up did the friends return to the police station and then to the deserted apartment on Morley Street.

There was no news about three-year-old Caitlynn Aine O'Hannigan and her father, Connor O'Hannigan. The earth had swallowed them, it seemed.

Emilee made the station commander contact the police in Dublin and send inspectors to Annagassan, but only after she had phoned Dr. Peter Jones at 6:03 a.m. from the police station and made him explain Connor's illness in graphic detail—only then did the police agree to alert their Irish colleagues.

The search remained fruitless.

The following Monday afternoon, Emilee received another call from the police station. She had to come to the station as soon as was convenient to identify a piece of clothing.

Emilee cried herself to sleep that second Monday night with Caitlynn's red jacket clasped to her chest. It had been found tucked among the reeds a mile down the same stream where Mary G had been found the week before. Caroline and Douglas were out of town when the news about the jacket had broken.

Tracy sat next to her on the bed, rocking her friend, stroking her face, murmuring endearments—anything, anything to make her stop weeping.

Emilee refused to let go of the soiled red jacket.

By daybreak, Tracy was convinced her friend had shed all the tears that were possible to shed in one lifetime.

CHAPTER 50

———— ✺ ————

Mr. O'Hannigan's letter.
Oxford. 29 July 2000.

"THAT WAS THE *last* time you saw Caitlynn?" Francois Moolman asked as he faced Emilee. He rubbed the dent in his chin and fanned himself with the letter that had caused all the panic.

Emilee nodded, not trusting her voice. She had waited three years back then, plus another four, only to mourn them then. Never to forget. Now this. She shook her head as if to free herself from the new calamity.

"Twenty-four years?"

Emilee stood, withdrew her hand from Francois's, and faced the river. "She would have turned twenty-seven in May: Caitlynn Aine O'Hannigan." She spun around and grasped his hands. "Do you think she looks *a little* like me?" She gasped. "Dare I even hope?" Her hands slipped from his as the bravado drained from her arms.

She gave a sob and muttered, "I want to show you something." With her hand clasped to her lips, she stomped from the room.

Francois followed her up the stairs to a guest bedroom where she rummaged in the closet and pulled out a cardboard box.

She opened the tucked-in flaps, turned back an old towel, and removed a small jacket. She gave it a firm shake and held it out.

Francois took the little red raincoat.

Emilee plopped down on the side of the single bed, pulled the garment from his hands, and clasped it to her chest. Her hooded eyes searched his face. He had to lean in closely to hear her murmur. "They found it the following Monday afternoon, about a hundred yards from my backyard dock on Castle Mill stream."

"Is that why you bought this house—here, next to the stream?"

"Perhaps." Her lips trembled. "I had it dry cleaned. It hung in my closet for seven years." Her eyes pleaded with him. "Then it was time to put it away. I have not . . . taken it out of here . . . until now." Her shoulders started shaking uncontrollably.

Francois kneeled in front of her and pulled her closer, almost crushing her against him to stop her shaking.

It was much later when she wriggled free from his awkward embrace, as he was still on his knees in front of her next to the bed.

She pulled the envelope from his hand, the letter from Slough. "Will you read it to me?"

Francois took the pen from his shirt pocket, pressed the button, slipped the tip into the flap of the envelope, and tore it open. He held it out to her, but she shook her head.

Danie Botha

He read.

26 July 2000
Emilee,

I would have loved to address you as "Dear Emilee," but I dare not. You must still hate me. I hurt you so much. I was ill. Actually—I still am. I was selfish. And yes, I guess I still am. I returned a month ago for my father's funeral. Mother tracked me down in Canada after his first stroke—asked me to come back to Annagassan. I was too late. He had a second stroke three days before I left BC.

Oh, I tend to forget. I have changed my name. Around these areas, I go by Peter Hamilton. That's another story.

I would not have bothered to make contact. How dare I? Even I couldn't sanction a second round of hurt. Even monsters have their limits. But I am ill. No, not the schizophrenia. That's still there—although, it is almost burnt out. I am dying. I have prostate cancer—it has spread to my liver and brain and bones. The liver part is okay—it's the brain that freaks me out. The spread to the bones hurt like hell. The Canadian doctors have been good to me. There's nothing more they can do, they said. They can't remove the growths in my head—it would leave me blind and paralyzed and only hasten my death.

You will not recognize me. I have put on much weight. The price of the medication. Although, I'm fast losing it now. Perhaps not fast enough. I have a beard. You guessed—it's gray. Oh, the tremors are the least of my worries. My voice— perhaps the only thing you'll find familiar.

328

How doesn't time change us, dear Emilee? As does our wickedness and all our self-inflicted burdens—our hatred and vitriol and self-interest.

I dare not expect your forgiveness, I have wronged you so many times over. But I must see you—if at all possible. I have to tell you about Caitlynn.

I have to do so in person.

I am so sorry.

Always in your debt,
Connor O'Hannigan. (aka Peter Hamilton)

PS 1. I was so jealous of the camaraderie and love between Caitie and you. And I was poisoned by my father. I'm not blaming him. But still.

PS 2. I don't know why I mailed the letter in Slough. Perhaps because I wanted you to move there with me long ago. I was happy there once. What is happiness? Forgive me— I'm rambling now. I'm returning to Mother in Annagassan. You'll find me there.

PS 3. Come quickly. I get seizures now almost every other day. And it hurts.

PS 4. How did I get your address? Ask Mother. You should forgive her. It was all my and Father's doing. I hope she will sprout again and blossom, after he's gone (and me perhaps too.) Father caged her spirit. I tried to escape from his reach. He was too strong. Perhaps I was too weak. Perhaps . . . (There's so much to forgive. There's also much to understand.) How can I ask this from you? (Do you still have Mother's phone number?)

PS 5. I want to go and show you where I walked and played when Patrick and I were little—before all the shit started. Long before then. I wish you'd known me then. I wish. I wish. You would have liked me better.

PS 6. I love you, Emilee. I know it is a little too late now for this. But 'tis true. Even in all my wickedness and brokenness. PS 6! My God. See? I told you I'm ill. I'm rambling again. It must be the brain swelling and the pain medication.

PS 7. My finances are somewhat screwed. I don't own a personal computer anymore. Where I'm going one doesn't need one. Pen and paper were easier to get hold of. Ah, yes . . . my handwriting. I hope, the one thing of me that has remained true—unblemished.

Always your Connor,
C. O'H. (P.H.)

Francois lowered the letter.

"That's *it?*" she whispered.

He nodded as he took her shoulders and leaned closer. He kissed first her wet eyelids, one after the other, savoring the salt, drying the shining trails over her cheeks with his thumbs, then he kissed the tip of her nose, then her lips. Her shivering wouldn't stop. He stood, scooped her up with great care, and carried her, along with the tiny red jacket and handwritten letter mailed in Slough, down the stairs and back to the living room, where he packed a fire.

Then he held her some more.

Epilogue

Annagassan. 2 August 2000.

Only when the taxi crossed the ancient stone bridge across the Glyde River did Francois stir. The rhythmic sweeping of the wiper blades and the incessant drizzle had lulled him to sleep. He rubbed his eyes.

"Your mother-in-law *is* expecting us?"

"She's *not* my mother—"

"Sorry . . . *Connor's* mother . . . Did you *phone* her?"

Emilee snorted as she stared at the grim strips of Irish Sea appearing and disappearing behind the dark houses. She shrugged and offered him a quick glance only to turn back to face the sea.

"I *dared not* speak to her." She tore the Kleenex in her hands to shreds. "It's been a *lifetime* since I last saw her—least of all spoken to her." She abandoned the scraps of paper and clasped Francois's hands. He cradled hers.

The cab crunched to a halt. Neither of them moved.

For the first time in her adult life, she didn't feel afraid. Not with Francois next to her. An unfamiliar awareness.

"Ma'am? Sir?"

Emilee paid the driver as Francois retrieved their single piece of luggage from the trunk.

The driver rolled his window down. "Ma'am . . . Should I *wait?*"

"*Pardon me?*" Emilee leaned closer. For the first time, she noticed the deep silver of the man's hair. The sparkle in his eyes was unmistakable. Was this the same man who had dropped her off and picked her up on her first visit to Annagassan?

Impossible.

The man smiled and touched his cap.

She sucked her breath.

"Then I'm leaving. Thank you, ma'am."

Emilee straightened and pursed her lips. "*Thank you*, sir."

It was him.

She tapped the roof of the cab as it pulled away.

The doorbell was a surprise. A new addition. Emilee glanced at the now-almost black stone walls. They were no less intimidating, unmoved in their solidity. They would outlive ten more generations. She hesitated.

Francois coughed and leaned forward. "Shall I?"

Emilee pressed the button.

Inside the mansion, the hounds were let loose. Emilee jerked her hand away and stepped back, right into Francois's arms. He laughed.

She mumbled under her breath as she struggled to regain her balance. "Shit! This is *not* funny, Francois. It must be the babies, or even grandbabies, of Saint and Dublin. Indomitable wolfhounds!"

They heard a woman's voice and then immediate silence. The dogs still had a mistress if no longer a master.

The front door swung open without a sound.

The two women seized up each other. Not a word was spoken. Francois held back.

Deirdre O'Hannigan moved first. A trace of a smile appeared in the now-wrinkled face as she stepped forward to touch her ex-daughter-in-law's hands, then she moved closer and hugged her, surprising them both.

"Emilee."

"Mrs. O'Hannigan."

Emilee broke the embrace and introduced Francois.

Deirdre O'Hannigan took her guests' hands. "Come. Connor told me about you . . . but that was *days* ago . . . He has deteriorated. We've made him comfortable in the clinic." She closed the front door behind them. "He refused to go to the hospital. We have nurses who are looking after him." She wiped her eyes. "Said he'd stay here with me . . . till the end." She spun around. "Come. Let's hurry." She faced Emilee in the walk. "It's a pity. I didn't have your phone number."

"How bad is—"

"He's in and out of a coma . . . He had much pain. They started him on a morphine infusion two days ago. The doctor was here this morning. His priority was to make Connor comfortable. The doctor talked of hours—"

Emilee increased her pace. Their urgent steps echoed as they turned down the narrow stone hallway, then down toward the clinic, away from the living quarters.

—∿—

Emilee entered the makeshift hospice room with caution. Connor had spoken the truth in his letter.

She did not recognize the person lying on the hospital bed: a mountain of a man covered with a single white sheet—whiter than the handkerchief he so loved to wear and open Mary G's door handles with. An intravenous line disappeared into his arm, and the thin oxygen tubing was dwarfed by his rich silver beard. She was reminded of Rip Van Winkle.

She stepped closer and watched his chest. It rose and fell, unhurried.

She sucked her breath.

Connor.

She squinted and wiped her eyes. His mustache was the only part of him that still had a carrot tinge, that was not entirely gray.

Even on tiptoes she had trouble reaching his lips. They were clammy. She murmured, "Connor."

The nurse smiled as she pushed a chair closer for Emilee, who plopped straight back into it and grasped his hand.

She squeezed it and said louder, "Connor."

She squeezed again, harder. "*Connor!*"

Muffled sounds escaped the patient as he thrust his arms about. Nurse, visitors, and parent all stepped closer.

Emilee leaned closer to his ear. "Connor, it's *me—Emilee.* Please speak to me! Open your eyes—"

"Emilee . . . ."

His voice croaked. Hoarse. Hesitant.

She pressed even closer to his ear. "Caitlynn. Tell me about Caitie. Please!"

"Caitie . . . ." A shudder shook his chest. His head rolled toward her and his eyes fluttered, but they returned to being closed. "She's not . . . Ask . . . Mother."

"*What* about Caitlynn?"

Connor became silent.

The rising of his chest slowed but didn't stop.

Francois led her away an hour later. The big man hadn't spoken since. He kept on breathing. The morphine infusion continued at the same slow rate. It seemed he was comfortable.

At the low garden gate leading down to the beach at the back of the house, Deirdre O'Hannigan waited on Emilee at sunrise the next morning.

Emilee was startled. She had expected to find Francois there.

The older woman had tied her hair down and turned her collar up. A crispness came off the bay. "May I walk with you? I started walking again after Doctor's funeral." She gave Emilee a rare smile. "I have forgotten how much I used to enjoy it."

The next moment, three young wolfhounds burst through the gate, brushed past them, and made for the surf. Mrs. O'Hannigan's feeble reprimand of "Slow down, Patrick! Careful, Lucky! Come back, Guinness!" was drowned by their yelping and barking as they rounded the wooden fence marking the end of the property, sending sand and gravel and shards of dune creepers flying.

The two women followed the dogs, who were already only small dots along the shoreline.

The older and the younger mother walked in silence. There was much to say. Much to ask. If only they knew how.

They had both first visited Connor in the clinic earlier that morning. He was unchanged. He had stopped responding but was still breathing.

Emilee stopped, bent down, and picked up a broken shell. She faced her host with slanted eyes, rolling the shell between her fingers. "Connor wrote me a letter a week ago. He asked me to meet him here in Annagassan. He wanted to tell me about Caitlynn—in person. But, if he couldn't, I had to ask *you*."

The older women took a sharp breath, her cheeks the color of writing paper.

"*Caitie?*"

Emilee nodded as she faced the sea. "He asked for my forgiveness in the letter. He must have sensed I might be too late—not get here in time."

"It's so long ago now, my child."

Emilee whispered as she grasped the other woman's hands, who winced. "She would have turned *twenty-seven* in May."

"What do you *want* from me?"

"The truth—"

The dogs had turned back when they noticed the women had stopped walking. They raced closer, yelping at a handful of gulls skimming the surf.

"The truth. Typical ... The two men ... They masterminded everything ... Now *I* have to explain." She shuddered.

They started walking again. Emilee tossed the shell away and increased her pace. "Masterminded?" she asked and kicked at the sand. "My God!" She halted abruptly and fell to her knees, grasping Deirdre O'Hannigan's hands. She shielded her eyes against the early sun. She had to see the older women's face, her eyes—get a glimpse of her soul.

"Did my child—did my baby—not drown?"

The mistress of Annagassan shook her head. "It was staged. They sent the girl away. *That* was Fergus's—Dr. O'Hannigan's idea. He poisoned our son's mind—"

"Then he was an *evil* man!"

"Fergus was ill."

"I thought he loved Caitie!"

"I told you—he was sick."

Emilee clambered to her feet, brushed the sand from her legs and hands, and stomped toward the water, muttering to herself. Five paces farther she spun around and hollered at her ex-mother-in-law. "Why didn't you *stop* them?"

"Fergus was a powerful man. He ruled the clan. He ruled Connor. He ruled me."

Emilee collapsed on the wet sand and rolled into a fetal position, rocking herself, wailing. "How *could* you?"

Deirdre O'Hannigan pulled her slumping shoulders back, placed two fingers in her mouth, and whistled at the dogs. The hounds obeyed immediately and came pounding back. She called at them. "Patrick, Lucky, Guinness! Go get the master at the house! Go!"

She dropped down next to Emilee and rubbed her shoulders. "I am so sorry." She wiped her eyes and sniffed.

Emilee turned onto her knees and glanced at the older woman, who was now openly weeping. Did this woman, after all, have a heart made of flesh and not out of moss-covered black stone?

"I have not cried since my son Patrick's death in seventy-one."
She grinned through her tears. "How silly I've become . . . I even
named one of my hounds after my son."

Emilee struggled to her feet as her host now dropped to her
knees. Emilee shivered uncontrollably. Hugging her shoulders
helped little. Her face contracted. She studied the pathetic bundle
at her feet, surprised at how little pity she felt for the woman.
How could she justify her complicity? Her silence of a lifetime.
How could it be nothing because it had happened long ago?

Caitie. My sweet, sweet child.

Emilee gave a dry sob and stormed in the direction of the
house, oblivious to the gulls and the dogs, who had returned
without the master, frolicking again in the crashing waves. She
could hear Mrs. O'Hannigan call her name. It only made her
walk faster.

—⟋⟍—

Emilee noticed him as he rounded the fence, close to the house.
He was barefoot and in a hurry.

She started running. "Francois!"

His face broke into a grin as he opened his arms.

"Why did you slip away without me?" He caught her in his
arms and spun her around to stop them from crashing into the
sand. They were both breathless.

Emilee leaned back in his arms and thumped his chest with
her fists, then pointed behind her, toward the sea. "I was kid-
napped by that witch—Connor's mother."

Francois laughed and kissed her protesting lips.

"Don't laugh. She had the help of three Irish wolfhounds. Protest was futile."

She took his hand as they started the sandy incline toward the small garden gate.

"I didn't know the two of you were pals."

Emilee scoffed.

"She couldn't find a priest, so I had to do. She confessed past sins."

Francois stopped and took both her hands. Then he tilted her chin. "Emilee, *what* happened out there? *What* is wrong?"

"My little Caitlynn never drowned in seventy-six." She sobbed, grasped him around the neck, and sought his lips. "Her red jacket on the river bank was a *decoy*."

"*No?*"

"It's *true*." She grabbed his hand and steered toward the stone mansion's back door. The dogs' barking became louder. Emilee accelerated her pace and pulled her companion along. "Hurry!" She was running by then. "I'll get the nurses to stop the morphine infusion. I have to speak to Connor O'Hannigan before he meets his Maker!"

END

Thank You for Reading!

Please consider leaving an online review for this novel. Reviews matter. By leaving a review more readers will gain access to the novel—hence enable the author to write more.

—∽—

ALSO BY DANIE BOTHA
Be Silent
Be Good
Maxime
Young Maxime

—∽—

Find more of my writing at https://daniebotha.com

Acknowledgements

Authors can't get their books out into the world on their own—it's a team effort. Granted, giving birth to the first draft is much of a solo-(ad)venture, after which the feedback from first (beta-) readers help shape the manuscript. A copyeditor is needed. A graphic designer for the cover art is indispensable. A printing and publishing house is required. And a launch team is crucial to help spread the word and help the book fly.

Thank you to my first readers, I could not have done it without you! Thanks to Isabella, Dean Gabrowski, Bernadette & Cassandra Mackenzie, Victor Duarte, Jackie Dutfield and Charlize Gatza!

Thank you to my siblings, Charlotte, Florence, and Dave, who keep inspiring me, reminding me it is possible.

Thank you to Blake Atwood, capable and patient copyeditor—hats off to you, Blake!

Thank you to my launch team of the previous novel, Maxime—It will be grand to have you rallying behind this one as well! Thanks to Isabella, Dean, Bernadette, Victor, Jackie, Charlize, Shelley Whitehead, Matt Legacé, Jay Ross, Jan Price, Diane Collings, John Pink and A.P. Maddox! And if I skipped a name: thank you, thank you!

Thank you to the graphic designer, Eleni Karoumpali from L1graphics. She was also responsible for the work on Maxime and Young Maxime.

And if there is nobody to read our work, why do we write? Thank you to all my readers and fellow writers and authors (many of whom have become friends), who keep inspiring and nudging me to keep writing and work and get better at my craft. Without your enthusiasm, feedback, support, teaching, and frequent challenging, it would have become a bleak, lonely, if not worthless venture.

References

My research has led me along numerous online resources which I will list as inclusively as possible.

The Guardian. January 30, 1972. https://www.theguardian.com/theguardian/from-the-archive-blog/2011/jun/01/guardian190-bloody-sunday-1972 (Accessed in 2016.)

BBC History. Several videos were also consulted to get a clearer picture of the events. http://www.bbc.co.uk/history/events/bloody_friday_belfast (Accessed 2016)

The Guardian. March 8, 1971. Women march for liberation in London. https://www.theguardian.com/theguardian/2013/mar/08/1971-womens-liberation-march-archive (Accessed in 2016.)

Video: 1971 First Women's Liberation Movement march – UCL students. Youtube.com (Accessed in 2016.) Several videos were researched and watched circa the early 1970s. (Accessed YouTube 2016.)

Poem by William Butler Yeates. https://www.poemhunter.com/poem/ephemera/ (Accessed 2016)

Oxford University. http://www.ox.ac.uk/ (Accessed 2016.)

Annagassan. https://en.wikipedia.org/wiki/Annagassan (Accessed 2016.)

Numerous online sources were researched on sweep boat rowing, including videos. https://en.wikipedia.org/wiki/Sweep_(rowing) [Accessed 2016]

You can find more of my writing at https://daniebotha.com